ALSO BY KRISTEN PROBY

The With Me in Seattle Series

The Love Under the Big Sky Series

SEDUCING
Lauren

KRISTEN PROBY

POCKET BOOKS
New York London Toronto Sydney New Delhi

Pocket Books
A Division of Simon & Schuster, Inc.
1230 Avenue of the Americas
New York, NY 10020

This book is a work of fiction. Any references to historical events, real people, or real places are used fictitiously. Other names, characters, places, and events are products of the author's imagination, and any resemblance to actual events or places or persons, living or dead, is entirely coincidental.

First Pocket Books paperback edition September 2014

POCKET and colophon are registered trademarks of Simon & Schuster, Inc.

For information about special discounts for bulk purchases, please contact Simon & Schuster Special Sales at 1-866-506-1949 or business@simonandschuster.com.

The Simon & Schuster Speakers Bureau can bring authors to your live event. For more information or to book an event, contact the Simon & Schuster Speakers Bureau at 1-866-248-3049 or visit our website at www.simonspeakers.com.

Cover illustration by Alan Ayers

Manufactured in the United States of America

10   9   8   7   6   5   4   3   2

ISBN 978-1-4767-5937-1
ISBN 978-1-4767-5939-5 (ebook)

For Dad

Acknowledgments

I'd like to thank my Pocket team for all of your hard work. I couldn't ask for a more dedicated, helpful, and professional group to work with.

Kevan Lyon, thank you for your persistence and encouragement.

I have to acknowledge my colleagues who have also become my dear friends. Thank you for challenging me, making me laugh, and having my back. Not only do I count you as friends, but I'm a fan too.

And finally, thank *you*, the reader.

SEDUCING
Lauren

CHAPTER

One

LAUREN

"Hey, Lauren."

"Hi, Jacob, what can I do for you?" I ask with a smile, and open my front door wider for the friendly county sheriff's deputy.

"Well, I'm serving you." He offers me an embarrassed smile and hands me a large envelope, then backs away. "Have a good day."

I move back inside, shut the door, and stare down at the envelope in surprise.

Served?

I rip open the envelope and see bright, flaming inferno red as I read the court document. And read it again.

"The fucker is *suing me*?" I exclaim to an empty room, and read the letter clutched in my now trembling hands for the third time. "Hell no!"

I grab my handbag and slide my feet into flip-flops, barely managing not to fall down the porch steps as I tear out of my house to my Mercedes and pull out of the circular driveway.

I live at the edge of Cunningham Falls, Montana. The small town was named after my great-grandfather Albert Cunningham. Ours is a tourist town that boasts a five-star ski resort and a plethora of outdoor activities for any season. Thankfully, summer tourist season is over, and ski season is still a few months away, so traffic into town is light.

I zoom past the post office and into the heart of downtown, where my lawyer's office is. Without paying any attention to the yellow curb, I park quickly and march into the old building.

The receptionist's head jerks up in surprise as I approach her and slam the letter still clutched in my hand on her desk.

"*This,*" I say between clenched teeth, "isn't going to happen."

"Ms. Cunningham, do you have an appointment?"

"No, I don't have an appointment, but someone had better have time to see me." I am seething; my breath is coming in harsh pants.

"Lauren." My head whips up at the sound of my name and I find Ty Sullivan frowning at me from his office doorway. "I can see you. Come in."

I turn my narrowed eyes on Ty and follow him into his office, too agitated to sit while I wait for him to shut the door and walk behind his desk.

"What's going on?"

"I need a new lawyer."

"What's going on?" he asks again, and calmly leans against the windowsill behind his desk. He crosses his arms over his chest. The sleeves of his white button-down are rolled, giving me a great view of the colorful tattoo on his right arm.

"*This* is what's going on!" I thrust the letter at him. "Jack is trying to sue me for half of a trust fund that he has no right to."

Ty's handsome face frowns as he skims the letter. "You came into the trust while you were still married?"

"Yes," I confirm warily.

"And you didn't tell him about it?" he asks with raised brows.

"I didn't even know the damn thing existed until after my parents died, Ty. Until *after* I kicked Jack out." I turn and pace away, breathing deeply, trying to calm down. "He doesn't deserve a dime of my inheritance. This isn't about money, it's about principle."

"I agree." Ty shrugs. "Have you talked with Cary?"

"I was just served with the letter," I mumble, and sink into a leather chair in defeat. "Cary's a nice guy, but I just don't think he's the right lawyer for this job." I glance up at Ty and my heart skips a beat as I take him in now that I'm calming down. He's tall, much taller than me—which is saying something, given that I stand higher than five foot eight. He has broad shoulders and lean hips, and holy hell, the things this man does to a suit should be illegal in all fifty states.

But more than that, he's kind and funny and has a bit of a bad-boy side to him too, hence the tattoos.

He's been front and center in many of my fantasies for most of my life.

I bite my lips and glance down as his eyes narrow on my face.

"Why do you say that?" he asks calmly.

"It took two freaking years for the divorce to be final, Ty. I don't want Cary to drag this out too."

"It wasn't necessarily Cary's fault that the divorce took so long, Lauren. Jack had a good lawyer and your divorce was a mess."

That's the fucking understatement of the year. "Will you take my case?"

"No," he replies quickly.

"What?" My dazed eyes return to his. "Why?"

He shakes his head and sighs as he takes a seat behind his desk. "I have a full load as it is, Lo."

"You're more aggressive than Cary," I begin, but halt when he scowls.

"I really don't think I can help you."

I sit back and stare at him, stunned. "You mean you won't." I hate the hurt I hear in my voice, but I can't hide it. I know Ty and I aren't superclose, but I've considered him a friend. I can't believe he's shooting me down.

He folds the letter and hands it back to me, his mouth set in a firm line and blue-gray eyes sober.

"No, I won't. Make an appointment with Cary and talk it over with him."

My hand automatically reaches out and takes the letter from Ty, and I'm just deeply embarrassed.

"Of course," I whisper, and rise quickly, ready to escape this office. "I'm sorry for intruding."

"Lo . . ."

"No, you're right. It was unprofessional for me to just show up like this. I apologize." I clear my throat and offer him a bright, fake smile, then beeline it for the door. "Thanks anyway."

"Did you want to make an appointment, Lauren?" Sylvia, the receptionist, asks as I hurry past her desk.

"No, I'll call. Thanks."

I can't get to my car fast enough. Why did I think Ty would help me? *No one will help me.*

All the connections I have in this town, all the money I have, and that asshole is still making my life a living hell.

I drive home in a daze, and when I pull up behind a shiny black Jaguar, my heart sinks further.

Today fucking sucks.

I pull my cell phone out of my bag, prepared to call for help if need be, and climb out of my car. I walk briskly past him and up the steps to the front door.

"Hey, gorgeous."

"I told you not to come here, Jack. I don't want to see you." *How can he still make me so damn nervous?*

"Aww, don't be like that, baby. You're making this so much harder than it needs to be."

I round on him, shocked and pissed all over again. "I'm the one making this hard?" I shake my head and laugh at the lunacy of this situation. "I don't want you here. The divorce has been final for weeks now, and you have no business being here. And now you're going to fucking *sue me*?"

He loses his smug smile and his mouth tightens as his brown eyes narrow. "No, I'll tell you what will make it easy, Lauren. You paying me what's rightfully mine is what will make it easy. You hid that money from me, and I'm entitled to half."

"I'll never pay you off, you sonofabitch." I'm panting and glaring, so fucking angry.

"Oh, honey, I think you will." He moves in close and drags his knuckles down my cheek. I jerk my head away, but he grabs my chin in his hand, squeezing until there's just a bit of pain. "Or maybe I'll just come back here and claim what's mine. You are still mine, you know."

My stomach rolls as he runs his nose up my neck, sniffing deeply. Every part of me stills. *What the fuck is this?*

"A man has the right to fuck his wife whenever he pleases."

"I'm not your wife," I grind out, glaring at him as he pulls back and stares me in the face.

He flashes an evil grin and presses harder against me. "You'll always be mine. No piece of paper can change that."

I don't answer, but instead just continue to glare at him in hatred.

"Maybe you should just go ahead and write that check."

He pushes away from me and backs down the stairs toward his flashy car, a car he bought with my parents' money, and snickers as he looks me up and down. "You've kept that hot body of yours in shape, Lo. It's mighty tempting."

I swear I'm going to throw up.

I can't answer him. I can only stand here and glower, shaking in rage and fear, as he winks again and hops in his Jag and drives away.

Jesus Christ, he just threatened to rape me. I might not be able to prove it, but I knew what his words meant.

I let myself into the house and reset the alarm with shaking fingers. I take off in a sprint to the back of the house and heave into the toilet, over and over until there's nothing left and my body shivers and convulses in revulsion.

How can someone who once claimed to love me be so damn evil?

When the vomiting has passed, I rinse my mouth and head to the indoor pool that my parents had built when I was on the swim team in high school. I strip out of my clothes, but before I pull my swim cap on, I dial a familiar number on my phone and wait for an answer.

"Hull." Brad is a police detective in town, and someone I trust implicitly.

"It's Lauren."

"Hey, sugar, what's up?"

"Jack just left."

"What did that son of a bitch want?" Brad's voice is steel.

"He threatened me." My voice is shaky and I hate myself for sounding so vulnerable. "I want it documented that he was here."

"Did you record it, Lo?"

"No. I wasn't expecting it. He's been an asshole in the past, but this is the first time he's come out and threatened me since he . . ." I pace beside the pool, unable to finish the sentence.

"That's because I put the fear of God and jail time in him." Brad is quiet for a moment. "Is there anything you need?"

I laugh humorlessly and shake my head. "Yeah, I need my asshole ex to go away. But for now I'll settle for a swim."

"Keep your alarm on. Call me if you need me."

"I will. Thanks, Brad."

"Anytime, sugar."

We ring off. I tuck my long, auburn hair into my swim cap and then dive into the Olympic-size lap pool. The warm water glides over my naked skin, and I begin the first of countless laps, back and forth, across the pool. Swimming is one of two things in this world I do well, and it clears my head.

I do some of my best thinking in the pool.

Is all of this worth it? I ask myself. When I married Jack almost five years ago, I was convinced that he was in love with me and that we'd be together forever. He'd been on my swim team in college. He was handsome and charming.

And unbeknownst to me, he'd been after my money all along.

My parents were still alive then, and even they had fallen for his charms. My father had been a brilliant businessman and had done all he could to convince me to have Jack sign a prenuptial agreement so in the event of a divorce, Jack couldn't stake any claim to my sizable trust fund.

But I stood my ground, blind with love and promises of forever, insistent that a prenup was unnecessary.

My dad would lose his mind if he knew what was happening now. If only I'd listened to him!

I tuck and roll, then push off the wall, turning into a backstroke.

The small amount of money that Jack is trying to lay claim to is nothing compared to the money I have that Jack knows nothing about. Since our legal separation, I've become very successful in my career, but I wasn't lying when I told Ty that it's not about the money.

This is my heritage. My family worked hard for this land, for the wealth they amassed, and Jack doesn't deserve another fucking dime of it. That's why the divorce took so long. I fought him with everything in me to assure that he didn't get his greedy hands on my family's money.

In the end he won a sizable settlement that all of the lawyers talked me into.

Jack wasn't happy. He wanted more.

I push off the edge of the pool and glide underwater until I reach the surface and then move into a front crawl.

After my parents died in a winter car accident just over two years ago, Jack made it clear that he didn't love me, had been sleeping around since we were dating, but expected me to keep him in his comfortable lifestyle.

When I threw a fit and kicked him out, he slammed me against the wall and landed a punch to my stomach, certain to avoid bruising me, before he left.

Thanks to threats from Brad, and Jack's knowing how well-known I am in this town, he's not bothered me since. Until now.

And now he's threatening me.

It's not worth it. Living in constant fear of seeing Jack around town, of finding myself in the middle of another humiliating scene. Seeing the pity in the eyes of people I've known my whole life.

And now, coming home to an ambush because he's feeling desperate?

I'm done.

I pull myself out of the water, exhausted and

panting, and resigned to see Cary in the morning to agree to a settlement.

It's time to move on.

It's early when I leave the house and drive to the lawyer's office. I don't have an appointment, and I don't even know for sure if anyone is there yet, but I couldn't sleep last night. I couldn't lose myself in work.

I need to get this over with.

When I stride to the front door, I'm surprised to find it unlocked. Sylvia isn't in yet, but I hear voices back in Cary's office.

I step through his door like I belong there, and both Cary's and Ty's faces register surprise when they see me in the doorway.

"You know, Lo, we have these things called phones, where you call and make what's called an appointment." Ty's gray eyes are narrowed, but his lips are quirked in a smile. He's in a power suit today, making my mouth immediately water. His shoulders look even broader in the black jacket, and the blue tie makes his eyes shine.

"Ha ha." I sit heavily in the seat before Cary's desk. "I'm sick of this shit."

"Ty told me you came by yesterday." Cary leans back in his chair.

"I was fucking served papers," I mutter, and push my hands though my hair. "But I think I want to settle."

Ty's eyebrows climb into his hairline. "I'll leave you two alone."

"You can stay," I mutter. "I could use both of your opinions. I'll pay double for the hour."

"That's not necessary." Ty's voice is clipped and he frowns as he gazes at me. "Why the change of heart?"

I lean back in the chair and tilt my head back, looking at the tin tiles on the ceiling. "Because Jack's an asshole. Because now he's decided to threaten me." I shake my head and look Cary in the eye. "But no payments. It's going to be in one lump sum and he needs to sign a contract stating that he'll never ask for another dime."

"Wait, back up." Ty pushes away from the desk and glowers down at me. "What do you mean he threatened you?"

"It doesn't matter."

"Lauren," Cary interrupts, "it does matter. What the hell happened?"

"When I returned home, Jack was at the house."

"Does he still have a key?" Ty asks.

"No." I shake my head adamantly. "I changed all the locks and installed a new alarm system the day he left."

"So he was waiting outside," Cary clarifies.

"Yes. I told him to leave, that I didn't want to see him and he isn't welcome at the house. He said I was making things harder than they need to be." I laugh humorlessly as Cary's eyebrows climb toward his blond hairline. "I reminded him that there's nothing difficult about this at all. We're divorced. It's over, and he can just go away." I shrug and look away, not wanting to continue.

"What did he threaten you with?" Ty asks softly.

I raise my eyes to his and suddenly my stomach rolls. "I'm going to be sick."

I bolt from the room and run to the restroom in the hallway, barely making it in time to lose the half gallon of coffee I consumed this morning. When the dry-heaving stops, I rinse my mouth and open the door, finding Ty on the other side.

"Are you okay?" he asks quietly.

I nod, embarrassed.

He reaches up and gently tucks a stray piece of my hair behind my ear. "What did he threaten you with?" He leads me back to Cary's office.

I swallow and cross my arms over my chest. I don't want to say it aloud. "He just threatened to be a dick."

"Bullshit," Cary responds, leaning forward in his chair. "Lo, the man wasn't afraid to put his hands on you when you told him to leave—"

"What?" Ty exclaims.

"—so you need to tell me what he threatened to do to you if you don't give him what he wants."

I shake my head and close my eyes, remembering the feel of Jack's nose pressed to my neck and the crazy look in his eyes when he wasn't getting what he wanted.

"Excuse us for a minute, Cary." Ty takes my hand in his and leads me toward the door.

"Uh, my client, Ty, remember?"

"We'll be right back," Ty assures him, and leads me into his office and shuts the door behind us.

"What did the asshole threaten to do to you, Lauren?"

"You said no yesterday, Ty. This isn't your case."

He shrugs, as if what I just said is of no consequence. "Answer me."

I simply shake my head. "It doesn't matter. Cary and I will figure it out. You don't have to stay in there with us."

I try to walk past him but he catches my hand in his, keeping me in place.

"Lauren . . ."

"Stop, Ty. You don't want me, I get it."

"Are you fucking kidding me?" His voice is deceptively calm. "Do you know why I turned you down yesterday, Lauren?"

I shake my head, my eyes wide and pinned to his.

"Because it would be a conflict of interest. I can't be your lawyer because I'm your friend, and I want to be a whole lot more than that."

If I thought I was stunned before, it's nothing compared to this. My jaw drops as he closes the gap between us. He doesn't touch me, but his face is mere inches from mine. His eyes are on my lips as I bite them and watch him, completely thrown by this turn of events.

"You have the most beautiful lips, Lo."

"What?" I whisper.

He takes a deep breath as he lays his thumb gently on my lower lip and pulls it from my teeth. I can't tear my gaze away from his mouth and I take a deep breath, inhaling the musky scent of him.

I've forgotten Jack and his threats, the lawsuit. Everything.

Ty clears his throat and backs away, watching me carefully. "Cary will remain your lawyer, but I want to know what the hell is going on, Lo. I can help."

I blink and continue to stare at him, completely dumbstruck. *He wants me?*

"And another thing, Lauren. You're not settling. Fuck Jack and his lawyer."

CHAPTER

TY

"Court is in recess until Monday," the judge announces as he leaves his bench. I smile reassuringly at my client, shake her hand, and grab my briefcase, ready to head out for the day.

It's been three days since Lauren's appearance in the office, and I haven't been able to reach her.

As I push through the courthouse doors, I pull my iPhone out of my pocket and dial her number, but it goes straight to voice mail.

Again.

I'm worried about her. She's not mine. She's not my girlfriend. She's not even my client, so I have no reason to be this worried.

She's a grown woman who can take care of herself.

But I'll be damned if I can stay away from her.

I bypass my office and head straight for home. I don't live far, so I typically walk to and from work. Summer is dragging on nicely, although a hint of the bite of fall is in the air. The tips of the maple trees lining the boulevards are beginning to yellow.

As I pause to pull my suit jacket off, a car honks as it passes. I wave and roll my sleeves, drape the jacket over my arm, and continue toward home.

Where is she?

If Lauren's ex-husband hadn't just threatened her the other day, I wouldn't be so worried.

But he did.

And she never did get around to telling me exactly what he threatened to do to her.

My first instinct is to drive to her house and check on her. What if she's fallen? Sick?

Or maybe she's just gone on vacation, you idiot.

I shake my head and cross the street leading to my house. The neighborhood is older, but the houses are well taken care of and nicely spaced. I approach my sister's home and smile when I see Jillian sitting on her porch, absorbed in a book.

"Hey!" I call out, and wander up her sidewalk.

She looks up in surprise and smiles when she sees me. "Hey, yourself. How was your day?"

I set my briefcase down and loosen my tie. "Long. You?"

"It was good." She gestures to the chair beside hers and I sink into it with a deep sigh. "Want some sun tea?"

"No thanks." I shake my head and push my hands through my hair, then glance down at the book in her hands. "What are you reading?"

Her eyes light up and she shows me the cover. "*A Spark of Passion* by Peyton Adams. It's the second in the series."

I raise my eyebrows and smirk at my little sister. Her dark hair is pulled back in her usual braid and she's in shorts and T-shirt, her new uniform since returning home from LA. She looks much younger than her twenty-eight years.

"You're reading porn now?"

"It's not porn," she sniffs. "Besides, they're gonna be made into movies, and I wanted to see what all the fuss is about."

"And?"

"They're so good. You should read them."

I laugh and hold my hands up as if in surrender. "No, that's okay. I'll leave the romance novels to you girls."

She shrugs and lays the book aside. "Your loss. You never know, you might learn something."

"I'll take your word for it. How are you settling in, brat?"

She smiles, reclines back in her chair, and lays her hands on her belly. "I love it. I'm so happy that Cara shacked up with Josh and let me live in her house."

"So kind of her," I reply sarcastically. Cara Donovan is Jill's best friend, and when Cara moved in with her fiancé, Josh King, she offered her house to Jill, who just moved back to town.

"So, what's up with you?" Jill asks, eyeing me carefully.

"Just a lot on my mind."

"No." She shakes her head and narrows her eyes. "You have that look you get when you have a woman on the brain."

"I don't get a look." I chuckle and cross my arms over my chest.

"Yeah, you do." She turns in her chair, facing me squarely. "Who is she?"

"I don't know what you're talking about."

"Don't lie to me, Tyler Sullivan." She shakes her finger at me, making me laugh. "Spill it."

"No woman." I shrug and watch a cat scurry across the road. "Just work stuff on my mind."

"Well, whoever she is"—Jillian ignores my sigh of exasperation—"she's not good enough for you."

"Of course she's not. She's imaginary because there is no woman."

"Okay." She smiles smugly. "Is it someone I know?"

"Oh my God!" I exclaim, and pull myself out of my chair. "I'm going home. I was going to take you out to dinner, but you fucked it up."

"Oh, don't be like that." She pouts, then lets out a belly laugh as I grab my briefcase and walk toward my own house just a few doors down. "You know you love me!"

"You annoy the hell out of me!" I respond over my shoulder with a laugh.

I jog up my porch steps and into my house, toss my keys on the coffee table and briefcase on the chair. I change into jeans and a T-shirt and saunter into the kitchen, open the fridge, and try to decide between leftover Chinese or pizza, then slam the door with a curse.

Unable to stop myself, I pull my phone out of my pocket and dial Lauren's number again.

Voice mail.

Fuck it.

I grab my keys and jog down to my car. I'm going to make sure she's okay. Her house is at the edge of town, so it only takes me about ten minutes to get there. I can't explain the pull I feel toward her. Hell, we grew up together, but it's only been in the past six months or so that I feel drawn to her in ways I can't put into words. My body yearns for her, I need to feel her, kiss her.

Protect her.

Jillian would laugh at me and accuse me of finding another broken woman to try to fix, but she's wrong. Lauren isn't broken, not by a long shot. The woman has more fight in her than just about anyone else I know.

Knowing her divorce was almost final, and seeing her around town, smiling shyly, trying to blend in—as if she ever could!—has had me in a permanent state of arousal since I saw her help a lost little boy find his mom on Main Street months ago. She's been in my head, and I can't seem to shake her loose.

Lo's Mercedes is parked out front when I pull into her drive, and I feel a surge of both relief and anger. Why the hell isn't she answering the phone?

I ring her bell and wait, my eyes moving over the house and property. There's no movement.

I ring the bell again and then pound on the door. She has to be here. Just as I'm about to back away and search the side of the house for another entrance, she pulls the door open, and the air leaves me.

Her big blue eyes are wide and glassy. Her gorgeous hair has been pulled on top of her head, but half of it has escaped out the back and is falling down her shoulders. She's in a skintight black tank top and yoga shorts. No shoes.

"Are you sick?" I ask, instantly concerned.

"What?" She scratches her head and frowns. "No, I'm working."

"Working?" I ask incredulously. I had no idea she worked. I assumed she lived off her trust fund.

"Yeah." She nods and steps back, giving me room to enter. I move past her, into her home. The house, the oldest one in town, is massive. The inside is lushly furnished in warm tones and inviting furniture. I look back to Lauren, to find her rubbing her forehead and blinking rapidly.

"Are you okay?"

"I'm fine."

"Are you sure you're not sick? When was the last time you had a shower, sweetheart?" I smile gently at her as she winces and her cheeks warm.

"I don't know." She scrunches up her nose in thought. "What day is it?"

"What day is it?" *What the hell is going on here?* "Lauren, what kind of work have you been doing?"

"I'm a writer," she responds immediately, then scowls. "Really, what day is it?"

"Friday," I say, and watch as her mind clears. It's fascinating. "How long have you been working?"

"Since Tuesday night."

"Since Tuesday?" I'm pissed off all over again. "Jesus, Lo, have you even eaten?"

"Why are you mad?" She scowls. "If you're gonna be mad, you can go be mad somewhere else. The story is flowing and I have work to do."

"You haven't been answering your phone, Lauren," I reply, consciously lowering my voice.

"I think it died two days ago."

"Two days ago?"

"Are you going to repeat everything I say?" She plants her hands on her narrow hips, pushing her perfect round breasts out.

Jesus, she's not wearing a bra.

She walks past me, through two open French doors into a large office. A wide dark desk dominates the room. Her laptop is sitting open with a Word file waiting for her to return to it. Yellow sticky notes cover every surface, and what looks like two-day-old pizza is sitting in a chair across the room. A plush chaise lounge sits under the big picture window, covered with pillows and a blanket, as though someone just woke from a nap.

"Is someone staying with you?"

"No, I sleep there for a few hours to recharge my batteries."

"Lauren, I had no idea you were a writer." I stand in her office and turn in a circle, taking it all in, and immediately feel overwhelming *pride*. "What do you write?"

She bites her lip and watches me, fidgeting. I can see the wheels turning in her head.

"What do you write, Lo?" I ask again, genuinely curious.

"I don't share this with anyone, Ty."

"Hey." I move to her and tuck a piece of her soft hair behind her ear, then pull her lower lip out from between her teeth. God, but I want to taste her. "I'm good at keeping secrets." I grin down at her. "Part of my job, remember?"

Her face relaxes into a soft smile, and my gut clenches. She's stunning. Jack is the biggest idiot on the face of the earth. If she were mine, I'd never let her go.

"I write books," she whispers.

"What kind of books?" I tilt my head to the side and watch her closely.

"Just books." She shrugs.

"Lauren." Her wary gaze finds mine. It looks like

she wants to tell me, but doesn't know if she should. "I promise, sweetheart, this is just between you and me. I'd love to know more about this."

She eyes me for a few more seconds, and just when I think she's going to refuse, she turns away from me and rummages around in her desk. When she returns, she shoves a dollar bill at me. "There, now you're my lawyer and you can't tell anyone."

I smirk down at her and shove the dollar back at her.

"I'm not going to tell anyone whether I'm your lawyer or not, Lauren." I take a deep breath. "You can trust me."

She walks to a closet in the corner, opens it, and pulls a book out of a box and returns to me, holding it out.

My eyes go wide. I'm stunned speechless.

I take the book from her and run my fingertips over the soft green cover.

"*A Spark of Passion*," I whisper, and raise my eyes to meet hers. "You're . . . ?"

"Peyton Adams." She holds her breath.

Jillian's words from not even an hour ago run through my mind. *They're going to be made into movies.*

"Lo, these books are huge."

She smiles proudly and nods and then frowns at me. "You read romance novels?"

"No." I laugh. "Jill is reading this book right now. Besides, they've been all over the news."

"Jill's reading it?" Lo smiles widely. "Does she like it?"

"Yeah, she loves it." I nod as Lo takes the book out of my hands and lays it on her desk. "So, you write those?"

"Yeah." She nods, her face somber again, and watches me carefully. "I can't tell anyone."

"Why?"

"Jack." It's a whisper, and it's all suddenly crystal clear.

I nod. "You're afraid that Jack would try to claim half and make your life a living hell."

Tears fill her eyes and she nods.

"Hey, come here." I pull her into my arms and hold her tightly against me, her head tucked under my chin. Her tall frame fits me perfectly. She takes a long, shuddering breath and leans into me, wraps her arms around my waist, and just holds on. I wonder how long it's been since someone just held her. "I won't tell anyone."

"I know," she murmurs.

"I'm so proud of you," I whisper into her hair.

She pulls back and looks up at me with surprised eyes. "Why?"

"This is amazing, Lauren. You're doing something you obviously love, and you're beyond successful at it. It's something to be proud of." My chest is full of pride and admiration for this amazing woman.

"Thank you." She smiles shyly.

"I have an idea." I pull away and take her hands

in mine, leading her out of the office. "You go have a shower and I'll make you dinner."

"Oh, you don't have to do that," she rushes to assure me, but I hold my hand up to stop her.

"I do." Despite her height, she looks so small standing here before me, still unsure and looking a little lost.

I need to take care of her.

"I'd love to spend the evening with you, learn more about your work, but I think I'd enjoy it more if you took a shower." I grin and can't help but tease her.

She blushes. "Smell that bad?"

"Not at all," I lie easily. "You smell like flowers on a spring day."

She laughs and heads for the stairs. "Okay, I'll take a break for a few hours. I can't guarantee what state the kitchen is in." She shrugs. "Hazard of the job."

"I'll muddle my way through." I wave her off and watch her long legs climb the stairs. "Take your time, sweetheart."

Her gaze lowers to mine in surprise at the term of endearment and my heart squeezes. Does no one show her kindness? Support?

Love?

"Thank you," she whispers, and disappears upstairs.

I grin as I head for her kitchen, pulling my phone out as I go.

I'm gonna owe Jill a favor.

CHAPTER

LAUREN

I stand under the water longer than I probably should, but damn, it feels so good. It's mortifying that it took Ty coming to my door to remind me that I haven't showered, or eaten really, in days.

It happens all the time when the words are flowing. I lose all sense of time as I fall into the rhythm of the story. Not to mention, it was a welcome reprieve this week, after the Jack mess on Monday.

And now Ty is in my house, looking all sexy in his Metallica T-shirt and faded blue jeans, making me dinner.

I have no idea the last time someone made me dinner.

After rinsing my hair for the third time, I step out of the shower and dry my body quickly, then pull on clean clothes and quickly dry my hair, brushing it briskly. Finally, I brush on a coat of mascara and smooth some clear gloss on my lips, then briefly stop before the mirror to check out the results.

Yep, major improvement.

At least I'm clean.

I cringe as I think of what I must have looked like when I answered the door, and I descend the stairs, finding Ty in the kitchen.

"I believe I smell better," I announce, catching his attention. He smiles at me and my feet pause as hot need sets up residence in my belly. Ty saunters to me, his eyes pinned to my own, and without breaking his stride, he pulls me easily into his arms for a big hug, rocking me back and forth. He buries his nose in my hair and takes a long, deep breath as his big hands glide over my back, from my shoulders to my hips. My nipples instantly pucker against him, and I thank the Lord above that I changed into a looser-fitting shirt.

"Mmm, you smell fantastic," he murmurs. "Are you hungry?"

"I might be dying of starvation," I mutter into his chest, earning a chuckle from him, and I calm. He makes me nervous, but in a good way. I'm happy he's here.

"It's a good thing we have provisions then. Come on, the table is set." He pulls away, but keeps my hand in his, linking our fingers, and leads me to the dining room.

The man seems to like to touch me.

I'm not complaining.

I can't help but admire the tattoos on his arm, the colors and lines that decorate his skin. I'd love to trace them with my tongue.

Seriously? He's just being nice!

He guides me into the dining room and I gasp. "Did I take a two-hour shower?"

"No." He chuckles and holds a chair out for me.

"How did you do all of this?" I gaze about the room. The long, black table seats ten. The large chandelier over the center of the table is lit, but on low. Ty found my candles and lit three of them at one end of the table. He set two places, and each is filled with delicious-looking pasta, salad, and bread.

But what shocks the hell out of me is the large bouquet of orange calla lilies in the center of the table.

I look at him in wonder. He chuckles again and kisses the top of my head before taking his own seat.

"The Italian restaurant delivers now?" I ask, recognizing my favorite bread.

"No." He winces. "I wanted to cook, but your cupboards are bare and I didn't have time to shop. I called in the order and Jill delivered."

"Jill knows you're here?" I ask, wide-eyed.

"Is that a problem?" he asks with a raised brow.

"No." I shake my head and take a bite of penne with red sauce. "I'm just . . . surprised."

"She dropped it off and tried to grill me with questions, but I cut her off at the pass." He winks at me and takes a bite of bread and then lifts a bottle of pinot noir. "Wine?"

"I shouldn't." I wrinkle my nose. "I have to go back to work later."

"One glass?" He grins, holding the bottle over my glass, and I cave.

"One glass."

"So, how long have you been writing?"

"My whole life." I sip my wine. "But I've been published for about eighteen months."

"That's fast."

"That's an understatement." I laugh and stab a tomato with my fork. "I feel like I'm caught in a hurricane. But it's been fantastic too."

"Why didn't you publish sooner?"

"I needed something after Mom and Dad passed and Jack left. So I absorbed myself in writing. It occupied my brain so I wasn't always so sad and lonely." I scowl.

"What?"

"That sounded pathetic."

"No, it didn't. I get it." He lays his hand over mine and squeezes reassuringly before returning to his food. "You've clearly found your calling. You're in high demand."

"It still doesn't seem real." He raises an eyebrow. "If you'd have asked me two years ago if I ever thought I'd sell tens of millions of books and have those books optioned for a blockbuster movie, I'd have had the guys with the straitjackets come get you."

He throws his head back and laughs, then pushes his empty plate away and leans his elbows on the table as he sips his wine, watching me with the look of a man who is confident in his own skin and enjoys watching the woman he's with.

I wish I had his confidence.

"Are you finished?"

"Oh my God, I'm so full." I push the plate away and lean back in the chair. "It was delicious. Thank you."

"You're welcome. Come on, let's take the wine and go sit on the couch." He rises, grabs the bottle and his glass, and motions for me to follow him. I can't help but notice how spectacular his ass looks in those jeans.

I flip the switch on the gas fireplace in the corner of the family room off the kitchen, then settle into one end of a long, soft sofa, pulling my bare feet up under me. Ty sits a few feet away, close enough to touch me. He sits facing me, one leg pulled up, and leans his elbow on the back of the couch, his head resting in his hand, and watches me with happy gray eyes.

"Thanks for coming by," I murmur softly, and sip my wine.

"Please don't let your phone go dead again. I'll worry." He exhales deeply, watching me for my response.

"I'll plug it in." I lean my head against the couch. Ty refills my wineglass, earning a mock glare from me. "I guess I won't be working any more tonight."

"Something tells me you could use a good night's sleep." He fills his own glass before setting the bottle on the floor.

"Tell me something," I begin, my confidence bolstered by the alcohol.

"Anything." He smiles.

"What do you have up your sleeve?"

"What are you talking about?" He frowns.

I shrug and look down into my glass. "Why are you being so nice to me, Ty? People don't do things like this just for the hell of it."

He pauses as his narrowed gaze travels over my face, not even bothering to pretend that he doesn't know what I'm talking about. He looks angry for a moment and rubs his fingers over his lips in agitation, and I can't help but wonder what I did wrong.

"I didn't mean to offend you. . . ."

"You didn't offend me, Lo. Is it so unbelievable that I just wanted to make sure you're okay and spend some time with you?"

"But why?" I ask again, confused. "What do you want from me?"

He stills, looking lost. "I don't want anything."

"Everyone wants something," I reply dryly. "Trust me."

He continues to watch me like I'm some kind of science experiment. "Lauren, the only thing I want from you is *you*."

My jaw drops. "Excuse me?"

He shakes his head and chuckles before taking

a sip of his wine. "I've been attracted to you for a while now, Lo."

"So you want to fuck me," I surmise with disgust. "We could have avoided this whole seduction scene, Ty. Thanks but no thanks." I move to rise, but he catches my arm, pulling me back to my ass.

"What the fuck?" He's pissed. "This wasn't a fucking seduction scene, it was me doing something nice for someone I like. And I didn't say I wanted to *fuck you*, although—don't get me wrong—I do. I want to get to know you, Lauren."

"You want to date me?" I squeak.

"I believe that's what I've been saying." He's completely exasperated, and I can't help but smile at him.

"Why now? Is it because of the books?" My heart sinks at the prospect that he's the first person in my life that I've confided in about the books and now he's just interested because of my newfound success, but it makes sense.

I've never had anyone in my life that was here without wanting something from me.

He scowls again and replies coldly, "I came here before I had any idea about your books, and now you're pissing me off. Don't ever insult either of us like that again."

I swallow hard and cringe. "Why now?" I whisper.

"It wouldn't have been right to approach you before, Lo. You had lost your parents and your marriage. You were sad, and hitting on married women just isn't my style."

I hadn't realized that I looked so sad on the outside, and that makes me just a little bit more self-conscious.

"To be honest, I just don't want to stay away anymore." My eyes find his again and he offers me a half grin. "I would very much enjoy getting to know you better, Lauren. If that's okay with you?"

I bite my lip and watch his finger glide around the rim of his glass.

"Lauren," he whispers.

"I'd like that," I reply softly.

He watches me lazily, sipping his drink, his temper calming. Finally, he sets his wine aside and takes my hand in his once again.

"You hold my hand a lot."

"You have beautiful hands. Does it bother you?"

"No, it doesn't bother me."

"Lo?" he whispers.

"Yeah?"

"I want to kiss you so bad it hurts."

I gasp and watch him with wide eyes as he reaches out and tucks my hair behind my ear, then gently runs his finger down my cheek. The air between us is full of anticipation.

"What's stopping you?"

I bite my lip, waiting for his response. He pulls my lip free with his thumb and brushes it along the tender flesh. Finally, he leans in, moving exquisitely slowly. He cups my cheek in his hand and lowers his face to mine. His lips nibble at the side of my mouth, making my eyes flutter closed as my hand glides tentatively up his arm, over his shoulder, and into his thick, black hair.

He's tender, gentle, as his lips sweep over my own to the other corner to tease and tempt some more.

I sigh as he brushes his nose over the tip of my own, then he sinks into me, his lips moving over me in the sweetest dance I've ever experienced. His tongue brushes over my lips, then slips inside my mouth, not to plunder but to simply tease and slide across my own.

All too soon, he backs away. I open my eyes to find his gray ones on fire. We're both breathing hard, and in this moment, I want nothing more than for him to strip me bare and take me right here on the couch.

But instead, he pulls me into his arms and holds me close, kissing my hair. "You taste better than I imagined." His hand caresses my back as he supports me against him, and we sit here, watching the fire.

"So do you," I reply softly.

His hand stills for a moment, then resumes its journey across my back.

"You're not staying the night," I inform him sternly.

"No, but I'll stay until you fall asleep."

I lean back to look at him, pulling my fingertips down his cheek. "You don't have to do that."

He pulls my fingers to his lips and kisses each one in turn. "It's my pleasure, sweetheart."

He tucks me under his chin, and we sit in silence. I don't want to fall asleep. I want to stay here in his arms, fully aware of him holding me, for as long as possible.

I'm not convinced this isn't a dream brought on by a caffeine crash and too much work.

Ty continues to caress my back and plant small kisses on my head until the warmth of the fire and wine lull me into a deep sleep.

I am not a morning person. Early-morning swim training during high school and college just about killed me. I'm a firm believer that nothing should ever happen before 9:00 a.m.

Ever.

I moan as I turn onto my back and realize that I'm on the couch, covered in the brown blanket from my office. I grin, brush my hair off my face, and stare sleepily at the ceiling, remembering my evening with Ty.

It was . . . surprising.

I can't believe I told him about the books. I haven't told anyone I know in fear of it getting back to Jack, giving him a whole new set of reasons to freak out and come after me for more money. Only my agent, publisher, and Cary know about my success as an author.

I can't explain why it was so easy to confide in Ty, except that I was still deep in a writing fog and he exudes safety. Confidence.

I naturally trust him, and that alone is enough to put me on edge, because trust isn't something I've ever given easily.

I sit up and toss the blanket aside, finding a note on the nearby ottoman.

Lo,

I hope you slept well. Thank you for letting me stay. Next time, you'll be waking up in my arms rather than to a damn note.

Ty

I fold the note with a grin and then make my way upstairs to pull on some jeans and a long-sleeved shirt, along with a green scarf to ward off the early-fall chill. If I'm going to be productive today at all—and I need to be with a deadline looming in just three weeks—I will need coffee.

The kind with chocolate and sugar, all in a really, really tall cup.

A smile hovers on my lips as I drive to the café in the heart of downtown. Drips & Sips is an early-morning hot spot in Cunningham Falls. Business-people stop in for pastries and drinks on their way to work, and others hold meetings or just pop in to sit and read the newspaper while they enjoy their coffee.

Things are in full swing when I saunter inside to the smell of freshly baked muffins and coffee. Just the scent of the place energizes me.

"Hey, Lauren." Cara Donovan is smiling widely as she joins me in line.

"Hey, Cara. How are you?" I grin back at her, but keep my walls firmly in place. Cara is a nice girl, but we don't exactly run in the same circles.

"I'm good. I thought I'd grab coffee before heading to the grocery store." Cara is a beautiful woman. She's much shorter than me, with pretty blond hair and hazel eyes. She and I grew up together. "Want to join me?" she asks, surprising me.

"Oh, I don't want to intrude," I murmur.

"Trust me, I'd love some company." Cara laughs as we approach the barista to order our drinks. "Now that I'm living with all those guys out at the ranch, I welcome girl talk whenever I can get it."

"How are things going out there?" I ask after we gather our drinks and pastries and make our way to an empty table by the window. Cara moved out to the Lazy K Ranch with Josh roughly two months ago.

"Good." She takes a bite of her huckleberry scone and sighs in happiness. "How are you?"

"I'm fine." I hesitate, then decide to forge ahead. "Cara, I'd like to clear the air."

"About what?" she asks, surprised.

"Well, I just want you to know that I'm sorry for all the hell Misty put you through when you were first dating Josh." I frown as I fiddle with my fork, not meeting Cara's gaze. "You didn't deserve that."

"Lauren, you have absolutely nothing to apologize for." Cara rests her hand on my arm. "Misty's a bitch. It doesn't make you one."

I shake my head in frustration. "Well, she's certainly not my friend anymore."

"Why was she your friend in the first place?" Cara takes a sip of her coffee.

"She really wasn't. She and Sunny work together, and Sunny's my cousin, so it's always felt natural to hang out with her." I shrug, not sure how to explain my poor choice in friends further.

"Well, I don't mean any offense, but Sunny is a bitch too."

I laugh, relaxing a bit as Cara and I share breakfast and girl talk. I don't remember the last time I felt this comfortable.

"Yeah, she is. I've cut some very toxic people out of my life recently." I can tell that Cara wants to ask me more, but she doesn't pry, and I don't offer any more of an explanation.

"I also have a question," I add.

"Shoot."

"I know you and Jill Sullivan are supergood friends, and I was wondering if you know her brother, Ty, well?"

Her eyes widen and she offers me a small smile. "I do."

"Do you know if he has a girlfriend?" I ask in a whisper, not willing to look her in the eye. *God, this is mortifying.*

"No, he doesn't." She tilts her head as she watches

me. "Jill called me last night, said she delivered dinner and flowers to your place at Ty's request."

I flush scarlet and stuff a bite of my scone in my mouth, not even tasting it.

"Trust me, if Ty had a girlfriend, he wouldn't have done all of that."

"He's been very nice to me this week," I murmur. "I don't know why."

"What do you mean?"

"I don't know why he's being so nice to me."

"Well, I think it's pretty obvious that he must like you."

It makes perfect sense when she says it. "I'm not used to receiving kindness with no strings attached." I clear my throat and chuckle ruefully. "That sounded so . . ."

"Horrible. I think you should just enjoy someone doing nice things for you, Lauren."

"Call me Lo," I say with a small smile.

Cara meets my smile with a wide one of her own. "Ty doesn't play games. He's not an asshole. Enjoy him."

I nod as I take a sip of my coffee. "Okay."

"Also, I'm going to give you my number so you can text me all the dirt that happens from here on out, and Jill and I can torture him mercilessly."

I laugh and shake my head. "I'll take your number, but can't confirm that you'll get the dirt."

"Oh, come on, throw us a bone once in a while." Cara winks. "It's our job to make his life a living hell."

"You love him," I observe quietly.

"He's the closest thing to a brother I've ever had. So, yeah, I love him. And it goes without saying that if you break his heart, Jill and I will have to kill you."

"Of course," I murmur. "But I have a feeling it's *my* heart that's in danger of being hurt."

CHAPTER

Four

"So, what are your plans today?" Cara asks as we exit the café.

"I was thinking about going home and getting to work." I take a deep breath of the crisp early-fall air. "But the sunshine is so nice, I might take a walk through town first."

"Work? What kind of work?"

Shit. What is up with my blabbermouth these days? "Oh, it's really more of a hobby." I wave her off, and just as she opens her mouth to ask more questions, her phone starts ringing. *Saved by the bell!*

"Oh, this is Josh! I better take it. Have a great day, and thanks for the chat." She smiles warmly and waves as she takes her call and walks toward her car. "Hey, babe."

I wave after her and set off on foot down the sidewalk. I've always liked Cara. She's a sweet girl, and maybe she's someone I could eventually be friends with.

It's a beautiful, sunny day on this Saturday morning. We are well into September, yet summer seems to be hanging on by the skin of its teeth, blessing us with chilly mornings, but warm days. I wander past the many gift shops, clothing stores, and restaurants that line Main Street, walking toward the residential side of town. Mrs. Blakely is sweeping the sidewalk in front of her little deli and offers me a wave as I walk past.

My phone vibrates in my pocket and I grin when I read the display.

"Hey, Em."

Emily Valentine is my closest friend. A fellow author, she lives on the other side of the country in Virginia, but we speak almost daily. We met at the beginning of our publishing journeys, and we spend many hours brainstorming new ideas for our stories as well as just talking about books, her kids, and my crazy ex-husband.

"Hey, girl. What are you up to?"

"I'm walking," I smile.

"Walking? Walking where?"

"Just going for a walk through town. It's a nice day."

"Huh." She's clearly stumped. "That's new. No swim today?"

"I skipped the pool this morning."

"Okay, hold up. Who the hell are you and what have you done with Lauren?"

I laugh at the sarcasm in her voice as I cross the street. "I thought I'd switch things up a bit today."

"You sound happy this morning." I hear her shuffling papers.

"I feel happy."

"Good. I'd feel happy too if these characters weren't pissing me off."

"What's up?" I frown.

"I hate it when I plan out exactly what I want to happen in the story and then the damn characters decide to be assholes and throw a wrench in it."

"Uh, Emily, you do know that *you* control *them*, right?" I grin widely.

"Don't accuse me of being mentally unstable, Lo. It doesn't become you."

For the next half hour we talk about the characters in Emily's story, brainstorming and working through the kinks.

"Oh, I like this so much better," Emily says excitedly. "Thank you so much."

"That's what we do."

"So, what's up with you? Who's the guy?" she asks almost casually.

"I can't just go for a walk and be in a good mood?"

"You're not just happy, you're chipper, and I don't think I've ever heard you say you were going for a walk in the time I've known you. Spill."

"See, this is why you write romance novels. You see a love story everywhere." My voice is dry, but she laughs.

"No, we write *erotic* romance, Lo. We see a love story and the potential for lots of sex everywhere. So tell me all about it and use all the dirty words."

"Oh my God, you're so funny!" I laugh loudly as I wave at Mr. Hart, who is mowing his lawn. "Okay, so there might be a guy."

"Is there might-be sex?" she asks excitedly.

"Not yet. Maybe eventually."

"Jesus, don't hold out for too long. Trust me, life's too short for that."

"You're a perv."

"You've read my books, Lauren. You already knew this."

I laugh again, enjoying my friend. "So, he's a guy that I've known most of my life. Grew up here in the same town as me."

She cuts to the chase. "Is he hot?"

"Girl, you have no idea."

"Pictures. I need pictures. Naked ones."

"I'll see what I can do." We both laugh. "He's a nice guy, which automatically makes me wonder when the other shoe will drop and his asshole side will shine through."

"God, you're so cynical. Maybe he's just a nice guy."

"Yeah, the last time I believed I'd met 'just a nice guy' I ended up divorced with a first-class jerk on my hands," I reply sarcastically. My breath is coming a little faster now, but my legs are loose and the exercise feels fantastic.

"There are kind people out there, Lauren. Does this guy have a reputation for being an ass? Is the town littered with broken hearts thanks to this person?"

"No." I chuckle as my stomach loosens. "I've never heard anything like that about him. And you could be right. After all, I met you."

"You did, but I'm not gonna have sex with you." A smile is in her voice.

"You're no fun," I tease.

"Have you been on a date with him yet?"

"No, but he said he's interested. We'll see. It might fizzle out." I shrug, although she can't see me, and turn down another long residential block. The sound of lawn mowers and children playing fills the air.

"Keep me posted." Emily pulls the phone away from her ear and speaks to her little one. "I have to go make lunch. Jamie's hungry."

"Okay, have a good day. I'm sure I'll talk to you tomorrow."

We hang up and I look around, realizing I'm walking down Ty's block. I didn't realize my feet were carrying me here. Maybe it was subconscious, since I was talking about him?

Or maybe I just want to see him.

He's probably not home.

As I approach his house, I see his Jeep parked in the drive, the hood up, and a tight, jean-clad ass bent over the side.

Okay, he's definitely home.

I tentatively wander around the other side of the Jeep and lean against the side, looking at the engine. He hasn't noticed that I'm here yet, and I'm not even sure how he'll react to seeing me here, but I can't seem to stay away. His dark head is bent low, his arms buried in the engine, tinkering with something. His arms are bare, as he's pulled off his T-shirt, which is draped over the windshield. A thin sheen of sweat covers his shoulders and back, and his entire sleeve tattoo, which runs from just above his wrist all the way up to the top of his right shoulder, is on full display, making my girlie parts all tingle and come to life.

Holy Jesus, Mary, and Joseph.

He's so fucking toned it's crazy. Jeez, his muscles bunch and stretch as he pulls on the wrench in his hand.

"Come on, you motherfucker," he mutters. I have to bite my lips to keep from laughing out loud.

"So, what seems to be the problem?" I finally ask when he doesn't notice me, keeping my eyes trained on the engine when his head whips up to look at me. I slowly lift my eyes to his and grin.

"I didn't hear your car," he murmurs with a smile.

"I walked." I shrug and look back down into the bowels of his Jeep. "What's wrong with your car?"

"You walked from your house?" he asks incredulously.

"No." I shake my head and chuckle. "From Sips. I had coffee with Cara this morning."

He stands up straight and leans his palms on the side of the Jeep, watching me. My eyes immediately fall to one drop of sweat slowly making its way down his hard chest.

"You had coffee with Cara?" He smiles.

"Yeah." I shrug shyly. "I'm sorry to just stop by like this. I was out for a walk and just sort of found myself here." I feel my cheeks heat and I back away, but he shakes his head and smiles widely.

"I'm glad you came by." He raises his brows as I continue to stare.

I shake my head and raise my eyes to his, then burst out laughing.

"Why are you laughing?" he asks with a wide grin.

"Because I don't think I've ever seen you without a shirt. I didn't realize the tats went all the way up your arm. Who would have thought that under it all you're just a bad boy?"

His eyes flash with heat as he narrows them on my face, watching me. He pulls a rag out of his back pocket and begins wiping off his hands, but his gray eyes stay on mine. Did I offend him?

"I'm not such a bad boy. Looks can be deceiving, Lauren." He smirks as he lowers the hood on his Jeep. "But from the look of you right now, you don't seem to mind the tats."

"I don't mind." I shrug nonchalantly and try to

ignore the way my heart picks up speed as he slowly saunters around the hood of the vehicle.

"Do you have any tats?"

"Yeah."

His eyes widen in surprise and then rake over me from head to toe.

"Where?"

I grin, enjoying this flirtatious banter. "Here and there."

"I have ways of making people talk, you know."

"Bright lights and rubber hoses?" I ask with a raised brow.

He tosses his head back and laughs, an all-out belly laugh. "I'm not a cop," he smirks.

"You might get to see them. Someday."

He closes the gap between us and kisses me gently on the forehead, not touching me anywhere else.

"I hope someday comes sooner rather than later," he whispers before pulling back and smiling softly down at me. "I would hug you, but I'm dirty."

I wave him off, as if it's no biggie, although I don't mind so much that he's a bit dirty and sweaty. "What were you doing?" I gesture to the car.

"Changing the oil."

"There are places you can go," I inform him with a perfectly straight face, "where you pull into this big garage, and then you leave your car and go into this small room with five-year-old magazines and stale coffee, and the people there will change your oil for you."

"Or, smart-ass, I can do it myself in my own driveway."

"Suit yourself." I shrug.

"Did you sleep okay on the couch?" he asks, changing the subject.

"Yeah, actually, I did. But I could always sleep just about anywhere."

"Hence the chaise in your office." He chuckles.

I nod and stuff my hands in my pockets. "I'm sorry that I interrupted your morning. I was just out for a walk and found myself here."

"I'm glad you did." He scratches his stomach, and my eyes follow the movement. His abs are just delicious. For being so dark haired, he has little hair on his chest and stomach, but a light trail of hair falls from his navel and disappears into his jeans. He's also sporting a V in the muscles on his hips that the heroes in my novels would covet.

"Lo?" he asks with a wide grin.

"Yeah?" I drag my eyes up to his again.

"I lost you for a second."

I blink rapidly and feel heat fill my cheeks. *Jesus, get a grip! You've seen hot men before, Lauren.* "Sorry, my mind wandered."

"I was asking you if you have plans on Thursday night."

I pull my phone out of my pocket and consult the calendar. "Nope."

"I'd like to take you to the charity gala with me." He reaches over the Jeep and grabs his T-shirt and quickly pulls it over his head. Part of me is disappointed that he's hiding all that hotness, but I also breathe a sigh of relief.

It's hard to think when there's so much to stare at.

"It's this Thursday?"

"Yes. I can pick you up at six."

Do I have anything to wear? My mind quickly takes a mental inventory of my closet.

"If you'd rather not, it's okay." He's clearly taken aback by my silence. "Jack will probably be there too."

"This is a small town. I will no doubt run into Jack from time to time. I was just thinking if I have anything to wear," I reply ruefully. "A girl usually needs a bit more lead time."

"I know, I'm sorry. The tickets fell into my lap and I'd really like for you to join me."

"I'd love to go." I realize that I mean it and grin. "I'll figure out the dress."

"Lauren, you could show up in a burlap sack and still be the most beautiful woman there."

"You are such a charmer." I laugh and then frown, remembering that Jack used to say the same things in the beginning.

"Don't," Ty whispers.

"Don't what?"

"Don't compare me to him. The difference is, I mean what I say, Lo."

I scowl at him, wondering how he can read my mind.

"So, six o'clock on Thursday," he confirms.

"I'll be ready. I can just meet you there if it's easier."

"This will be a date, sweetheart. I will pick you up."

Butterflies take flight in my stomach and I can't help the cheesy grin that spreads across my face. "Okay." I close the gap between us and rise on my toes to kiss Ty's cheek. "Thank you for inviting me."

He growls and reaches for me, wraps his arms around my waist, and pulls me to him in a bone-melting kiss. His hands spread over my back and hold me against him while his mouth sinks over mine, tasting and teasing, nibbling my lips. I brace my hands on his shoulders as I inhale deeply. He smells of sweat and oil, but he also still smells like Ty, and damn if it's not the best smell in the world.

Just as I soften against him, he pulls back, still holding me close, and leans his forehead against mine. "I'm sorry, I smell," he whispers.

"Nah." I smile. "You smell like flowers on a spring day."

He chuckles and plants his lips on my forehead, takes a deep breath, then backs away from me.

"I should go get my car and get to work." I bite my lip and watch him as I back down his driveway. "I'll see you on Thursday."

"Do you have plans tonight?" he asks to my surprise.

"I'm under deadline," I reply regretfully. "I have to

write half of this book in three weeks. That's why I was so deep in the writing cave this week."

"Writing cave?" He laughs. "Is that anything like the Batcave?"

I shrug and smirk. "Maybe."

"You have to eat sometime. And I owe you a home-cooked meal."

"You don't owe me anything," I reply honestly. "But if you showed up, I wouldn't turn you away." *Did that just come out of my mouth? What is it about this man that makes me say things that are so out of the ordinary for me?*

"I'll remember that. Hey, what did you and Cara talk about this morning?"

I just laugh and wave at him as I set off down the block back toward downtown. "Have a good day!"

"I'll find out sooner or later!" he calls after me.

The sound of his laugh follows me down the block, and I smile in anticipation. I wonder, will he show up for dinner tonight?

He doesn't show up that night, but at around seven thirty, my phone pings with a text, pulling me out of my writing rhythm and alerting me that it's dark outside and the only light in the room is from my computer screen.

Ty: **I'm sorry, can't make it over tonight. Jill is having a crisis. Don't lose yourself in the cave and forget to eat!**

I smile widely and then reply, **No problem. Hope Jill's okay. Have a good night.**

I stand and stretch, reaching for the ceiling, then bend over and touch my toes before walking to the doorway and flipping the light switch.

Just a few moments later, my phone pings again.

Ty: **You're not going to eat, are you?**

I laugh and then respond, **I will eat.**

There's no response and I lose myself back into the story. It's been flowing well ever since I returned home earlier today. The walk back was nice. It cleared my head, and I've decided to follow Cara's and Emily's advice and give Ty the benefit of the doubt. He's a nice guy.

And he's handsome.

I shake my head and settle back in my chair, re-reading the last paragraph and picking up where I left off, losing myself in my characters and their world.

Suddenly, my doorbell rings. I frown as I pad across the floor. Did Ty change his mind?

I open the door with a wide smile, but instead of Ty, I find a tall, young boy standing on my porch holding a large pizza box.

"Hi, Miz Cunningham."

"Hi, Jordan. I didn't order a pizza tonight."

He shifts on his feet. "I know, but Mr. Sullivan called it in and asked us to deliver it to you. He said to send you whatever your favorite is."

Oh my. "Oh, okay. Thanks, Jordan."

He nods and skips down to his beat-up Toyota as I set the alarm and walk back into the office. The pizza smells heavenly. I didn't realize how hungry I was.

When I reach my desk, my phone pings.

Ty: **Did dinner arrive?**

Rather than answer, I call his number and chew on my bottom lip while it rings.

"Hey." His voice is strong yet tender.

"Thank you."

"I don't want you to waste away. You need to eat." I hear the smile in his voice. "And since I couldn't be there, this is the next best thing."

"It's very thoughtful, Ty."

"Hold on," he mutters, then pulls the phone away from his mouth but doesn't cover the receiver, allowing me to hear everything that's happening. "No, I'm not going to tell you who I'm talking to. Shut up, I'll be right there."

He brings the phone back to his mouth and sighs in exasperation. "I have a sister for sale."

"I heard that!" Jill yells in the background.

"Good!" he replies. "Sorry."

"It's fine." I chuckle. "I'll let you go. I have a delicious-smelling pizza to dig into."

"Enjoy it. I'll talk to you tomorrow."

My eyebrows climb into my hairline in surprise. "You will?"

"Yes, Lauren, I will. Sorry about tonight. Jill had car trouble."

"It's fine, Ty. Have a good night."

"Good night."

He hangs up and I reach for the pizza box.

Hawaiian with olives.

A girl could get used to this.

CHAPTER

Five

TY

"You canceled on a date to come help me change my tire?" Jill asks with surprise.

"You're my sister. Of course I did. Besides, we didn't really have a date. There were no concrete plans." I pocket my phone and drop into Jill's couch with a sigh.

"So, how long have you been seeing Lauren?" She grins smugly.

"It's new." I glare over at her. "I suppose Cara called you."

"Of course she did." She waves me off and rolls her eyes. "I like her."

"You do?" I'm surprised.

"Yeah. I don't know her very well, but she seems nice." Jill narrows her eyes and focuses on something over my shoulder.

"You and Cara always said that you hated that group of girls."

"Oh, she hung out with bitches, that's for sure."

"But how do you really feel?" I ask sarcastically.

"I guess we can't judge her for her inability to choose better friends. Besides"—Jill smiles—"I hear that events from this past summer made her take stock of the people in her life and get rid of the toxic ones. Good for her."

I scowl and cross my arms. "Just what did she say to Cara?"

"Oh, nothing bad. I wish I'd been there." Jill's blue eyes go wide, then she claps her hands in excitement. "Maybe Cara and I can take her out for girls' night!"

"Slow down there, cruise director."

"It would be fun."

"Actually," I reply as I think about it, "you're right. You should ask her."

"Okay." Jill nods, as though it's been decided. "I will. So, what else is on your mind?"

"I invited her to the charity thing for the athletic department at the high school on Thursday."

"Did she say yes?"

"Yeah, but it's short notice, and she's really busy. I was thinking about maybe buying her a dress."

Jill just sits in her chair and blinks at me, her face completely sober.

"What?" I ask irritably.

"You really like her," she murmurs.

I nod and stand to pace around the room. "I do."

"Well, do you know her size?"

"Uh . . . she's slim. How am I supposed to know her size?" I stop and prop my hands on my hips.

"Ugh, men. Okay, here's what we're going to do. I will call Louise Sumners and ask her to let us into her shop tomorrow so we can look around. I think Lo shops there. Most of us do." Jill shrugs and pulls on her lip as she thinks. "We'll find something. I think it's kind of romantic that you want to buy her a dress."

"You do?"

"Yeah. I never would have guessed you have it in you."

"I can be romantic," I grumble.

God, this was a stupid idea.

What if she thinks I'm being a controlling bastard and throws me out?

I take a deep breath and then ring her doorbell. I can hear loud, booming music inside, surprising me.

She listens to loud rock music while she writes? How can she think with that much noise?

Knowing she most likely can't hear the doorbell over the music, I walk around the house to the family-room area, which has French doors that open onto a wide patio. The scene before me surprises the hell out of me.

Lo is painting the walls of the family room while shaking her amazing ass, dancing about the space in time with the music.

She's so fucking gorgeous.

Her auburn hair is pulled back into a ponytail and she's wearing another of those tight black T-shirts, showing off her perfect tits, and black yoga shorts.

Jesus, her legs go on for miles.

When she turns around to load her paint roller with more paint, she squeals when she sees me, then blushes furiously as she lays the roller in the paint and comes to open the door.

"Hey!" she yells over the music.

"Hey, yourself," I shout back.

She grins and lowers the volume on the sound system.

"I tried the doorbell," I inform her dryly.

"Sorry, I couldn't hear you."

"Shocker." I laugh and hold up the white garment bag and the shoebox in my hands. "I come bearing gifts."

Her mouth forms a little O in surprise. "It's not my birthday."

"I know you're under deadline, and I didn't want you to worry about what to wear on Thursday, so I took the liberty . . ." My voice fades in uncertainty.

She just stares at me, lost, and to my horror tears fill her eyes.

"I'm sorry, it was a bad idea. You probably want to buy your own dress."

"Oh my gosh, no." She chuckles and blinks her eyes furiously as she takes the dress and shoes from me. "Thank you so much for this."

"You're welcome. What are you doing anyway?" I turn in a circle and take in the chaos.

"Painting."

"You haven't taped anything off, Lo. And you don't have anything covering the floor."

She blushes furiously. "I know. I bought all the stuff"—she gestures to the bags of supplies in the corner—"but it was an impulse decision and I didn't want to take the time to tape and stuff. That's not the fun part."

I laugh and shake my head at her. "You go put that stuff away. I'll be here."

She smiles softly, then turns on her bare heel and hurries up the stairs, yelling, "Thank you!"

I dig into the supply bags and pull out a drop cloth, brushes, and tape and set to work, running the tape along the baseboards, molding, and fireplace. Just as I spread the drop cloth on the floor, Lo returns to the room.

"What are you doing?"

"Well, if we're going to do this, we're going to do it right."

"You're helping?"

"Like I would just leave you here to do this alone? Besides"—I brush my finger down her soft cheek, over a spot of mocha-colored paint—"I think you need to be supervised."

"Okay, you're recruited." She giggles and my gut clenches.

We dig in, dipping our rollers in the tray of paint, then smoothing it over the walls. "Why are you painting and not writing?"

She scrunches up her nose and turns the music back on, the volume low. "Because I got stuck. The characters are pissing me off, and Emily isn't around to talk."

"Who's Emily?" I reload my roller.

"She's an author and a good friend of mine. We usually brainstorm together, but she had to go to some family thing today, so I didn't have anyone to talk it out with. Swimming didn't help." She sighs and drops her roller to her side, tilts her head, and stares blankly at the wall, as if in deep thought. Then she turns to me and, as calm as can be, raises her roller and coats my left arm in paint.

"Did you just *paint me*?" I ask with a raised brow.

She nods and grins, then starts singing with the song and shaking her hips while painting her wall.

She's adorable. "I'm going to get you back for that."

"I figured." She shrugs as if it's of no consequence.

"So, tell me about your characters. I'm no Emily, but maybe I can help."

She shoots me a surprised glance and bites her lip in concentration. "Well, they're in the middle of a fight right now."

"What are they fighting over?"

"Another woman." She rolls her eyes and shakes her head, as though she's gossiping about real people. "It's ridiculous. He's not cheating on her. He's completely gone over her, and she *knows* that, but she has so much baggage from her past that it's difficult for her to trust." Lo picks up more paint on her roller and turns back to the wall.

"Who is the other woman?"

"His ex-wife." She grimaces. "The ex has photos and videos of her having sex with the hero. Unbeknownst to the heroine, those were all taken years and years ago when they were still married, but the bitch is making it look like it's all happened recently."

"She's a gem," I comment lightly.

"Oh, I hate her. Her name is Misty." Lo throws her head back and laughs. "If the real Misty ever reads this book, she will claw my eyes out."

"She'll have to get through me first," I mutter calmly, watching Lo's beautiful face as she talks about her work. Her eyes are shining and her cheeks are glowing. She's excited about her writing.

"Anyway, I haven't figured out how the hero is going to convince the heroine that the ex is just being a vindictive bitch." Lo begins to sway to the music again, and I just can't keep my hands off her for one more second.

I lower my roller to the pan and stalk over to her, wrap my arms around her middle from behind, and bury my nose in her neck, hugging her close. Her body tenses and her hand stills, the roller braced on the wall. "You smell fantastic."

She sighs and leans into me, tilts her head back to rest on my shoulder, just as a slow song begins on the stereo. I begin to move slowly, swaying from side to side, enjoying the feel of her firm body in my arms. She lays her free hand on my arm and moves with me.

I inhale her sweet scent and drag my nose down the slope of her neck before pressing my lips to the soft skin where her neck and shoulder meet. My hands begin to roam across her tight belly.

"Your stomach is so firm. I don't think I've ever known a woman with washboard abs before," I murmur into her ear. *I want to see her abs.*

She chuckles lazily. "It's the swimming. Great for your core."

"I might have to take it up."

"Nothing wrong with your abs," she mutters.

I smile against her neck. Yeah, I know she appreciated the show she got in my driveway yesterday. Remembering the way her eyes glassed over as they made their way down my chest and stomach makes my dick twitch against her firm ass.

Just as the song reaches the bridge, her body tenses and she pulls out of my arms, her eyes wide, and drops her roller in the pan, splashing paint onto the drop cloth.

"That's it!" she exclaims, and runs from the room toward the office.

I frown after her and stare around the room, wondering what in the bloody hell I'm missing, then follow her down the hall. When I reach the doorway to her work space, she's already sitting in the desk chair, her feet pulled up under her, and she's typing furiously on her computer, her lips clamped between her teeth and a crease on her forehead as she concentrates.

I guess she figured it out.

I chuckle and return to the family room and finish the first coat of paint, then go back out to my car and unload the groceries I brought with me. I'll make her dinner while she works her ass off.

It still stuns me that she's the author of some of the most well-loved novels in the world. Her books are a sensation. Millions are in print, and when I dug deeper, using Google and Facebook to find out more after being with her last week, I learned that not only has she sold the movie rights, but the film is moving forward. The movie company is currently casting the characters, and millions of women have nothing better to do than hang out on social media discussing who should play whom.

It's amazing.

It seems that Lo, or Peyton Adams, is also something of an enigma. She won't release publicity photos and won't give live interviews, which has fans and industry people alike in an uproar.

I pray to God she has a good entertainment lawyer.

I walk out onto the deck off the kitchen and fire the propane grill to life, clean the grates, and let it burn while I go back inside to season two rib-eye steaks and throw together a large green salad.

I whisk together a vinaigrette dressing, then carry the steaks out to the grill and lay them on the grates with a loud sizzle.

There's nothing like red meat on a grill.

It's a guy thing.

While I stand outside, enjoying an early-autumn evening, my phone rings in my pocket.

"Hello?"

"Well? Did she like it?" Jill asks.

"I don't know if she pulled it out of the bag. We're painting her house."

The line goes silent and I pull the phone away from my face to make sure I didn't lose the call.

"Jill?"

"I'm here. You're painting her house?"

"Well, one room of it. She was working on it when I got here."

"Huh."

"What did that mean?" I check the steaks.

"When I asked you to help me paint my house, you hired a company to come do it."

I smile and shake my head. "I told you then, I didn't have time to paint your house. What are you bitching about? You got out of doing it yourself."

"I just find it interesting, that's all."

"Shut up, Jilly."

She laughs. "Have fun painting. It might be fun to paint each other, now that I think about it."

"I'm hanging up now." I press the off button and pull the medium-rare steaks off the grill, kill the gas, and saunter inside.

Just as I finish plating the steaks and salads, ready to carry them to the table, Lauren comes barreling into the kitchen and, without saying a word, launches herself into my arms. She jumps up onto me, presses that sweet body against mine, wraps her legs around my waist, her arms around my neck, and plants a kiss on me that would make the gods weep. I plant my hands on the globes of her ass, holding her up to me as her mouth moves confidently yet softly against my own. She slides her tongue along my lips, nips my bottom lip with her teeth, and sinks into me again.

Impatient to touch her, I prop her on the island countertop and glide my hands up her sides to cup her breasts and brush my thumbs over her nipples.

She inhales sharply, pulls back, and stares at me, panting, eyes wide. My hands slide up to hold her face as I turn the tables and take her mouth, softly at first, nibbling at her lips. My fingertips brush down her cheeks to her jaw and around her neck to thread the silky strands of her hair around my fingers and hold her tightly.

A soft moan escapes her lips and her hips circle as she pushes her center against my cock. She's on fire, and I know without a doubt that she wouldn't object to my ripping these flimsy shorts off her and sinking inside her, losing myself in her for the rest of the night.

She pulls back to catch her breath and I lean my forehead against hers, count to ten, and find the strength to not fuck the hell out of her here on her kitchen counter.

This is not how the first time is gonna go.

"What was that for?" I whisper.

"You saved my life." She grins.

"I did?" I cock my head to the side.

"Yeah. I finished the scene." Her eyes drop to my lips as she sticks out her little pink tongue and runs it over her bottom lip, tasting me there.

I have to take a deep breath and lower her to the floor and back away. "Good."

She frowns at me.

"What?"

"Why did you stop?"

"Lo." I reach up and brush my thumb over the apple of her cheek. "When I make love to you for the first time, it won't be on a kitchen counter.

We'll do that another time." I grin and wink at her, then lift the plates and lead her to the table off the kitchen. "Are you okay with a less formal dinner tonight?"

"This is amazing." She eyes the steaks the way a lion eyes a wildebeest.

"Hungry?"

"So hungry." She takes a seat.

"Did you eat today?" I narrow my eyes.

She laughs and waves me off. "Yes, food master, I did. But working makes me hungry."

"I hope you eat red meat." Before I join her, I move back into the kitchen. "Wine?"

"I love red meat. No wine for me." She shakes her head. "I'll just have water. I have to get back to work after dinner."

I pour us both a glass of water and join her, digging into our dinner.

"So you figured out the scene?"

"Yes. And I figured out what happens next." She smiles smugly and takes a bite of her steak. "Oh, sweet Jesus, this is delicious."

"So what happens next?"

"You'll have to read the book." She winks at me and stabs a cucumber.

"I plan to," I respond truthfully.

"Really?"

"I've already started *Ignited Lust*." I take a sip of water, watching her surprised face.

"And?"

Fucking sexy as hell. I want to try every single kinky thing you've written in that book with you. "It's fantastic."

A shy grin spreads across her face. "Thank you."

"You're welcome."

She finishes her plate and takes it into the kitchen.

"Leave the dishes." I follow her, take the plate from her hand, and lower it into the sink. "I'll clean up."

She bites her lip and looks like she feels almost guilty. "I'm sorry, Ty, I have to get back to work. This deadline . . ."

"It's okay, sweetheart." I pull her into my arms and hug her to me, kiss her head, then lower my lips to her forehead. "Go work."

She pulls out of my arms and squeezes my hand before letting go. "You're pretty cool, Ty Sullivan."

"I'm glad you think so. I think you're pretty cool yourself."

She grins and turns her back on me to return to her work. Cleaning the kitchen doesn't take long. When I poke my head into the office to let her know that I'm leaving, she's back in her spot, legs pulled up under her in her chair, typing like mad on the keyboard.

Rather than interrupt her, I move up behind her and kiss her head. "Don't work too late," I murmur.

"M'kay." She barely registers that I'm here.

I glance at her screen.

*...pulls her into his arms and kisses her with a
ferocity to rival an angry storm...*

I grin and back away, leaving her to her work. I
set her alarm and let myself out, already looking forward to Thursday night.

CHAPTER

LAUREN

The doorbell rings just as I make one final turn before the mirror. Ty sure has good taste. This dress fits me like a glove, and the shoes are just plain sexy.

I have no idea how he pulled off buying the right sizes, but I'm not complaining. The dress is blue, the color of the sky on a clear summer day. It's completely backless, leaving everything from my neck to the top of my butt bare. You can even see the dimples over my ass, which makes me grin. I'm not so self-involved as to think that I'm the most beautiful woman on the planet, but I've worked hard to get my body in the shape it's in.

My back looks fantastic in this dress.

You can also see my entire tattoo.

I pulled my hair up into an intricate knot and am wearing my mother's diamond chandelier earrings.

The shoes are sparkling silver heels, and I bet when I stand next to Ty, I will be able to look directly into those sexy gray eyes of his.

I snag my silver clutch off my vanity and descend the stairs to the front door.

"Holy shit," I whisper as I take in the sight of Ty. He's in a fitted black tux that makes his shoulders look wide and his hips narrow. His inky-black hair has been tamed into a sleek style, and he's holding a bouquet of red roses in his hands.

I bite my lip and step back into the foyer so he can come inside and shut the door.

"Turn around," he murmurs softly. His eyes are on fire as they rake over me from head to toe.

I toss him a sly smile and slowly turn in a tight circle.

"Dear God, stop," he mutters, and approaches me from behind. The flat of his hand glides down my spine, from my neck to where my tattoo ends, right above my rear. "This is the most beautiful ink I've ever seen."

I smile softly and glance back at him over my shoulder. "Thank you."

I have a line of brightly colored flowers that fall down my spine on vines.

"What kind of flowers are they?" he asks softly, his fingertips tracing the lines of the vines up and down my spine, sending goose bumps all over my body.

"They're rose of Sharon."

"What do they mean to you?"

"I'll tell you later. It's a long story." I turn to face him. My breath stutters at the primal lust burning in his eyes. "Thank you for this dress."

"Oh, sweetheart, I think I need to thank you for wearing it. I knew the color would make your eyes shine, and it does. But I had no idea that little treat was waiting for me on your back."

"You look completely hot yourself, counselor."

He smirks and holds the flowers out for me. "These are for you."

"They're lovely." I bury my nose in the soft, fragrant blooms and take a deep breath, fussing over them. "Mmm, they smell great."

I turn and head for the kitchen to put the flowers in water.

"Are you ready?" I ask as I return to the foyer.

"When you are."

"We're not taking the Jeep?" A classic red convertible Mustang is parked in the drive.

"It's a beautiful night for a drive in the 'Stang."

"Uh, I worked on this hair for a long time, Ty. It's not convertible-safe."

He laughs and presses a button in the car and the roof closes smoothly. "Better?"

"Thanks." I sit in the soft vinyl seat. "I didn't know you were into classic cars."

"I like to tinker." He shrugs as he pulls onto the highway. "It's a hobby, not an obsession."

"Ah, so that's why you like to change your oil yourself."

"Yeah, I suppose so." He nods, smiles warmly, and takes my hand in his, then pulls it to his mouth. "You are stunning, Lo."

"It's the dress." I smooth my free hand down the soft skirt.

"It's the woman wearing it," he murmurs, and kisses my hand again. "Are you okay with coming to this thing tonight, given that Jack will be there?"

"We live in a small town, Ty. I see Jack here and there. I can't avoid it even if I want to." Jack is the athletic director for the school district, and given that this is a fund-raiser for the high school athletic department, Jack will be there.

"I'll be by your side all night."

My gaze turns to his profile as he pulls into the recently built O'Malley Center, which houses a five-hundred-seat theater and a grand ballroom for special occasions. "He won't threaten me here. It's too public."

"You still haven't told me what he threatened you with last week." Ty turns his gaze to mine, but I just shake my head and look away. "You will tell me eventually, you know."

Not if I can help it.

The valet opens my door and offers me a hand, helping me from the car. Ty is quickly by my side.

"You're tall in those shoes," he murmurs in my ear. I'm just the right height that all I have to do is tilt my head up slightly and my lips will meet his.

So I do.

I press my lips to his in a chaste, simple kiss before he presses his hand to the small of my back and ushers me into the ballroom.

Round tables are covered in black tablecloths with white place settings. Simple centerpieces of orange fall flowers grace each table. At the head of the room stands a podium, and along one wall is a long line of tables full of silent-auction prizes.

Ty snags two glasses of champagne from a passing waiter and hands me one. "Shall we go browse?" He gestures to the auction tables.

"Sure."

The auction items range from spa days and handmade quilts to ski packages and trips for two to Mexico.

I sign my name on a trip for four to Disneyland, and Ty raises his eyebrows. "Are we going to visit Mickey?"

"No," I giggle. "My publicist and her family could use a vacation."

His eyes soften as he runs his hand down my bare back. The man can't keep his hands off me, and it's quickly becoming addicting. "That's nice of you."

I shrug as he leads us farther down the tables. He bids on a few things before we decide to go find our seats for dinner.

"Ty! Come sit with us!" Cara is waving from a table smack-dab in the middle of the room. Josh is sitting next to her, looking hot, but uncomfortable, in his suit.

"Shall we sit with Josh and Cara?" Ty asks, linking his fingers through mine.

"Sure." I nod and smile at Cara as we approach.

Josh stands and shakes Ty's hand, then shakes mine. "You look lovely, Lauren."

"Thanks. You both look fantastic." Cara's dress is gray and fitted, showing off all of her curves. Her blond hair is loose and hanging in big curls. Josh's black suit and gray tie look magnificent on him.

He pulls on his collar and fidgets in his chair with a grimace. "I hate wearing a suit."

"Suck it up." Ty laughs as he pulls a chair out for me. "It's only for a few hours."

"Maybe we can find something fun to do with your tie later," Cara suggests, and bats her eyelashes at Josh. He looks down at her with such tenderness and affection it takes my breath away.

Ty finds my hand under the table and links our fingers again, giving me a gentle squeeze.

The room is filling with beautifully dressed people, and soon two more couples join us, completing our table.

"Where is Jill tonight?" I ask Cara.

"She said, and I quote, 'I would rather walk through the bowels of hell without sunblock than go to that thing,'" Cara replies with a wide smile.

"So, how does she really feel?" I ask with a straight face, making everyone laugh.

"I think she had a date tonight," Cara confides, wiggling her eyebrows.

"On a Thursday?" Ty asks with a scowl. "With who?"

"We're all out on a Thursday," I remind him.

"She didn't say who." Cara shrugs. "I'll get the dirt later."

Conversation flows around the table while our dinner of chicken cordon bleu with pilaf is served and devoured. I glance around the ballroom and spy Jack near the front of the room, laughing with a group of his colleagues. His eyes catch mine and he offers me a smug smile before rising and moving to the podium. I automatically stiffen at the sight of him and just pray that he's smart enough to stay away.

He can be so embarrassing. He rarely cares what he says or who hears him.

"Excuse me," Jack speaks into the microphone, calming the conversation around us. "First, I'd like to thank you all for coming tonight to support the athletics department here in Cunningham Falls."

Ty threads his fingers through mine and leans in to whisper in my ear, "You okay?"

I just nod, and he squeezes my hand in silent support, and I'm thankful to have him here with me. He grounds me, which surprises me. I'm growing to really like him.

To trust him.

"Each dollar raised tonight will go toward buying new uniforms and equipment for our athletes, as well as help pay for lodging and transportation to events out of town." Jack clears his throat and gazes about the room. "I'd also like to take just a moment to thank you for so graciously welcoming me into this community. I'm proud to work for a school system that continues to produce such amazing athletes. As most of you know, I was married to one of the best athletes Cunningham Falls has ever seen, and I'm confident that with your help we can continue to make you proud of your students."

Ty growls low in his throat as Jack's eyes seek me out in the crowd. *That son of a bitch! He did that on purpose, and we all know it.*

I make an effort to maintain my composure, not letting my face show the horror or embarrassment of being linked to Jack. I will never give him that satisfaction.

"What an asshole," Josh murmurs.

"All of the winners of tonight's silent auction will be contacted by phone before the end of the month. I hope no one outbid me on that golf package in Monterey. I have a feeling I'll need a celebratory vacation soon. We are about to start the dancing portion of the evening. Have fun, everyone." Jack flashes that charming smile of his that turns my stomach and returns to his table.

I turn to face Ty, surprised to find his eyes glittering in anger.

"Hey," I murmur, and pull my fingers down his face. "It's okay."

"Don't let that jackass ruin your night, guys." Cara

pats Ty on the arm and smiles over at me. "You're way too pretty for him, you know. You are one hundred percent his loss."

I laugh and shake my head, some of the unease lifting from my shoulders.

Ty relaxes and his face softens as he gazes over at me. "She's right. And thank God he's an idiot and didn't know what he had when he had it." Ty plants his lips on my forehead in a soft kiss and pulls me to my feet. "Let's dance."

The DJ queues a slow song, the same song that played in my house while Ty and I painted last weekend. Ty grins and pulls me into his arms as other couples join us on the dance floor. He holds my right hand close to his chest and rests his other hand on the skin at the small of my back and begins to sway to "Beneath Your Beautiful."

"You look magnificent in this dress," he murmurs into my ear. "And I love how tall you are in these shoes. Tall enough that I can whisper anything I want into your ear without bending in half to reach you."

I grin and inhale deeply, enjoying the musky scent of him, enjoying being pressed against his firm body. My fingers comb through the soft, inky hair at the back of his head and he sighs deeply.

God, his body wakes mine up in ways it hasn't in a long, long time.

"That feels good," he whispers.

"This tux is nice," I murmur, running my hand up

and down his arm. "It's definitely not something off-the-rack."

"I like nice suits." He shrugs. "I'm in them almost every day."

"Custom?" I ask with a raised brow. He nods with a smirk. "Very fancy, Mr. Sullivan."

He chuckles softly. "I'm just as happy to wear an old shirt and jeans."

"I like that about you. It makes you . . ." I narrow my eyes and tilt my head, trying to find the right word.

"Human?" he asks with a chuckle.

"I was thinking approachable." I run my hand down the lapel of his jacket over his chest, then trace down his arm with my fingertips. "And what's beneath here," I whisper, "is damn hot."

His breath catches and his eyes blaze as he watches me. "Keep that up, Lauren, and I won't be responsible for fucking you right here on the ball-room floor."

It's my turn for my breath to catch, and then I smile, a slow, wide smile. I love that I've turned him on as much as he does me. "I'll behave for now."

"Damn," he mutters.

I rest my head on his shoulder, enjoying the feel of his strong arms wrapped tightly around me. I don't care that many of the members of our community are watching us, including my asshole of an ex-husband. All I know is that this song is romantic and this man is a breath of fresh air.

We stay on the dance floor for two more songs. Ty is an excellent dancer, twirling me about and leading me effortlessly around the room.

When the third song ends, he dips me low and then ushers me back to mingle with our friends. He keeps one hand on me at all times, whether it be on my back, on my neck, or holding mine, brushing his thumb over my knuckles. He introduces me to anyone I don't already know, which aren't many, and engages me in conversation.

He's looking out for me. Who said chivalry is dead?

Warmth that has nothing to do with the three glasses of champagne I've consumed tonight settles on my skin and I just can't stop smiling.

Finally, we circle back around to Cara and Josh.

"How is the school year going so far, Cara?" I ask, and sip a fresh glass of champagne.

"Pretty well." Cara nods. "I have some good kids this year."

"Ah, hell," Josh mutters as he looks over my shoulder. I follow his gaze and my heart sinks when I see Jack making his way toward us.

Ty immediately grabs my hand, catching Jack's attention. Jack's eyes narrow on my face as he stops before me.

"Can I help you?" I ask, maintaining my composure.

His mouth tilts up in a perfect smile, showing off his straight teeth. "That's a loaded question, baby."

"Don't call me baby," I reply quietly.

His smile fades and his eyes shift to Ty before landing on me again. "I see you're doing the right thing by pinching pennies."

"What are you talking about?"

"Fucking your lawyer rather than paying him," Jack replies softly so only our small group can hear him.

God forbid he causes a scene.

Cara gasps, but I just smile at Jack and squeeze Ty's hand when I feel his body tighten in anger. "Anything and any*one* I choose to do is my business, Jack."

"Just remember what I told you the other day." He winks at me.

My heart lodges directly in my throat. *Damn him!*

"You might want to watch your language, Jack," Ty murmurs. His hand is holding mine like a vise and I can feel the anger coming off him in waves.

"Or what?" Jack challenges.

Ty steps forward into Jack's space and replies calmly, "Or I will make your life a living hell."

"Are you threatening me?" Jack demands.

"I didn't hear him threaten you," Josh replies coldly. "I think he made his intentions pretty clear."

Jack's nostrils flare and he pins me in another glare before turning on his heel and stalking away.

"Does he always talk to you like that?" Josh asks from behind me. I turn to him and nod, my face flushing now in embarrassment. Ty tucks me against his side and kisses my cheek.

"What did he mean about what he said to you the other day?" Cara asks with a frown.

I shake my head, but Ty catches my chin in his fingers and makes me meet his gaze. "Answer the question, Lauren."

I bite my lip and hate myself for letting my eyes fill with tears when I whisper, "He just threatened more of the usual. He's an ass." *I refuse to tell these people that my ex-husband threatened to freaking rape me!* How humiliating.

"Motherfucker," Josh bites out.

Ty's eyes narrow on my face for a long moment, and then without looking away he addresses the other two. "I'm taking Lo home."

"Drive safe," Cara says. "Lo, please call me if you need anything. I have two good ears." She folds me into a hug and it's almost my undoing.

"Thank you," I murmur.

Ty grips my hand again and leads me out to the valet. He doesn't speak as we wait for the car. He doesn't even look me in the eye.

His body is humming with tension. He swears under his breath and pushes his free hand through his hair, and when the valet returns with his car, he doesn't wait to help me inside before he stalks around to his side, slips in, and drives toward my house.

Why is he so mad?

I don't know what to say. He's so damn angry, and I'm not sure what I did to earn it. Not telling him about Jack's threat? Jesus, I can't even think about it without losing my lunch.

He pulls up to my house and leads me to my porch, waits for me to unlock the door and disarm the alarm system.

"Thank you for joining me this evening." His voice is stiff and formal.

"Would you like to come inside?"

"I shouldn't." He begins to back away, but I stop him.

"Ty, what did I do?"

"What are you talking about?"

"Why are you so mad at me?"

He watches me for a moment and then deflates like a balloon, exhaling and letting his shoulders and head fall.

When he looks up at me, his eyes are sad and worried, confusing me even more.

"I'm sorry, I don't know what made you so angry, but I really don't want to be alone tonight." The last few words are whispered and I'm embarrassed again. "It's okay." I back into the house, ready to make a hasty retreat. "I'm being silly. I'll see you around."

I'm suddenly swept up in his embrace. He pulls me against him, tucks my face against his neck, and rocks me back and forth soothingly.

"Ah, sweetheart, I'm not mad *at* you, I'm mad *for* you."

"Okay," I whisper.

"Are you sure you want me to stay?" he whispers back.

I nod and he lifts me effortlessly into his arms. He locks the door behind us and moves up the stairs, raising his brow at me in silent question.

"Over there." I point to my room.

Ty sets me on my feet by the bed and cradles my face in his hands. He kisses my lips softly and then backs away. "Go get ready for bed, and I'll meet you back here."

I admit that I'm thrown. He's not going to tear this dress off me and make love to me?

Silently, I grab an old T-shirt and march to the bathroom to wash my face and brush out my hair.

When I return in just my shirt and panties, my face clean and hair down, Ty is already in the bed, his torso bare, sheet and blanket gathered at his waist.

"Come here."

I comply and climb in bed next to him. He pulls me into his arms, my head on his chest, and tucks us down into the bed.

He's not going to attack me? I know he's as attracted to me as I am to him. I can feel it against my hip right now, for the love of Christmas.

He laughs and pushes his fingers through my hair, slowly pulling until it falls onto my back, and repeats the motion. "Your gorgeous brain is working a mile a minute."

My head comes up in surprise. "What do you think I'm thinking?"

"I think you're wondering why we're settling in to go to sleep rather than making love." His finger slips down my jawline. "I'm desperate to have you, Lo, but we have time. For now I'm happy to hold you."

He turns us both onto our sides so he can see my face, but continues to touch me. "I would love it if you'd tell me about the gorgeous ink on your back."

I smile softly and turn my gaze to his own tattoos on his arm. I begin tracing the lines with my fingertips and softly tell him the story.

"My dad was crazy about my mom." My finger traces a skull as I swallow over the lump forming in my throat. "They loved me very much, but they loved each other fiercely. Watching them together was like watching a fairy tale. I know that sounds trite, but there's no other way to explain them." I smile up at Ty. "When I was young, my dad planted lines and lines of rose of Sharon bushes along the property. He planted them himself," I stress. "He didn't have a gardener do it for him."

My finger follows the circle of a yin-and-yang symbol as I remember the look on my mother's face when the flowers would bloom in late summer.

"The flowers are colorful and delicate, just like her, he used to say. So when they died, it made sense to get the flowers for both of them."

"Thank you," he whispers. My eyes meet his. "For telling me about them. It makes the tattoo even more beautiful."

"I miss them," I whisper.

"I know. I'm sorry, baby." He pulls me back into his arms and holds on tight. "Now, about Jack."

I tense and try to pull away, but Ty keeps me in his grasp. "There's really nothing more to talk about."

"Yes, there is. I want you to file for an order of protection with the court."

I stare up at him in surprise and then shake my head. "I can't prove anything. All he does is threaten."

"That's what an order of protection is for. It's to protect you from abuse, and that includes harassment and intimidation."

"Ty," I sigh loudly. "I appreciate that you want to protect me, but honestly . . ."

"I don't know your whole history yet, Lo, but I can feel that he's put his hands on you before." I bite my lip, unable to answer him. "I want a legal document in place stating that he can't come near you."

"I don't think it'll make any difference. But if it'll make you feel better, okay."

He kisses my forehead and relaxes under me. "Thank you. Let's sleep, baby."

Baby.

"Hey, beautiful," Ty whispers as he kisses my forehead. I pry my eyes open to find him smiling down at me.

"Hey, yourself," I murmur. "Time is it?"

"It's early. I have to go home and get ready for work, but I didn't want to leave without saying good-bye."

I push up to my knees and wrap my arms around his neck, bury my nose against his warm cheek, and squeeze him. "Thank you for last night. I had a great time."

"I'm glad." He pulls back and kisses my forehead and then my lips. "If I don't leave now, I won't leave at all."

"Okay, stay." I smile.

"You're too tempting." He chuckles. "But I only have to work half the day today. You'll hear from me later."

"Looking forward to it," I reply.

He settles me back onto the bed and waves as he leaves the room. "Go back to bed, and don't forget to eat today."

"Yes, sir!" I call after him.

I hear him laugh as he descends the stairs.

CHAPTER

Seven

When my doorbell rings at noon, I've finished writing two chapters, caught up on my e-mail, and signed five hundred books for my publisher.

Apparently, a good night's sleep helps productivity.

When I open the door, a huge bouquet of red roses with pink Stargazer lilies greets me, along with Mr. Feldman from the flower shop.

"I have a delivery for you, Lauren." He grins and passes the large vase with the heavy blooms over to me. "Have a nice day." He tips his hat and skips down to his van as I take the fragrant bouquet to the kitchen and pull the card from its plastic holder buried in the blooms.

Last night was amazing. The gala was fun too. Meet me at Frontier Park, north side of the bridge, at 5:00. —Ty

What does that man have up his sleeve? Aside from that sexy-as-hell tattoo?

With a quick check of the clock, I realize I have plenty of time to take a quick shower and drive to the courthouse to file the order of protection against Jack before walking over to the park. It's not far from my house.

The process at the courthouse is quick and smooth, and Susan, the court clerk, doesn't even bat an eye when she hands me the appropriate paperwork to fill out and submit to the judge. Relieved that it's over, and a bit nervous about what Jack's reaction is going to be, I return to the house, park, and set off on foot for my date with Ty.

It's a beautiful day again today. I wonder how long we'll continue getting these sunny fall days before Mother Nature decides the gig is up and gives us cold and rain instead.

The walk to the park is short. It borders my property at the edge of town and sits next to a small river. A large stone footbridge arches gracefully over the water. I love this bridge. I came here often as a teenager to sit and watch the water, read a book, or just think.

As I pass over the top of the arch, I move to the side of the bridge and look over to watch the water move quickly below, then I continue down the other side. This park has no playground equipment for kids. It's full of meandering paved paths for runners and cyclists, tall trees, and picnic tables sprinkled here and there.

I turn a corner and see Ty sitting at a picnic table, his head bowed as he types away on his phone. He's spread out a red cloth on the table, and a large brown paper bag is sitting on top.

He doesn't see me as I approach, so I take a moment to watch him. His brow is creased in concentration, his gray eyes narrowed on the device in his strong, lean hands. He's changed out of his work clothes into jeans and a plain, black T-shirt. A hoodie lies on the bench beside him.

I've never seen anyone else as handsome as he is.

"Mind if I join you?" I ask with a smile.

His head whips up and he smiles widely as he rises from the bench and crosses to me, pulling me in for a big hug.

I'm quickly becoming addicted to Ty's hugs.

"I'm happy to see you," he murmurs against my hair.

"Thank you for the ridiculously gorgeous flowers." I grin as I pull away. "And for this." I gesture to the table.

He smiles shyly. "Who knows how many more pretty days we'll have?" he asks, mirroring my thoughts from just a few moments ago. "Might as well take advantage of it. I hope you're hungry."

"I'm always hungry." I laugh and sit on the bench next to him.

"Well, I didn't have time to throw something to-gether, but I brought Mexican."

"How did you know that I have an addiction to guacamole?" I ask with wide eyes, teasing him.

"How do you know I have guacamole?" He raises an eyebrow as he unloads the bag.

"Mexican without guacamole is just . . . wrong."

He laughs as he sets aside the bag and begins to pull the tops off the foam containers. "You're in luck. We have the guac, along with carne asada, *pico de gallo*, and all the trimmings."

"Where's yours?" I dig in with gusto, not at all shy about eating in front of him.

"You're funny." He laughs and joins me, piling his plate with delicious food. "How was your day?"

"I had a good day. I filed the order of protection." I shrug and bite into a chip with dip and sigh in plea-sure. "So good."

"Here." He touches his index finger to the corner of my mouth, coming away with a dab of guaca-mole. With my eyes on his, I grip his wrist in my hand and pull his finger into my mouth, licking it clean.

His eyes darken and narrow. "Lauren," he whis-pers.

"Yeah?"

"Eat your dinner." He turns away and digs into his plate and I grin at him. "You should have called me. I would have gone to the courthouse with you."

"It was easy." I wave him off and shake my head.

"The hard part will be when Jack is served. That won't go over well."

"It doesn't matter what his reaction is, Lo. I'm relieved that you filed. I still would have liked to be there with you."

"I'm fine. How was your day?" Ty holds a forkful of Spanish rice to my mouth. "Mm . . . good."

"It was pretty good. I left at around one." He takes a bite of his steak. "Oh! Here." He pulls a thermos from under the table and fills two red Solo cups. "We can't have Mexican without margaritas."

"I didn't realize they let you take liquor to go," I reply dryly.

"They don't, smart-ass."

"Why, counselor, I do believe you're breaking the law. There is an open-container law in Montana, you know." I bump his shoulder with mine and then take a sip of the sweet drink.

"It's our secret. I won't tell if you don't."

"Deal." He feeds me another bite of rice. "So your day was good?"

"Busy," he confirms. "But good. I'm glad it's the weekend."

"I wish I had weekends." I frown down at my food.

"You have to take days off now and again."

"I do, but the story is always in my head. And lately, I don't have time to take days off. Not whole days, anyway." I shrug and stuff more delicious guacamole in my mouth. "I'm not complaining, though. It's a fun job."

He holds another bite up for me but I shake my head and wipe my mouth with a napkin. "I'm full. That was great. Thank you."

"You're welcome." We pack up the leftovers and empty containers.

"Let's go sit on the bridge for a little while," I suggest.

"Sounds good." He nods and rises from the table, holding his hand out for me to join him, and we stroll slowly down the path to the bridge.

"I love this place." I take a deep breath, enjoying the musty smell of the leaves. "I used to come down here almost every day after school in the fall and the spring to do homework or read or just think."

"What did you think about?"

We approach the top of the bridge and lean against the railing, taking in the tall mountains ahead that are sprinkled with yellow and red trees. A breeze has picked up, making the limbs above sing.

"Oh, normal teenage-girl stuff, most likely." I turn my back to the rail and lean on my elbows, watching Ty as he leans his hands on the rail next to me. "You know, boys, clothes, school. Swimming."

"Do you still swim?"

"Every day."

"Really?" His brows rise and he reaches up to tuck my hair behind my ear. "That must be how you stay in such great shape."

"It is." I nod. "I'll never stop swimming. My parents built the pool house when I was a freshman in high school and took an interest in it."

Ty slides closer to me. His hand glides over my stomach and around my waist, holding my side against his stomach, and he lowers his mouth to my temple. "Thank you for bringing me to this spot."

I turn to smile at him, and my breath catches. His lips are mere inches from mine. I can feel the heat of his skin, and I know without a doubt that I want him.

I trust him.

I need him in my bed.

I turn into him and wrap my arms around his shoulders. His nose brushes against mine. I take a deep breath and whisper, "Ty?"

"Yeah, beautiful?" he whispers back.

He sweeps his lips across mine and settles those lips on the corner of my mouth, nibbling lazily, before moving down my jawline.

I tilt my head to the side, giving him more space. He cups my face in his hand, his lips hovering over mine again before he pulls back to gaze down at me. We're both panting now, eyes bright with lust, and my stomach is clenched, my center pulsing in need.

"Let's go to my place, Ty."

He smiles softly, his breath still coming hard. "You need to be sure, Lo. I won't share you. So you need to be completely sure that this is what you want."

I stare up at him, my mouth open. *His?* His. "That means you're mine too. It goes both ways."

He smiles triumphantly and kisses me long and hard, his mouth demanding and urgent. He finally backs away, grips my hand in his, and guides me back to the picnic table to gather our things before leading me to his Jeep.

The ride to my house is short. We arrive in just a few minutes.

"Wait for me," he murmurs. He kisses my hand before leaving the car, walking to my side, and opening the door for me.

"You're so chivalrous."

"Is that a good thing?" He leads me up to the house.

"Yeah, it's good. Different."

"Get used to it, beautiful."

He runs his hand down my hair and waits while I unlock the door and key in the alarm code, then simply takes my hand and leads me to the stairs.

"Every instinct I have," he begins as he climbs ahead of me, "is telling me to take you right here on these steps, but I want to make love to you all night, and I don't think the stairs will be comfortable for long."

He tosses a smile over his shoulder at me and leads me to the bedroom. He turns to me and pushes his finger into the waist of my jeans and pulls me against him. "I need to get you naked."

"Back at you."

Suddenly we are a tangle of arms and clothes and laughter as we strip each other down. When the offending clothes are gone, Ty lifts me and, with one arm wrapped around my waist, climbs to the middle of my king-size bed and lowers me gently. His hands glide up my arms. He threads his fingers through mine and pins my hands to the bed above my head as he lowers his head and kisses me softly. He settles his pelvis against mine, his cock nestled against my folds, and he just kisses me until we're both breathless.

"I want to touch you," I whisper against his lips. He frees my hands and they roam down his smooth back to his firm ass and up his sides. "Love the way you feel."

He growls and kisses down my neck, across my collarbones, then licks his tongue over a nipple. I gasp and shove my hands in his hair as he pulls the nub through his lips and sucks it into his mouth, worrying it with the tip of his tongue. His hand finds the other breast; his thumb moves back and forth over the nipple, making it pucker.

I arch my back, pushing deeper into his embrace.

"You're so fucking sweet," he growls, and switches breasts, tasting and biting the other nipple almost painfully, but I can't get enough.

My hips tilt, pressing my core against his stomach as he continues his journey south. His hands slide from my sides down to my hips, and that amazing, talented mouth of his nibbles its way down my stomach, over my navel, and lower still to the bare, sensitive flesh below.

"God, you're so beautiful." His hand glides over my flat stomach and his eyes watch the movement. I push my hands through his hair gently, needing to touch him, to be connected to him.

He spreads my legs wide as he shimmies farther down the bed and brushes his tongue over my clit, just barely touching it.

"Holy shit!" I exclaim as my hips leave the bed.

"Shh." He grins and spreads my lips, then lowers his mouth to me again, softly brushing his lips over me, then he sucks my clit into his mouth and pulls in tiny pulses.

"Fuck, Ty."

"Oh, we will, beautiful. Trust me." He pushes a finger inside my wetness and groans. "God, you're so wet."

"I'm kinda turned on here."

He pushes my legs up toward my chest and spreads them so he can still see my face. His dark hand against the white flesh of my thigh is a huge turn-on. A second finger joins the first in my pussy, and he begins moving them rhythmically in and out, swirling them and pushing in again. His tongue returns to my clit, and my whole body tightens and heats. Goose bumps spread as I climb higher and explode around him, shamelessly pushing my pussy harder against his mouth as I have the most intense orgasm of my life.

I can feel his lips and tongue move up my body, and he reaches for a foil packet that I didn't even see him throw on the bed earlier.

Once he has the condom in place, he leans on his elbows above me, his hands buried in my hair, and kisses me deeply. I can taste myself on him, and it makes me crazy with want for this sexy, kind, funny man. My hands can't stop roaming over him, feeling him. I rake my fingernails lightly over his shoulders and he groans deeply.

"Ah, sweetness, you feel so good."

"I'll feel better when you're inside me." I smile breathlessly. He grins and pulls his hips back, nudging my opening with the head of his erection. He slowly slips inside me, his eyes intense and pinned to my own, and when he's completely buried in me, he rests his forehead against mine. I lift my legs up around his hips, opening myself up further to him, and he moans.

"Fuck, you're amazing," he whispers.

I roll my hips, urging him to move. He curses and begins to rock his hips against me in shallow thrusts.

"I won't break, Ty."

He finally begins to move in earnest, sliding most of the way out and slamming back in, and suddenly it's as though he's been unleashed and can no longer control himself. His thrusts are urgent and hard. His hand closes around my breast, squeezing and tugging on my nipple as his mouth makes love to mine.

I'm building again, my body tightening around him.

"That's it, Lo, come again." He bites my shoulder,

and I feel his own muscles tighten under my hands, and I know he's close, beyond the point of return.

"Come with me," I reply breathlessly as the orgasm consumes me, sending electricity shuddering through me. He growls and stiffens, his own release shooting through him.

As our bodies calm, he pulls away and discards the condom, but instead of joining me back on the bed, he holds his hand out for me and pulls me from the bed with him.

"Where are we going?" I ask drowsily.

He grins and leads me toward the bathroom. "I'm not done with you yet."

"No?" My heart flutters at the primal look in his eyes.

"Not even close." He lifts me onto the vanity and kisses me like he's never kissed me before and never will again. "Stay here." He turns away to start the shower. When the room is filling with steamy, hot air, he lifts me off the vanity and into the shower.

"I'm a dirty girl," I tell him with a perfectly straight face.

He grins and lathers his hands with my shower gel. "You are that. I've read your books."

"Well, now I know what all the fuss is about," I reply without thinking, watching his semi-erect dick sway with his movements.

"What do you mean?" He glides his soapy hands over the tops of my shoulders and down my arms.

"I've never had an orgasm while having sex before."

His hands still on my stomach and his eyes whip up to mine. "Repeat that, please."

"I'd rather not, thanks." I duck my head in embarrassment. Seriously, I have no filter.

"You've never had an orgasm?" he asks incredulously.

"Oh, I've had them, just not when I was having sex with a man."

"Have you had sex with a woman?" He grins.

"Well, I'm a woman, and I've had sex with myself, so, yes, technically I have."

His finger tilts my head up so I can't avoid his gaze. "How can you write such sexy stories and you don't know what your characters are feeling?" he asks softly.

I shrug and frown. "I have a great imagination. I've also never been a serial killer, but I've written about those too, you know."

"Oh, sweetness." He kisses my forehead and then smiles devilishly down at me. "Oh, the fun we're gonna have."

My thighs clench at his delicious promise. He continues to wash me thoroughly and lazily, then he steps aside so the water rinses the suds away. I reach for the soap and return the favor, examining every inch of his glorious body.

"How did you get this scar?" I trace a thin scar along his right thigh.

"Sledding accident."

"The sled won?"

"A tree won." He laughs. "Zack, Josh, and I went sledding on the ranch when we were about nine. I slid right into a tree."

"Poor baby." I kiss the scar gently.

"You have the most amazing mouth, Lo."

I kiss the scar again and grin as I continue to explore Ty's body. My hands glide up the opposite leg and over his hip. "No tattoos besides the ones on your arm?"

"Nope." He shakes his head.

"What do the ones on your arm mean?"

"I'll tell you later. It's hard to talk when your hands are roaming over me, baby."

I laugh and stand, and just when he's going to back away, I grip his cock in my hand and pull up and down, reveling in the smooth velvet over the hardness.

"You have a gorgeous dick," I say as calmly as if I were talking about the weather.

"Enough," he mutters, and pins me against the wall of the shower. "Between your hand and your dirty mouth, I can't take any more." He lifts me effortlessly and I wrap my legs around his hips and my arms around his neck and smile down at him.

"Fuck," he growls, and leans his forehead against my shoulder. "I didn't bring any condoms in here."

"Um, well, I'm on the pill, Ty. I haven't been with anyone in almost three years."

"Three fucking years?" he asks in shock. His head whips up and his eyes search mine. "Oh, sweetheart."

"I'm fine," I reply dryly. "The point is, as long as you haven't been a man-whore, and don't plan on being one in the near future, we should be good to go."

He laughs and slides inside me, leans against me, and stays still as his hands cup my ass, holding me up.

"Fuck, you're tight," he growls. "I've never not worn a condom, Lauren."

His mouth takes mine as he begins hammering into me against the wall. I don't want him to be gentle this time or worried about hurting me.

I want him to fuck the hell out of me.

And he does.

He's like a man possessed, pushing violently against me, squeezing the breath from me. "Not gonna last, sweetness." He grinds his pubic bone against my clit. "Come with me."

My head falls back and I cry out as we both come apart. He kisses my cheek and my lips softly before lowering me to the floor.

"I'm hungry," I murmur with a grin.

"Let's go raid the kitchen."

CHAPTER

TY

I turn over and reach for Lo, but she's not there. I open one bleary eye and scan the room, but she's nowhere to be found. The bed is still warm where her delectable body was curled up beside me, so she hasn't been gone long.

It's only seven in the morning on a Saturday. If she's already downstairs working, I'm going to drag her ass back up here and bury myself in her for the next few hours.

On second thought, I think I'll do that anyway, no matter what she's doing.

I sit up and scratch my head and then notice the note in her pretty handwriting.

Ty,
> *I'm down at the pool. It's just off the mud-*

*room out back. Feel free to come down when
you wake up.*

   Lo

She's swimming. She told me yesterday that she
still swims every day, and given how tight her body
is, it shows. I've never been with another woman
whose muscles are so toned, yet she's still soft and
curvy in all the right places. Her abs are defined, but
she still has round breasts. Her thighs are toned, but
not hard.

She's fucking amazing.

I jump out of bed, not bothering to throw on my
boxer briefs, and go in search of her.

The house is cold this morning, just one more
reminder that winter is just around the corner. I pad
through the kitchen and the mudroom and see the
door leading to the pool house.

It's enclosed in glass. The pool is Olympic length,
and three lanes wide, so it's perfect for swimming
laps. A few chairs border the side, along with an
open stand-up shower in the corner.

It smells of chlorine and the air is humid and
warm.

But what catches my utmost attention is the
stunning woman swimming nude.

She's swimming away from me. The ink on her
back is moving back and forth with each stroke, and
her ass pokes up through the water in the rhythm
of her movements.

She has her hair tucked in a white swim cap.

When she reaches the end of the pool, she tucks down and pushes off the side, then turns into a back-stroke. Her perfect breasts surface out of the water as she moves her arms gracefully and quickly over her head toward me. Her eyes are closed and her breathing is even.

She's breathtaking to watch.

I wonder what she thinks about when she's in this space.

She tucks and pushes away from the wall again, back into a front stroke, showing me glimpses of her back and ass.

Not wanting to interrupt her, I sit at the side of the pool and dip my feet into the warm water, watching my woman move gracefully back and forth before me.

In the time I've been here, I've counted twenty-five laps.

She finally stops and stands in the pool, bouncing on the balls of her feet, her breasts peeking over the waterline. She's panting. She pushes the water off her face and pulls the cap off her hair, letting it fall around her shoulders.

The attraction is swift and hot, like lightning in a night sky.

She turns and sees me sitting at the side of the pool.

"Good morning." I smile and push off the side into the water.

"Hey, I'm sorry, have you been here long?"

"Long enough to be staggered by your graceful body in this water."

Her big blue eyes go round. She stands still as I approach her and pull her into my arms.

"You're beautiful in the water," I whisper.

"You look pretty hot in here yourself," she whispers back with a grin.

Unable to resist her delicious lips for another second, I cover them with my own. She tastes of chlorine and toothpaste and Lauren.

I'm addicted to her sweet mouth. I pull her legs around my hips, easily moving her through the water to the edge of the pool. Her hot pussy molds around my cock. I didn't think I could get harder, but I just did.

One touch of her, and she undoes me.

I brace her against the pool so I can touch her face, her breasts. Her skin is so smooth.

"Ty?"

"Yes, beautiful?" I kiss the soft skin below her ear.

"Please." She hitches her legs higher on my hips and I know she wants me to push inside her and fuck her blind here in the pool.

And I fully intend to.

But I can't stop kissing her.

I scrape my teeth along her jawline to the corner of her lips, cup her tight ass in my hands, and slide into her waiting heat.

"Fuck me, you're so damn tight," I growl against

her mouth. She moans, leans her head back against the lip of the pool, and moves her hips rhythmically with mine as I pump in and out of her, slow and steady.

I don't want this to be over too fast.

Her breasts are cresting the water, begging for my mouth. One of her nipples tightens in my lips as I suck on it, becoming a hard nub.

God, I love her tits.

She cries out and grinds her hips against me, wanting more friction.

"Harder, Ty, please."

"You want it rough, sweetness?"

"God, yes!"

I pull out of her and turn her away from me. "Grip the side of the pool." She follows my command, and I loop one arm around her lower belly, holding her up in the water, and push inside her, hard, in one swift motion.

"Yes!" she cries, and I pull out and slam back inside her, hard, setting a new rhythm. Slower but harder, burying myself balls-deep with each thrust.

My free hand glides from the nape of her neck to the small of her back, over the bright tattoo between her slender shoulders, as the water splashes loudly around us, waves rippling over the side of the pool. Our moans and sighs are bouncing off the glass around us, echoing in the sexiest song I've ever heard.

I feel her body tighten; her grip on the pool intensifies, her fingertips white with exertion. Her pussy pulses around me, those tight muscles ripple and milk me, until my eyes roll back in my head.

"Ah, fuck, Lo, I'm not gonna last if you keep doing that."

She laughs and squeezes me harder, the little vixen. I grip her hair in my hand and pull back, exposing her neck to my mouth as I lean over her body and pound harder, sending the water around us into a frenzy.

"You want me to come inside you?" I growl.

"God, yes," she moans as I sink my teeth into her shoulder. The base of my back tingles, and I feel my balls tighten and lift, and just as she cries out and grips my dick like a fucking vise, I explode inside her, jerking my hips uncontrollably.

Fucking hell, I just took her in the pool like a fucking animal.

And damn if I don't want to do it again.

I slide out of her and turn her into my arms. Her lips seek out my own and I happily oblige her silent request, kissing and nibbling her beautiful, plump lips.

"Come on, beautiful." I climb out of the pool with her steady in my arms. "Let's get in the shower."

"Okay." She curls up against me, her face buried in my neck. "I think that was the best morning workout of my life."

"Definitely not a bad way to start the day." I chuckle and kiss her forehead softly. She curls up in my arms and rests her head on my shoulder as I carry her upstairs. "Can I stay with you this weekend?"

"I have to work." She frowns and looks up at me with worried eyes. "But I want you to stay."

"I can run home and grab some work of my own, pack an overnight bag, and bring back some breakfast if you like."

Her smile is wide and brighter than the sun in Tahiti. "I'd love that."

"Okay, shower first."

"Good idea."

The sound of Lauren's fingers clicking on her keyboard is surprisingly soothing. I'm sitting in her chaise lounge with my own laptop on my lap and a pile of paperwork beside me on an end table.

We've been working for the better part of the day, taking breaks to eat and stretch before jumping back in. Her work ethic staggers me.

I've watched her smoothly move from her Word document to her e-mail, answer a phone call, answer a question on social media, and then dive back into her project.

I have no idea how she doesn't lose her concentration.

She also talks to herself and her characters while she writes, which I find absolutely hilarious.

"No, damn you, I don't want you to say that until the next chapter," she murmurs, then groans in frustration.

Completely adorable.

"I'm going to go outside and make a phone call, baby."

She mumbles and waves me off, not paying attention to me as I chuckle and leave the room, then step out onto her front porch and call my friend Brad Hull, one of Cunningham Falls' police detectives.

"Hull," he answers immediately.

"Hey, it's Ty."

"What's up?"

"I need a favor." I take a deep breath, gazing out over the trees bordering Lo's property. "I want to know everything there is to know about Lo's ex-husband, Jack."

"Did something happen?" Brad asks, his voice hard.

"He was an asshole at the charity gala, and Lo has said that he's threatened her. I talked her into filing an order of protection, but I don't trust the fucker. Just because there's a piece of paper that says he can't come near her doesn't mean he still won't."

"So, the rumors are true." Brad's voice softens, taunting me. "You've got a thing for Lauren Cunningham."

"We're seeing each other."

"I'm glad you talked her into filing the protection order, and that she has you looking out for her. I don't have to run his background check. I already did that when she first separated from him."

"What's on it?" I prepare to hear the worst.

"Not a fucking thing," he replies with frustration.

"You're kidding."

"Nope. Never been arrested, no abuse or harassment suits. He's squeaky-clean."

"Not anymore." I lean on the porch railing, scowling.

"He's not going to be happy when word gets out around town that she filed that order and embarrassed him. Not to mention, he works with kids, so it could threaten his job."

"Good," I reply immediately. "We'll keep our eyes open."

"Thanks for the heads-up."

I end the call and scrub my hand over my face. *Fuck.* It didn't occur to me that the order could jeopardize Jack's job at the school, but Brad's right. Not that it matters. She needed to file, for her own protection.

We'll deal with any aftermath together.

I return to Lo's office and grin when I see she's still sitting exactly as she was when I left. I turn my attention back to my own work, responding to e-mail and drafting letters to clients.

Suddenly my phone vibrates with an incoming text.

Lauren: **You look hot sitting over there.**

I glance up to find her staring at her computer screen, smiling while biting her lower lip.

"I'm right here, you know."

She doesn't respond and I go back to my e-mail. Within seconds, I have another text. She must be using iMessage on her Mac.

Lauren: **I think you should work naked.**

"I'm sitting in the same room. There is no need to text me." My voice sounds stern, but I'm grinning. She is so funny. I love her playful side. She still doesn't acknowledge my words, just pretends like she's still working.

Lauren: **Don't be a killjoy. Take off your shirt. We'll call it research.**

I laugh and shake my head, then respond to her text: **Heads up.**

She looks over at me as I throw a pillow at her, making her laugh out loud uncontrollably.

"You did not just throw that pillow at me," she laughs.

"I'm right here. Talk to me."

"Okay." She wipes tears of laughter from the corner of her eye. "Take off your shirt."

"I will if you will."

She raises her eyebrows in surprise and tilts her head in thought. "Hmm, that could be interesting. Okay." She whips her T-shirt over her head, leaving her in a lacy white bra. "Your turn."

I reach over my head and pull my T-shirt off and throw it on the floor before leaning back against the cushion. "Happy?"

"Mmm." Her blue eyes rake up and down my torso. "Very happy." Then she turns back to her computer and continues to tap her pink-tipped nails on her keyboard.

"Seriously?" I laugh.

"What?" She doesn't even look my way, but her lips are set in a smug line.

"I just got half-naked and you're going back to work?"

"I told you, I needed you to strip for research."

"Research for what?" I ask curiously.

"My character has tattoos up and down his arm, and I wanted to see yours."

Well, what in the hell am I supposed to say to that?

"Of course," she continues with a perfectly straight face, "I have yours memorized. I just wanted you to be half-naked."

She's so fucking funny.

I laugh and stand, setting my computer aside, and pull her out of her chair and into my arms, carrying her back to the chaise lounge. I settle her in my lap and nuzzle her neck. "I think we need a break."

"I was hoping you'd say that." She sighs, relaxes against me, and brushes her fingertip over the ink on my arm. "These are sexy."

"I had no idea you were into tattoos."

"I didn't either." She laughs. "I like them on you."

I love the way she touches me.

"What is this one for?" She traces the yin and yang on my biceps.

"It's Zack and Josh."

She purses her lips. "That's appropriate."

"I think so." I smile. Zack and Josh King are identical twins and have been my best friends since early childhood.

"And this one?" She traces the crown across my shoulder.

"It's for Jilly." I kiss Lo's forehead and breathe her in. She smells like peaches and cream.

"Why a crown?"

"I've always called her princess." I shrug and smile down at Lo. "She's always acted like one. She's the baby, and we all spoiled her."

I frown and Lo sees it immediately. "What?"

"I am pretty protective when it comes to the women in my life."

Lauren chuckles and continues to softly slide her fingertip over my skin. "You don't say," she murmurs dryly.

"She had a bad marriage," I reply softly, my gut tightening in anger when I think of the asshole who hurt my baby sister. "She doesn't talk about it, and she won't tell me what happened, but she got hurt."

"And that pisses you off," Lauren whispers.

"Hell yes, it pisses me off. I was just thinking that we all spoiled her, and the one person who was supposed to take care of her was a douche bag."

Lo cups my cheek in her hand and I instinctively turn my face into her touch and kiss her palm.

"She's home," she croons, and kisses my shoulder.

"Yeah, I'm happy she's home."

Lauren goes back to concentrating on my ink. I

have a feeling our whole break is going to be consumed with talking about each tat.

When what I wanted to do was make love to her here on this chaise.

"This?" Lo asks with a chuckle.

"It's a skull, Lo. It's because I'm badass, naturally."

"Naturally." She laughs loudly.

I nod and hug her close.

"I'm assuming this one is for your mom," she says sarcastically, pointing to the heart with MOM written though the middle of it.

"Safe assumption."

"Okay"—she trails her finger down my forearm, sending chills through me—"what's with the bluebird?"

"It's Cara."

Lo's head snaps up and she narrows her eyes on my face. "Why?" Her cheeks have reddened and she looks . . . pissed.

"Because she's important to me. She's been in my life a long time, and she was there for me when some bad shit went down."

"How was she there for you?" Lo asks quietly.

Well, fuck me, she's jealous. "She just offered me the comfort I needed in a really difficult time in my life."

Lo stiffens, and I cradle her face in my palm, tilt her head up to meet my gaze. "Cara is like my sister, Lauren. She's never been in my bed, I've never had a romantic relationship with her."

Lo deflates in my arms, but she says simply, "I didn't ask."

God, women are so fucking difficult. "Okay, well, I'm letting you know anyway."

She nods and buries her face in my neck, hugging me tight. I wrap my arms around her, press my hands to her back, and hold her close to me.

Finally, she backs away and grins. She scurries off my lap and snatches my shirt up off the floor, slipping it over her head as she saunters back to her desk chair.

"Hey," I protest. She can have the fucking shirt if she'll wear it for me every time I'm here.

She's sexy as hell in it.

"You need to stay naked, not me," she smirks, and turns her attention to her computer.

"What if I'm cold?" I ask with a laugh.

"Man up, Sullivan," she retorts.

My phone vibrates at my hip. "I'm right here, Lo. Seriously, you don't have to text me."

"I'm not." She frowns.

I glance at my phone and see a text. "Speak of the devil, it's Cara."

Her eyes narrow on my face.

I just chuckle and open the message: **Bring Lo out to the ranch tonight. Jill and I are having 'ritas on the deck.** My eyes meet Lo's across the room.

"What is it?"

"Do you feel up to going out to Josh and Cara's tonight? Jill's gonna be there, and the girls are planning to have drinks on the deck."

Lo looks shocked at the invitation, and part of me softens. Does she never receive invitations to hang out with friends? *Probably not, now that she's finally cut that bitch Misty out of her life.*

"Do you want to go?"

"Sure." I shrug, trying not to sound too eager. I'd love for her to become friends with the people who mean the most to me. She means the world to me and I don't ever plan to let her slip through my fingers. "But we don't have to, if you'd rather not. Although I think you'll have fun."

"Where will you and Josh be?"

"There is plenty for us to get into trouble with out at the ranch, sweetness. I won't be far."

A shy smile moves across her face and she nods happily. "Yeah, let's go."

CHAPTER

Nine

LAUREN

"You're here!" Cara exclaims when she opens the front door of the ranch house she shares with Josh. "Come on in."

We follow her into a large, open space. A large rock fireplace dominates one wall of the living area, with brown leather couches covered in brightly covered throw pillows arranged around it. The kitchen and the dining area are open to each other, giving the house a wide-open, inviting feel.

Cara leads us through to the kitchen, where Josh, his twin brother, Zack, and Jillian are all gathered.

"Hey, guys." Jill greets us with a grin and a twinkle in her eye as she pulls me right into her arms for a big hug.

"Hi," I murmur in return. The guys exchange their usual weird handshake-man-hug thing and a margarita glass full of blended deliciousness is shoved into my hand.

"We are about to kick the guys out so you and I can drill Jill about her date the other night, Lo," Cara announces, and sips smugly on her drink.

"There's nothing to tell," Jill insists.

"I wanna stick around for this conversation," Ty adds, glaring at Jill.

"I definitely do *not* want to be here for this," Zack mutters, scowling at Jillian fiercely. She won't meet his gaze.

Interesting.

"Come on." Josh motions for the guys to follow him. "We can go down to the barn for a while. There are a couple new foals out there."

"The girls get margaritas on the deck and I have to go hang out in your barn?" Ty asks in disgust as he follows the guys out the front door. "I'm getting the shaft."

The door closes behind them.

"Finally, they're gone!" Cara grabs a platter of chips with a bowl of salsa and leads us out to the deck, where it seems the party has already begun.

"You started drinking without me," Jill accuses Cara.

"Josh and I had one drink before you all got here." She grins and plops into a hanging porch swing.

Jill and I drop our handbags in a chair and join Cara.

"So, how are things with Ty?" Jill asks.

"God, you're so subtle," Cara mutters with a dis-approving scowl.

"I'd like to hear about your date," I reply before licking the salt on the rim of my glass.

"Yes, spill it!" Cara exclaims.

"Fine, but if I talk, you talk." Jill points her white-tipped finger at me accusingly.

"Deal," I agree with a nod.

"I went out with Brad."

"The cop Brad?" Cara asks with wide hazel eyes.

"Yeah, that Brad."

Cara looks at me and then back to Jill. "Why?"

"I like Brad," I add. "What's wrong with him?"

"Nothing." Cara shakes her head. "I just had no idea that Jill was into him."

"I don't think we'll go out again." Jill growls in frustration and leans her head back against her chair. "I screwed it up."

"How is that?" I ask, still shell-shocked to be here with these two women.

"I did it on purpose. I'm a bitch."

"You're not a bitch," Cara insists, shaking her head furiously.

"I don't think you're a bitch," I reply.

"That's because I've never had sex with you," Jill mutters.

"You had sex with Brad?" Cara squeals.

"No." Jill scowls. "It was a first date. I'm not a hooker."

I snort at that, worried that the margarita might come out my nose.

"I'm so confused," Cara whines.

"Brad's a nice guy. We had dinner. I'm not interested in seeing him again. That's it." Jill pins me with her ice-blue eyes. "Your turn."

"Things are good." I shrug, hiding my grin as Cara and Jill both scowl at me.

"We need more details than that, sweetie," Cara informs me. "Do you need more liquor?"

"Yes," I reply gratefully. Cara pours more into my glass from the blender pitcher.

"Are you sleeping with him?" Jill asks.

"Hey!" Cara exclaims with a laugh. "Dude, really?"

"You want to know too," Jill points out diplomatically, and I feel my cheeks heat.

"Good point." Cara turns to me and pulls her feet up under her, settling in for a good story. "Are you?"

"She is. She's blushing." Jill is grinning widely. "I don't want details because, ew, he's my brother."

Now that I have a few drinks in me, I decide to play with her a bit. "He's really hung."

"Oh, God, stop," Jill groans. Cara bursts out laughing.

"And, boy, does he know how to use it," I continue with a straight face. "He's got this one move where he grabs my leg and turns me so—"

"I don't want to know this!" Jill laughs and covers her ears with her hands.

"You asked." I shrug and sip my drink smugly.

"Speaking of good sex, Jill, are you still reading that book I gave you?" Cara asks.

"Dude, it's so good!"

"What book are you reading?" I frown down into my almost-empty glass.

"You have to read it!" Jill jumps from her seat and digs into her handbag, pulling a familiar green-covered book out of her bag. "It's called *A Spark of Passion* by Peyton Adams. Have you read this series?"

I'm struck dumb. I don't know what to say. I've never been in this position before.

"They're going to be made into movies," Cara continues, and grabs the book from Jill's hand. "How far are you?" she asks Jill.

"I'm almost done." Jill grins at me. "They are supersexy."

"Oh my God, that's an understatement." Cara laughs. "Do you want me to read you some of it?"

"Sure." I watch them with rapt attention. *They love my books!* "What are they about?"

"They're about three brothers, Julian, Marco, and Stephan. This is Stephan's book."

"So, each brother has his own book?"

"Yeah, and oh my God, they're all so hot." Jill fans her face with her hand and rolls her eyes. "They are all sexual dominants, which I didn't think I'd be too into, but holy hell, they are just so fucking amazing."

"Oh! Here's a good part." Cara tucks her hair behind her ear and smiles widely. "Excuse my language in advance. Stephan has a dirty mouth."

"I fucking love his dirty mouth," Jill sighs dreamily.

I can only laugh. I love this so much!

Stephan tied my hands above my head to the metal headboard of his bed. I was already sweaty and heaving in exhaustion from the two orgasms he'd given me with his mouth.

His mouth was bloody fantastic. His lips and tongue were made to give a woman pleasure.

With my hands secured above me, Stephan smiled softly and dragged his hand down my torso, between my breasts, and rested it on my stomach, rubbing his thumb back and forth on my skin.

"Do you know how gorgeous you look tied to my bed, Elizabeth?" he asked.

I couldn't make words form. Speech completely left me as his hand journeyed lower to my hip and the inside of my thighs.

"Answer me," he admonished.

"No, sir," I responded softly.

"I had no idea calling a guy *sir* could sound hot," Jill informs me, interrupting Cara.

"Shh, I'm reading!"

"Sorry. Continue." Jill grins and bites on her straw.

"You're so fucking beautiful, baby," he whispered, and leaned down low to pull my nipple into his mouth. "I'm going to fuck you, all night, with you chained to my bed." His nose glided over

my chest to the other nipple, and he pulled it deeply into his mouth. "You're mine, Elizabeth. Do you understand me?"

"Yes, sir," I responded breathlessly.

"Holy hell, this is hot," Cara murmurs.

"Don't stop now!" Jill complains.

"No, by all means, keep reading," I agree. I've never had a reader read my work to me before. It's amazing. It's humbling.

It's freaking hot.

He spread my legs and clasped leather bands around each ankle, holding me wide-open to do with as he pleased. I'd never felt so exposed, so helpless, and yet so sexy in all my life.

Stephan stepped back away from the bed and his eyes warmed as they traced the lines of my body, from my head to my feet. He still had his slacks on, unbuttoned. His large hands unzipped and let them drop to the floor, pooling around his ankles.

He wasn't wearing underwear.

"God, I love a man who goes commando," Jill mutters, and I can't help but nod in agreement as I sip my drink, listening intently.

"Hmm, what shall I do to you first?" he murmured as he joined me on the bed. He crawled over

me and lined his perfect, long, smooth cock against my mouth. "Open your pretty mouth, sugar."

I immediately complied, and he slipped just the head of his dick between my lips.

"Suck," he whispered.

With my eyes pinned to his, I closed my lips around the crown of his cock and sucked hard, pulling him deeper into my warm, wet mouth. He bared his teeth in a grimace and swore under his breath as I began to move my mouth more vigorously against him. He fisted the base of his erection and reached for my nipple with his other hand, twisting and pulling on it as I squirmed beneath him.

"You like that, don't you, baby?"

"Hell yes, I like that!" Jill agrees with a giggle, and refills her drink.

I nodded vigorously and moaned in agreement, then sucked his velvety flesh to the back of my throat and swallowed, massaging the head with my muscles.

"Ah hell, honey," he groaned as I felt the first stream of hot cum bathe the back of my throat. He pulsed against me, threaded his fingers into my hair, and held me still while he came, long and hard, into my mouth.

"You're going to be the death of me," he whispered raggedly.

"Wow," I mutter, and blink at Cara. Her cheeks are flushed as she stops reading, fanning herself with the book.

"I'm telling you, all three books are this hot," Jill assures me.

I watch both of them soberly and bite my lip. *Should I tell them? Can I trust them?*

Ty trusts them implicitly, and I would trust Ty with my life.

And honestly, I'm dying to share this part of my life with people who know me.

"Lo?" Cara frowns, watching me. "What's wrong?"

"Can you guys keep a secret?" I cringe. *Shit, am I doing the right thing?*

"When we're together for girls' night, this is a vault. Nothing will be repeated," Jill assures me, all kidding aside. "Honest, we don't spread rumors, Lauren. You're part of Ty's life, and that means that you're a part of ours too. We would never intentionally hurt you. Any of us."

"She's right." Cara nods. "We are your friends."

I scrape my hands over my face and take a deep breath, still disbelieving what I'm about to tell them.

"I wrote those books," I say in a quick rush, the words coming fast, as though I'm tearing off a Band-Aid.

"What?" Jill asks with a frown.

"*You* wrote these?" Cara asks.

I nod and watch their faces carefully.

"But your name isn't Peyton Adams," Jill points out.

"It's a pen name," I reply softly. "I don't know how I can prove it to you." I shrug and look out over the back pasture to the tall mountains behind the Lazy K.

"You wrote these," Cara repeats, her voice more excited now.

I nod, not quite ready to meet their gazes. "I did."

There's a long, silent pause. I'm sure they're trading glances and staring at me like I'm a crazy liar. *Why did I say anything?*

Suddenly, I'm tackled in a big hug and pulled out of my chair.

"You wrote these amazing books!" Jill exclaims, and holds on to me, her arms wrapped around my torso, my own arms pinned to my sides, and jumps up and down excitedly. "That's so cool!"

"Lo, this shouldn't be a secret!" Cara exclaims, and hugs us both.

"It *has* to be a secret." My eyes are wide with fear as I pull out of their embrace. "No one can know."

"But why?" Jill asks.

I rub my fingertips over my forehead. "Jack can never know."

"Oh," Cara sighs, and scowls. "I hate that asshole."

"What will happen if Jack finds out? You're divorced."

"But they weren't divorced when she released them," Cara guesses correctly.

"I sold them and released them after we were legally separated, but I don't know what he'd do or how far off the handle he'd fly if he found out," I whisper, embarrassed.

"Has he hurt you before?" Jill asks, and fills my glass. I should stop drinking. I tend to talk too much under the influence.

"Yeah," I whisper.

"What? What did he do?" Cara asks angrily.

"He knocked me around a bit when I kicked his ass out." I shrug. "We're in the middle of a legal mess, and I just don't need to add this to it."

"Our lips are sealed." Jill's smile spreads widely across her pretty face. "I know a famous person!"

"I'm not famous." I wave her off with a laugh.

"Uh, Lo, yeah, you are." Cara pats my shoulder. "Your books are being made into huge movies."

"I guess." It's still weird to think about.

"Do you know who the actors are gonna be?" Jill asks.

"No." I shake my head and laugh. "The producers have that job."

"Don't you have a say?" Cara asks.

"They asked who my dream cast was, and they do consult me, but at the end of the day, it's their decision. It's their movie."

"Wow." Cara grins. "Do you get to go watch the filming?"

"Can we come too?" Jill hops in her seat like a teenager.

"Where are we going?" Josh asks as the guys join us on the deck. Ty's eyes meet mine. They're warm and happy, and my body immediately warms, and I know it has nothing at all to do with the alcohol.

"Can we tell them, Lo?" Jill asks.

"Ty knows." I shrug.

"You told them?" Ty asks me softly, and kisses my forehead.

I nod shyly. "They were reading it to me, and I couldn't help it."

"I'm fucking lost," Zack complains. "What are we talking about?"

"Well?" Jill demands, her body quivering in anticipation.

"Okay, but first, let me just say, it's really important that this stays between the six of us. Please."

Josh tilts his head to the side, watching me carefully. "Okay."

"Of course," Zack replies. "Who are we going to tell?"

"You know these books Cara and I have been reading?" Jill asks the guys, showing them my book.

"The smut books? Yeah." Zack rolls his eyes.

"Hey, don't knock the smut books," Josh informs his brother, wiggling his eyebrows. "They're really good inspiration."

I giggle and turn my face into Ty's chest, embarrassed. He rubs his hand over my back and kisses my head.

"She writes them!" Cara exclaims, pointing at me.

"Really?" Josh asks with raised eyebrows.

I nod and bite my lip. "I do."

"Why doesn't everyone know about this?" Zack flips through my book, reads silently, then swallows hard and closes the book carefully, making us all laugh.

"Jack," Josh murmurs. "That fucker."

"It's okay," I assure them all. "I'm fine. I don't need to go public to be happy. I'm proud of them, and now my friends know, and that's all that matters."

"I'm so excited for you!" Jill exclaims happily. "Can I have sex with the actor who plays Stephan in the movie?"

"Jesus, Jill," Zack growls.

"What?" She blinks at us innocently.

"Uh, I'll see what I can do." I laugh and shake my head at her. She's nice.

And she's my friend.

"Did you have fun?" Ty asks, and kisses my hand as he drives us back to my place.

"I did." I pull my hand from his and push my fingers through his soft hair. "They're really cool and they make me laugh."

"And they love your books, so that must be good for the ego," he adds dryly.

"Tonight was good for my ego. It was fun to hear them talk about the books. About what they like about them, and when Cara read from it, I thought I was dreaming."

"Don't you ever interact with readers?" Ty frowns.

"I do online," I reply thoughtfully. "And it's fun. But this was the first time face-to-face. It was really fun."

"I'm glad." He squeezes my thigh affectionately as we pull into my driveway.

"Shit, is that my alarm going off?" I ask in panic as he comes to a stop.

Headlights fill Ty's car from behind us.

"Stay in the car." His voice is firm as he jumps out of the car, and a second car joins the first behind us.

Thank God, it's the cops.

But I'll be damned if I'll stay in the car and sit idly by while my house alarm is going off.

I jump from the car and stomp over to the guys.

"I told you to stay in the car." Ty's voice is exasperated.

I just shake my head. "No way. I want to know what's going on."

"Your alarm went off about ten minutes ago," Dan Teller informs me. He's one of the newest cops on the force in our small town. "Will you please key in your code and we'll look around?"

"Sure."

"I don't want you going anywhere near that house until we know it's safe."

"I have you and three cops with me, Ty." I gesture to Dan, and to Kyle and Adam, who pulled in behind Dan. "I'm safe."

As Ty swears under his breath about stubborn women, I lead the guys up to the front door and key in my pass code, silencing the alarm.

"The alarm company said it was a breach in the windows in the back of the house." Kyle pulls a flashlight from his belt and gestures to the other two. "Each of you circle the house and I'll go through the back."

"I'm coming too," I begin, but Ty grips my upper arm in his hand and pulls me against him.

"No."

I frown up at him but he just raises a brow, daring me to defy him.

Talk about stubborn.

The officers are gone for what feels like forever and I'm just about to tell Ty where he can shove it and go find them when they come through the house to the foyer, where Ty and I are waiting.

"There's no one here, but we need to show you something." Adam's face is grim as he gestures for us to follow him to the pool house.

"Motherfucker," Ty growls when we reach the pool. All of the windows in the pool house have been broken. Large rocks from my garden litter the cement floor, along with shattered glass.

"Don't walk in there," Kyle warns me as I take in the destruction around me. The bottom of my pool is full of glass as well.

"My pool," I whisper.

Ty pulls me against him and hugs me tight.

"Who would do this?" I ask.

"That's what we were just about to ask you," Dan replies with a soft smile. "Any ideas?"

"I know who did this," Ty replies. "Her ex-husband."

"How do you know?" Kyle asks.

"No one else would do something like this." I pull out of Ty's embrace, keeping his hand firmly in my own, grateful that he's here with me. "It's definitely Jack. He knows how much I love this pool."

"He must have been served with the protection order today," Ty agrees grimly.

"Can you prove it?" Adam asks.

"That's your job," Ty responds coldly.

I shiver as I glance around the room again. This took *work*. These windows are strong, and the destruction is extensive.

"How could he have done all of this in five minutes?" I ask.

"He couldn't have," Kyle replies, his head tilted in thought. "There had to be at least two people doing this."

I shake my head, at a loss.

"What do we do now?" Ty asks.

"Well, for tonight, we need to secure the house. The door between the mudroom and the pool doesn't lock, so I'll have someone come out and change the doorknob," Adam replies.

"We'll stay at my place tonight," Ty informs me.

"No, absolutely not."

Ty scowls at me as I shake my head stubbornly.

"We're going to make some calls and wrap this up for tonight," Adam continues. "Someone will be out tomorrow to check on things and continue the investigation."

"Thanks, man." Ty shakes all of their hands and

leads me into the house and up the stairs to the bedroom.

"Lo, I really think we should stay at my place."

As the adrenaline from the night begins to wear off, I start shivering. I wrap my arms around my stomach and shake my head. "I will never let Jack scare me out of my own home, Ty. I won't give him the satisfaction."

He frowns and pulls me into his arms, wraps his arms around me, and runs his hands up and down my back, as though he's warming me up. "It pisses me the fuck off that he did that with the intention of hurting you."

"I'm rather pissed myself," I reply softly, and sigh as I lean into his embrace. "Stay with me?"

"I'm not letting you out of my sight, sweetness. You're stuck with me."

I grin against his chest and nuzzle him, relishing the scent of him, his strength surrounding me. "Thank you."

CHAPTER

Ten

"Come on, beautiful, let's have a bath," Ty suggests after the police and the locksmith have left.

My heart sinks. *He wants to have sex now?* I step away and frown up at him. "Really?"

He smiles softly and cups my face in his hands, pulls me in for a soft, gentle kiss, then pulls back. "As much as I would love to make love to you right now, I think I can restrain myself, Lo. You need a bath to relax. Let me take care of you."

He leads me to the bed and, with his hands gripping my shoulders, lowers me to the side. "I'll be right back."

He disappears into the bathroom and I hear the water running in my large soaking tub. It's big enough for two. I wonder, will he join me?

I'm too numb to get up and take my clothes off, and surprisingly, hearing Ty bustle about in my bathroom is strangely soothing.

He returns a few minutes later, shirtless, and my mouth goes dry.

"It should be illegal for you to walk around shirtless."

He smirks and pulls me to my feet. "Why is that, baby?"

"Have you *seen* you?" I instinctively reach out and brush my fingertips over his chest, drawing a sharp inhale from him.

"Lo . . ." His voice is a warning, but I ignore him and continue to explore his chest, abs, hips, with my fingers.

"You're so handsome."

He takes my hands in his and brings them to his lips, kisses them softly, and watches me with hot gray eyes. "Come on, before I forget that you've had a traumatic evening, spread you out, and fuck you until the bed breaks."

Well, doesn't that sound delicious? Maybe I've changed my mind from earlier.

"Rain check," he whispers, and leads me to the bathroom. Not only did he run the bathwater, but he lit several candles and poured my favorite bath oil into the water as well.

It's soothing and soft and thoughtful.

He helps me undress and holds my hand while I step into the steaming-hot water. I lean back against the edge, close my eyes, and sigh deeply.

"Feel good?" I can hear the smile in this voice.

"Hmm. Join me."

"I will in a minute. I want to check the house one more time. You soak."

He kisses my forehead and is gone, and I let the heat of the water seep into my muscles, relaxing me. I'm suddenly beyond tired.

"No sleeping in the bath, sweetness."

I open my eyes to find Ty standing over me, his arms crossed, gazing down at me with a half smile.

"I'm not sleeping," I lie. "Join me."

"Don't mind if I do." He quickly shucks his clothing. "Scoot forward."

He slips into the bath behind me, then pulls me against him. "How do you feel?" He kisses my neck and reaches for a washcloth, lathering it up with body wash.

"Better."

"Good."

"Everything okay downstairs?"

"Yes. It's quiet down there. The locksmith added a locking knob and a dead bolt." I nod and am about to ask more questions when he leans in and whispers in my ear, "Relax. There's nothing more you can do tonight."

We sit in silence as he washes my arms, my back, my chest, and down my stomach to the juncture of my legs, never touching me in a sexual way, but in a soothing, cleansing manner that makes me melt against him.

Finally, he sets the washcloth aside, and while I'm still soapy, his hands glide to my shoulders and begin to knead the muscles there.

"Dear sweet Jesus, keep doing that and I'll marry you." The words slip out before I can stop them, before I even realize I'm saying them, and I bite my lips and cringe, hoping he doesn't notice.

But rather than freaking out at the *M* word, he simply chuckles and continues to spoil my shoulders and neck. "If I knew the way to your heart was rubbing your shoulders, I would have done it long ago." He rinses the soap from my skin and tugs me back into his arms to rest against his chest. I curl up against him and sigh deeply as he continues to gently caress my arms and shoulders, kisses my temple, and nuzzles my ear.

When the water cools and we're both wrinkling up like prunes, Ty pulls me from the bath, wraps a towel around his waist, and then slowly and thoroughly dries me off, his eyes warm as they roam over my skin.

"You're gorgeous."

I smile softly as he sets the towel aside and leads me to the bedroom and tucks us both in the bed. He pulls me against him and holds me tightly.

I've never felt so pampered in my life.

I don't realize that I've spoken aloud until Ty whispers, "Get used to it, sweetness."

I'm sitting in my office, my laptop set up before me, sending out e-mails and responding to requests on social media. It's early in the morning, and I should be writing, but I just can't concentrate.

I tossed and turned last night and gave up any hope of falling back to sleep at around five this morning and came down to work, leaving Ty to get as much rest as possible.

Jack destroyed my pool house.

I hear bare feet pad up behind me, and Ty's strong arms circle me as he buries his face in my neck and inhales deeply. He drags his nose up to my ear, sending shivers through me.

"Good morning." I push my fingers into his messy hair.

"I'm getting tired of waking up to an empty bed," he responds softly. "I'd rather wake up with you under me."

"I couldn't sleep."

Ty kisses my cheek, sets a mug of hot coffee on the desk for me, and shuffles over to my chaise lounge, giving me a prime view of his bare back and boxers-covered ass.

God, he has a nice ass.

"I made coffee." He shoots me a sleepy grin. "Why couldn't you sleep, beautiful?"

"Just a lot on my mind." I lift one shoulder in a shrug and lean back in my chair, watching him. "Since I couldn't swim, I decided to get up and get an early start on work."

"Working on a Sunday?" He raises a brow.

"I work every day, Ty."

"I think you need a day off." He scrubs his hands through his hair with a wide yawn.

I laugh and turn my attention back to my computer screen. "After I meet next week's deadline, we'll talk."

"Hmm . . ."

I glance up to find him tapping his lips with his forefinger.

"What are you thinking?"

"What would happen if you were cut off from your computer and phone for a whole day?"

"I'd most likely be set behind."

"But it wouldn't kill you."

"No." I tilt my head and watch him as he takes a sip of his coffee. My phone rings on the desk at my elbow.

"Hey, babe." Ty's eyebrows climb into his hairline at the term of endearment and I mouth the word *Emily.*

"Hey, whatcha doin'?" she asks.

"I was working, but now I'm chatting with Ty."

"Tell him I said hello."

I pull the phone away from my face and grin at Ty. "Emily says hello."

Without responding, he unfolds from the chaise, approaches my desk, and holds his hand out, silently asking me to pass the phone.

I pull it back to my ear. "Uh, I think Ty wants to speak with you. Hold on."

"Thank you." He winks at me. "Hi, Emily, this is Ty Sullivan. . . . Oh, good, she's told you about me." He sends me a wide, happy smile. "I wanted to let you know that Lo will be unavailable for the rest of the day. I'm taking her hostage."

I feel my jaw drop as I sit numbly and listen to his side of the conversation. "Ty, I can't . . ."

He shakes his head at me and laughs at whatever Em has said on the other end of the line. "I agree, she deserves a day off. . . . Yes, I'll take good care of her, and she'll call you tomorrow. Thank you, Emily."

He presses END on the phone, powers it off, and lays it across the room from me, out of my reach. Before I can respond, he grabs my laptop, closes it carefully, and lays it out of my reach too.

"You're taking away all my toys?" I ask sarcastically.

"No, I'm giving you the day off." He walks to me and pulls me out of the chair. "I want to spend some quality time with you today."

"I figured I'd be able to work while you did the guy thing and watched football all day. It is football season, isn't it?"

He laughs as he pulls me through the house to my bedroom. "Yes, it's football season, but you're more important."

"Wow, more important than football?" I chuckle. "You must be smitten."

"I think I'm more than smitten," he whispers as he gathers the hem of my shirt in his hands and pulls it over my head, tossing it on the floor. "I'm intrigued."

My nipples pucker against the cool air and his nimble fingers as he brushes his knuckles over them lightly.

"I'm captivated," he whispers, hooking his thumbs in my panties and pulling them down my hips, letting them drop to the floor. I reach out to touch him, to pull his shorts down, but he grips my hands in his and pulls them up to his lips. "Trust me?"

"Of course."

He grins and cups my face in his hands and pulls me in for a long, deep, wet kiss. He pushes his hands back into my hair, combing through it rhythmically. He has such amazing hands, I just want to purr.

He softens the kiss, nibbles my lips, and nuzzles his nose against my own. "Lay on the bed, please."

I move onto the bed, to the middle, and lie on my back. "Now what?" I ask breathlessly, already so turned on I can barely stand it.

"Raise your hands over your head."

His gray eyes are on fire as they roam over my body. He moves to the head of the bed and pulls a red necktie from the back of a nearby chair, loops it through the iron rungs on my headboard, and ties one hand, then the other, giving me room to move, but not enough to pull my hands down to touch him.

"I don't get to touch you?" My body tightens at the sensation of being tied to the bed, at Ty's mercy, open to his every sexual whim.

"Not for a little while." He grins as he tests the restraints on my wrists. "Feel okay?"

"Yes." My voice is harsh. Ragged.

I don't care.

Morning light filters in through the blinds on the window, across the bed, across my body, sending shadowed lines over me. Ty walks to the end of the bed and watches me for a long moment, his arms crossed over his chest, gliding his finger over his bottom lip. His biceps are bunched and his stomach is tight, and I want nothing more than for him to take those damn shorts off and join me on this bed.

"Do you have any idea how much you make me ache?"

"If it's anything like the way I'm aching right now, yes."

He smirks and circles to the other side of the bed, his eyes still pinned to my body, making me squirm and rub my thighs together to try to ease the ache between my legs.

"Ty, please touch me."

"Oh, I plan to, sweetness. I'm going to touch you all fucking day."

My breath catches at his promise. I bite my lip and watch him as he moves onto the bed and kneels between my legs.

"I love losing myself in you, beautiful. But I realize that I haven't taken my time to explore you like I've been craving. I am going to slowly worship every inch of this amazing body, Lauren. Do you have any issues with that?"

I shake my head no, entranced in the heat in his eyes.

Finally, *finally*, he touches me. His hands settle on

my feet and glide up my calves to my knees and my inner thighs, his touch light and soothing.

"Your skin is so soft." He plants soft, openmouthed kisses to my inner thighs, working his way higher. I pull on the tie holding my hands, wanting desperately to touch him. "You're going to have to be patient, baby. This is going to take a while."

"You're trying to kill me."

He smiles against my thigh and then bites me gently. "But what a way to go."

I chuckle, then moan as his tongue drifts up my inner thigh to my core, making me shudder.

"God, you're good at this," I whisper.

"I can't get enough of you, Lo." He wraps those amazing lips of his around my clit and gently pulls, brushing the tip of his tongue over the nub until I'm writhing, chasing the unbelievable sensation of his mouth on the most sensitive part of me.

He slides down to my lips and kisses them, then slides his tongue inside me with a rolling motion and pushes his nose against my clit, and I come up off the bed in a wave of sensation.

His hand settles on my stomach, over my navel, holding me still as he continues to lap at me, his lips dancing over my pussy, making me mad.

"God, Ty."

"Watch me, Lauren."

My eyes open and find his as he slides his tongue up and down my slit, his mouth glimmering in my juices.

"You taste amazing."

"Breakfast of champions," I mutter.

His eyes smile up at me, then he plunges a finger into my pussy and pulls up against my G-spot, sending me spiraling into a crazy orgasm, pushing my pelvis against his face and pulling on the ties, longing to hold his head against me.

He kisses each thigh, my smooth pubis, over to my left hip bone.

"Your body amazes me." His nose skims over to my belly. He presses a soft, wet kiss to my navel, then raises himself up on an elbow and traces my abs with his fingertip. "Your muscle tone is amazing."

I grin down at him as my stomach flinches under his light touch.

"Ticklish?" He grins.

"Yes."

"Hmm, I'll have to remember that for later." He settles on his stomach, his chest at my pelvis, eyes level with my breasts, and he continues to gently caress my skin, trailing a path around my breasts, beneath them, between them.

My nipples are peaked and screaming for his mouth.

He lowers his head and sweeps his tongue over one, then the other, leaving them wet. "I love your breasts."

"You're a boob man?"

"I'm a Lo man." He chuckles and pulls a tight peak into his mouth, licking and sucking lazily.

Finally, he climbs up me and kisses my arm, then moves to my mouth, hovering above me, gazing down at me.

"You're so beautiful, Lo."

"Thank you," I whisper.

He settles his lips on mine, and I can still smell and taste myself on his mouth. It just turns me on more. I wrap my legs around his hips, grind my core against his hard erection, still covered by the cotton of his shorts.

"Please make love to me," I whisper against him.

"I will."

"I want to touch you."

"You will."

"Have I mentioned that I'm not a patient person?" I growl.

He chuckles and unties my hands, kisses me once more before pulling off me completely.

He effortlessly flips me over. "Hold on to the head-board."

I immediately comply, reaching up and gripping tightly on the metal of the bed. Suddenly, Ty is covering me with his body again. Heat is rolling off him. His erection is pressing against my ass.

He leans in and whispers in my ear, "I've been wanting to do this since the first time I saw this ink."

He kisses my shoulder and over to my spine, then kisses all the way down my back, over my tattoo.

When he reaches the bottom, he starts up again, but this time trailing over the ink with the tip of his tongue. I squirm beneath him, delighting in the feel of the soft sheets against my sensitive breasts and bare pussy, silently begging him to finally slip inside me.

His hands cup my ass, squeeze, then glide down my thighs before finding my ass once more.

"Your ass is perfect. Firm, round. It fits flawlessly in my hands."

Dear God, his words are as sexy as his body, as the delicious things his hands are doing to me. I've never had my body explored so thoroughly.

"Your back is slender, and with your arms up over your head like this, your muscles are spectacular."

I feel him slip his hand down my spine over my bottom, and he pushes his fingers into my pussy again.

My hips buck, pushing back against his hand, needing to feel him deeper.

"You like that, baby?" he whispers against my skin.

"God, yes."

I feel him shimmy behind me, pushing his shorts down his thighs and legs, and suddenly he's blanketing me with his hard body and his bare cock is pressed to my opening.

He slides in slowly, lazily, until he's buried balls-deep. I try to pull my knees under me, to lift my ass in the air, but he holds me flat, plants his hands on the cheeks of my butt hard enough to leave handprints for days, and begins to ride me.

"I can't hold back any longer, sweetness, I'm sorry."

"God, it feels so good, Ty."

His thrusts quicken. His breath is harsh. "Give me one more, Lo. Come with me."

I shake my head and push back against him.

"Yes, Lauren." He leans down, braces one hand on the bed at my hip, and pushes the other beneath me, between my legs, to circle my clit.

My toes curl.

The world shatters around me as I come hard, clenching around him and milking his hard cock with my pussy.

"Ah, fuck, Lo." He pushes once, twice, then stills, rocking hard against me as he spills inside me.

Finally, he kisses me softly, right between my shoulder blades, and pulls away. He pads into the bathroom, where I hear water running.

I love that he always wants to take care of me after he makes love to me.

"Turn over, beautiful."

"I don't think I can move," I mutter into the pillows.

He laughs and lowers my arms to my sides, massaging them firmly, then nudges me onto my back. He brushes my hair off my face and kisses me softly. "Hi."

"Hi."

"Okay?"

"So okay."

He cleans me up and joins me on the bed, pulling the covers over us both.

"Ty, it's late. We should get up."

"Rule number one when you've been held hostage is you don't get to make those decisions. You didn't sleep last night. Get some rest."

"You don't have to stay with me," I whisper, and settle against him, my head on his chest, arm and leg draped comfortably over him.

"Well, it looks like I'm trapped."

I start to back away, but he pulls me closer. "I'm here, baby. Sleep."

Before long, the rise and fall of his chest and his fingers brushing up and down my back lull me to sleep.

"Bullshit." Ty's voice comes from another room, pulling me from sleep. I stretch and glance at the alarm clock, shocked to see it's after four in the afternoon.

I slept all day!

Rain is pounding against the bedroom window and the room is cast in gray, dark because of the storm working its way through.

"I don't care if we can't prove it, Brad." Ty's angry. I move from the bed, wrap the sheet around me, and walk down the hallway toward the upstairs living room, where Ty is standing before the large picture window, looking out into the storm. He's dressed in jeans and a white T-shirt. He's barefoot and his hair is still a mess. I lean against the wall, listening shamelessly. "No one else in this world would have done that to her house. A kid would have thrown one rock, not destroyed the whole fucking place."

He listens and pushes his hand through his hair. "I want her place patrolled regularly. This fucker isn't going to hurt her."

Brad must agree, because Ty nods. "Good. Thanks, man. Let me know if you hear anything else."

Ty hangs up and turns around, then stops short when he sees me. His face softens and he smiles. "You're awake."

I nod and cross to him, wrap my arms around his waist, and lean into him. "How's Brad?"

"Grouchy." Ty laughs and kisses my head while running his hands up and down my back, hugging me tight. "Pissed that we can't pin the vandalism on Jack."

"No proof?"

"None." Ty's voice is thick with frustration. "But the windows will be replaced by Wednesday. Brad was here earlier while you were asleep to check for any other evidence and clear the scene to be cleaned up."

"Oh, good. I'll have to call my pool boy and have him come take care of the pool."

"You have a pool boy?" He raises his eyebrows at me and his lips twitch as he tries to hold his laugh in.

"Of course I do. I have a pool." I grin and kiss him chastely. "Michael is very thorough."

"Do I have to kill him? Lawyers don't do well in prison, you know."

I laugh as I pull away. "Nah, he's very gay." I sniff the air. "You're cooking."

"I owe you a home-cooked meal." He brushes his

knuckles down my cheek before taking my hand in his and leading me down to the kitchen.

"Shouldn't I get dressed?"

"You could, but it would be a waste of time because I plan to just get you naked again."

"So today is just a naked day, then? Why aren't you naked?"

He cocks a brow and smirks.

Arrogant ass.

"Sit here." He motions to a stool at the breakfast bar, where I can watch him move about the kitchen. I like seeing him in my kitchen.

"Do you like to cook often?" Ty sets a plate of tiny-sliced bread with tomato and mozzarella cheese on the counter and I dig in, ravenous. "I'm starving."

"I'm not surprised. You didn't eat all day."

"I know, I slept all day."

"Not all day," he reminds me with a smile. "Wine?"

"No thanks, just water. Where did all of this come from? I know I didn't have it in my fridge."

"Jill delivered."

He pours me a glass of water and then sets about whipping potatoes and grilling asparagus.

"I'll have to start paying Jill mileage. This is quite a production." I take a sip of water and scoop up another piece of bread. "And delicious."

He takes my wrist in his hand and pulls my food to his mouth, taking a big bite.

"Mmm, you're right. Not as delicious as you, though."

I feel my cheeks heat and realize that I've never been given the opportunity to taste *him*. I tilt my head and watch him bustle about the kitchen.

"What are you thinking?"

"That I'd like to suck your cock."

He stops with a lamb chop gripped in the tongs in his hand and his head whips up to gape at me. "Excuse me?"

"You heard me." I shrug and take a bite of bread. "I've only done it once in my life, and I'd like to try it again."

He sets the food on the countertop and braces his hands on the granite, watching me. "Right now?"

"Maybe after dinner. I'm hungry."

His eyes are hot as he watches me. "Unless you want me to bend you over the breakfast bar, don't bite your lip."

I release my lip and lick it slowly where my teeth were buried in it.

"Damn it, Lo," he whispers.

"What?"

He shakes his head and paces away, pulls the asparagus out of the oven, and plates our meal. "I have a permanent hard-on when I'm with you."

"Is that bad?" I laugh.

"It's new. It's never been like this for me, and we've only just begun."

Wow.

He smiles softly and gestures to the dining table. "Come on, sweetness, let's eat so I can get you back to bed and bury myself in you for the rest of the night."

"Maybe I'm tired."

"You slept all day."

"Maybe I'm sore."

"We'll soak in the tub for a while." He frowns over at me as I join him at the table. "If you don't want this, all you have to do is say no, Lauren."

I grin and rise up on my toes to kiss his cheek. "I'm teasing you."

He pulls me to him, wraps his arms around my middle, and buries his face in my hair. "You're not funny."

"I'm hilarious."

CHAPTER

"Why didn't you call me Saturday night?"

Cary is furious as I sit across from him in his office. I should be working, and instead I'm here for a meeting late Monday morning. "There was nothing you could do, Cary."

"It had to be Jack."

I grin at him and shrug. "Obviously, but there is no proof. No prints, nothing left behind."

"He's such a prick. I'm sure the protection order pissed him off. Word has gotten around town, and I heard that he's been suspended from work." Cary shakes his head and leans back in his chair, watching me. "Is Ty staying with you?"

I nod slowly, maintaining eye contact. "Is that a problem?"

"Nope, he's not your attorney." Cary rubs his fingers over his mouth, deep in thought. "Lo, I know that Jack roughed you up when you kicked him out in the beginning, and now he's destroying your house. You never did tell us what he threatened to do to you that day at your house."

I drop my eyes and bite my lip.

"I understand if it makes you uncomfortable to talk about it around Ty, but I'm your attorney, and I need to know what's going on, Lo. Jack's pissed off, and if he continues like this, he could really hurt you."

I pull in a deep breath and push my fingers through my hair and blurt out, "He didn't use the exact words, because he's too clever for that, but he essentially threatened to rape me."

"What the fuck?" Cary leans forward and slaps his hands on his desk.

"He just wanted to scare me."

"I would have agreed with you last week, but he just destroyed your pool house, Lauren. He's obviously not stable."

"I have an alarm system on the house and Ty's been staying with me." Cary shakes his head and is ready to interrupt me. "Seriously, Cary, there's nothing more we can do when we can't prove that he's done anything wrong."

"I want everything documented from here on out. If he contacts you, you record it with your phone and you call me and Brad at the station."

"Okay."

"I mean it, Lauren. I don't trust this asshole."

"I agree."

"It sounds like we'll get a court date regarding the matter of the trust in November."

"November?" I stand and pace about Cary's small office. "Jesus, Cary, that's a month away!"

"I know. We were lucky to get in then."

A whole month of living like this will make *me* crazy.

"Keep Ty close by, your alarm set, and your eyes open, Lauren."

"I will." I check the time and grab my purse. "I have to go. I have an appointment."

Cary stands and shakes my hand. "I'll be in touch."

I nod and step out of his office and walk to Ty's door. It's open, so I walk in and close and lock it behind me, taking in the dark-haired man sitting behind his desk, his phone at his ear. *God, he's amazing.*

His eyebrows climb when he sees me.

"That all sounds good to me, Bill. I have to go. I just had something important come into my office. I'll be in touch next week."

I dump my purse in his visitor's chair, walk around his desk, and climb in his lap as he finishes his call.

"This is a nice surprise," he murmurs, and kisses me softly. My hands travel up the sleeves of his white shirt and wrap around his neck. I tangle his hair in my fingers and hold on as he takes the kiss deeper and then softens it again.

"I'm here to treat you to lunch."

"Oh, I wish you'd called." He plants his lips on my

forehead and takes a deep breath. "I have an appointment in five minutes."

"I know." I grin up at him and feel my cheeks flush as I admit, "It's me."

He lifts his cell phone off his desk and checks his calendar. "You're Jenny Fisher?"

"Yeah. That's one of my characters' names."

He's grinning at me like I just told him I won a Pulitzer. "Where are we going to lunch?"

"Right here. It's being delivered in"—I check the time on his computer—"a half hour."

"What are we going to do for the next thirty minutes?" He buries his face in my neck, nibbling my skin softly and sending shivers through me.

"Well, I have this fantasy."

"Oh?" He leans back to look me in the eyes. "Do tell."

"Last night"—I slide off his lap and to my knees—"I told you that I wanted to kiss you here." I pull my index finger down the seam of his zipper and feel the hard ridge of his erection beneath his black slacks.

He pulls in a deep breath and watches me with narrowed, heated gray eyes. "You did."

"I want to do it here."

"In my office." It's not a question.

I nod and pull his belt open, then unfasten his slacks. His lips curl into a half smile as he watches me open his pants, reach into his boxers, and uncover his hard-as-hell cock.

"You have a beautiful dick."

"I don't know if a guy wants his dick to be referred to as beautiful." He laughs.

"But it is." My hands slide up and down his length in long, easy motions. "It's big and smooth." I lean in and lap my tongue over the sensitive underside of the head and around the crown. "Delicious, just like I thought."

"God, baby." He leans his head back for just a moment, then continues to watch me. "Your hands are so fucking amazing."

He lifts his hips so I can shimmy his pants down to his thighs, giving me better access to his hard cock and tight balls.

I cup his sack in my hand, massaging gently, and wrap my lips over his dick, pulling him into my mouth and pushing down until he reaches the back of my throat. I grip him with my lips and pull all the way back up before sucking on the head while brushing my tongue over the tip.

"Damn, you're good at that." He's panting now; his voice is rough and his hands clench and unclench where they lie on his armrests.

I grip the shaft in my hand and work him firmly as I suck and lick on his gorgeous cock, reveling in how his hips gently thrust against me, pushing deeper inside my mouth.

Finally, one of his hands grips the back of my neck and he sets the pace, fucking my mouth in a steady rhythm.

"Lo, I'm gonna come soon, so if you don't want me to do it in your mouth, you need to stop now."

I moan and increase the pace, suck harder, pump my fist faster. His balls tighten and lift as he steadies my head, pulses into me, and erupts inside my mouth. I swallow quickly, massaging the head of his cock with my mouth as he shudders and convulses around me.

He gentles his grip and combs my hair with his fingers as I tuck him away, help him shimmy his pants back up his hips, refasten his pants, and sit back on my heels, smiling up at him smugly.

"That was fun."

"I would have to agree." He chuckles and pulls me back up onto his lap. "You're good at that."

"I haven't had much practice." I shrug, still smiling. "I like it."

He chuckles and kisses me deeply. "I can taste myself. You taste better."

His phone rings and I make a dive for it. "This is Ty Sullivan's office."

He cocks his head to the side, watching me with curiosity.

"Good, I'll meet her at the door." I hang up the phone and scramble off Ty's lap and around his desk toward the door. "She's a little early."

"What are you up to?"

"Lunch." I grin back at him and open his office door. "Did you get the extras I asked for?" I grin at Mrs. Blakely, who hands me a bag full of goodies from her deli, along with an armful of flowers and a bottle of wine.

"Good luck, dear." She smiles wide, winks, and walks away.

I take a deep breath before turning and carrying our lunch back to Ty's desk.

"Can you please move your laptop?"

He complies and stands to help me, but I stop him with a shake of my head. "Just relax. I got this."

"Lo, what did you do?"

"Well"—I spread a tablecloth over his desk—"you do a lot for me. Probably more than anyone besides my parents."

I pull boxes out of the bag, but rather than eating out of them, I plate our food on the nice plastic plates that Mrs. Blakely sent along.

"So, I thought it would be nice to do something for you."

I set the bag and boxes aside and open the wine, pour us each half a glass, and sit down opposite him, finally meeting his eyes to see what his reaction is.

"How did you know that pastrami on rye is my favorite?"

"I asked."

I can't read him. His eyes are warm, but they look kind of scared too, and I can't figure out if he's happy or if this is all a bit too much on a Monday afternoon.

"Is this too weird?"

"You bought me flowers."

Now I feel ridiculous. I simply nod and glance over at the pretty bouquet of lilies. "They brighten up your office."

"Come here."

I stand and walk around his desk to where he's sitting in his chair. He holds a hand out for mine and pulls me onto his lap, wraps his arms around me, and kisses me ferociously, deeply.

Finally, his lips slip over my cheek to my ear. "You brighten up my office. Thank you."

"My pleasure."

He hugs me close and then pushes me abruptly to my feet. "I'm hungry."

We munch happily on our sandwiches and chips and sip our wine as I look around his office, taking in the walls of books and the diplomas on the wall by his desk.

"So, why law school?"

"Why not?" He shrugs and takes a sip of his wine, watching me.

"You know, you never tell me much about you. You know all there is to know about me." I push my half-eaten sandwich aside, finished with it.

"Do I?" He raises a brow.

"Pretty much. So talk. Why law school?"

He sighs, wipes his mouth with a napkin, and tosses the wadded paper on his empty plate before sitting back and watching me from across the desk, his gray eyes troubled.

"Jill and I had a shitty childhood."

That shocks the hell out of me. I had no idea.

"Our mom is doing better now. She's down in Florida with Cara's parents, and she's happy. But our dad was a scary son of a bitch." Ty shakes his head and takes a sip of wine. "He typically beat on Mom; sometimes he'd beat on me. It didn't really matter once he was drunk and pissed enough, as long as he got to smack someone around."

I don't know what to say, so I just sit and let Ty talk.

"Do you really want to hear this story?" he asks quietly.

"Keep going," I murmur softly.

He rubs his lips with his fingers and shifts in his chair. "I didn't want to go away to college because then there wouldn't be anyone here to make sure that Mom and Jilly were okay. But I got some scholarships, and Mom insisted I go. She swore that she and Jill would be fine. Dad had sobered up some and hadn't pulled anything in about two years, so I went."

Dread fills my stomach at the look of guilt and anger on Ty's face.

"I came home for Thanksgiving my freshman year to find my mom's face covered in bruises and Jill hiding in a closet." He raises his eyes to me. "I almost killed him."

"What do you mean?"

"I beat the fuck out of him. I discovered that he hadn't knocked Mom around my last few years of high school because I'd gotten bigger than him, and he was a pussy. He knew he couldn't take me anymore."

Ty laughs humorlessly and fiddles with an unused plastic knife. "He came at me, drunk and yelling and throwing things, and managed to land a few punches, and then I saw red. I beat him unconscious."

"Did your mom file charges against him?" I'm sitting on the edge of my seat. How did I never hear about this?

"No, she filed them against me at the time because she was too afraid of what Dad would do to her if she put him in jail."

"You have got to be kidding me!" I gape at him, sure that I've just heard him wrong.

"Nope. Put me in jail. Of course, I got off. It was purely self-defense. But the public defender said something to me that changed my life."

"What did he say?"

"*She* said, 'Take a long, hard look at your life. You can either become your father, or you can do better. It's up to you.'" Ty's gaze finds mine. "I chose to be better."

"And your mom?"

He shakes his head and sighs. "She was with him until the day he died five years ago. There was nothing anyone could do to make her see that she could leave him. But I took Jill out of there. She lived with Cara and her family until she graduated from high school."

I just sit and watch him, so unbelievably proud.

"You're not saying anything. Rethinking this whole being-with-a-guy-from-the-wrong-side-of-the-tracks thing?"

"Don't piss me off when I'm sitting here thinking how proud of you I am."

He smiles halfheartedly, and I come around the desk to sit in his lap again. Cupping his face in my hands, I kiss him softly and deeply. "I think you're pretty cool."

He chuckles and pulls his knuckles down my cheek. "I'm nothing special, Lo." His eyes turn sad as he watches me. "I couldn't even save my mom from the bastard who beat her."

"That wasn't your job," I insist. "Ty, I know I was lucky to have parents who loved each other and were respectful of each other, but I was married to a man who loved nothing more than making me miserable." I shake my head and try to come up with the words to help him understand. "He didn't hit me, not until the very end. But taking verbal jabs at me, beating down my self-esteem, made him very happy. And I knew that what he was doing was abusive, and I didn't leave."

"You didn't—" he begins with a shake of his head, but I interrupt.

"I did have my parents and friends that I could have turned to, but *I* didn't leave, Ty. You need to understand, when a woman is being abused, no one can save her but *herself*. She has to be the one to decide that she won't live that way anymore. It was shitty of your mom to choose to stay with your dad rather than take you and Jill out of there. But it was *her* choice."

He exhales deeply and closes his eyes, then leans his forehead against mine. "Thank you for that," he whispers.

"I can't bear the thought of you blaming yourself for something that isn't your fault."

"I always felt like protecting Mom and Jilly was my job. I know my dad was a pitiful excuse for a man, but Jill and I spent more time at Zack and Josh's house than we did at home. Jeff King showed me what it was to be a real man, and he never would have stood for anyone treating his wife like that."

"I'm glad you had a place to go."

"I remember one time, Zack told his mom to shut up, and Jeff had Z up against the wall by his collar so fast, he didn't see what was coming."

"Good for him." I grin.

"Yeah, he never made that mistake again." Ty sighs again. "That's why it was so hard for me to watch my dad with Mom. I'd tell her over and over again to leave the bastard, and she would just shake her head and walk on eggshells around him."

"It's not your fault." I hold his face in my palms, making him look at me. "You got Jill away from there and you did the best you could."

"It's always been in my mind, you know? What if I'm more like him than I think I am?"

"You are nothing like that, Ty."

"I take care of the women in my life, and I know I'm sometimes overprotective, but I just need to know that they're safe. And now that I have you, that includes you. No one will ever touch you in anger again, Lauren. Never." His arms tighten around me, pulling me into the safety of his embrace, and I know that no matter what kind of shit Jack throws my way, I can stand up to him. Ty will be right there by my side.

And for the first time since my parents died, I feel . . . *safe.*

I bury my face in his neck and pull in a deep breath. God, he smells so good.

Finally, I check the time and sigh in resignation. "My hour is up." I clean up our mess and walk to the door.

Ty is right behind me. "Wait." He stops me before I open his door and instead of kissing me like I expect, he drops a soft kiss on my forehead. "Thank you, sweetness."

"You're welcome."

"I'll see you tonight."

"Have a good day, dear." I wave and wink, then saunter out of his office to the sound of his laughter.

"I'm way behind deadline," I moan into the phone. "I have to have this draft to the editor by next week."

"Okay," Emily replies. "What's the problem?"

"I've been a little distracted," I reply dryly. "Between sexy lawyers and psychotic ex-husbands, I've been a tad busy."

"Well, you're not busy right now and you're talking to me rather than writing."

"You're not helping!" I laugh and twirl in my office chair. "Seriously, I'm worried."

"Ask for an extension."

I wrinkle my nose and shake my head. "I can't."

"Because you're the only author in the history of the world to ask for a deadline extension."

"Shut up," I grumble. "I seriously can't ask for the extension. The publishing date on this book has been moved up because of the movie release, so I don't have any wriggle room."

"Okay, do you need any help?"

"Yes. Why are my characters determined to fight in almost every chapter? They are supposed to be falling in love and having lots of sex, and instead they fight like cats and dogs."

"Makeup sex?" Em asks with a smile in her voice.

"Oh, there's been plenty of that." I worry my lip between my teeth and rock back and forth in my chair. "Maybe they should go on vacation and loosen up a bit."

"I know! Send them to Tahiti! Lots of sun and water sex and they're not required to wear much clothing, so your heroine can ogle the guy's hot body a lot."

"You might be onto something." I nod and smile. "Maybe he has a private jet."

"Plane sex!" Emily laughs, and I can hear her clapping. "I bet he does have his own jet. He's rich as fuck."

"Yeah." The idea is taking shape in my head and I grin. "I like it. I like it a lot."

"Okay, you go write the fun plane sex. I have to write a murder scene."

"I like mine better."

She laughs and says good-bye and I dive back into my story, spending a few hours with my characters. The plane sex and sunshine are good for them, softening the mood of the story, making it fun and sexy.

I decide to stop at the end of the chapter, and when I glance at the clock, I'm relieved that I haven't missed my weekly date with Mr. Darcy at the hospital.

I've gone to read to Mr. Darcy every Monday afternoon for the past year. He is eighty-five, and blind, but he once wrote amazing political and mystery novels. He was our neighbor when I was growing up and was a friend of my father's. As an only child, I found things to keep me busy, and sometimes that included walking over to his house when he was doing yard work to talk his ear off or to listen to his stories. He used to tell me all about the books he was writing, and I never tired of listening to his ideas.

When my parents died, he was one of the few people who continued to check in with me, to make sure that the house didn't need to be repaired and that the yard work was getting done.

He was widowed young and never remarried. His children all live on the West Coast and don't visit often, which is why when his eyesight finally failed due to his diabetes, they put him in convalescent care at the hospital, rather than take him home with them.

I wave at the nurses as I walk past to his room and knock gently on the door, in case he's napping.

"Come in, darlin'."

I push inside and grin at him. He's seated in his favorite La-Z-Boy chair by the window, in a University of Montana sweatshirt with a blanket covering his lap, the newest James Patterson book resting in his lap, waiting for me.

"What if it wasn't me?" I kiss his cheek.

"I know your knock by now, girl." His voice is rough, but he's smiling. His hand clasps mine firmly. "How are you?"

"I'm good."

"Aren't you under deadline?" Until I met Ty and his friends, Mr. Darcy was the only one who knew about the books, although he doesn't know just how racy they are or how popular they've become.

"Yes, but I wouldn't miss our date for the world."

"You should be raising a family. Making babies. Writing books. Not wasting your time on an old man like me."

"Stop that." I take the book from his hands and sit in the wooden rocker across from him. "I like wasting my time on you."

He laughs and shakes his head. "Sassy as ever."

"So I take it this is the new book we're reading?" I flip the book open and turn to chapter one.

"Unless you have something else you'd rather read."

"Nora Roberts?" I grin.

"I have nothing but respect for that woman, but I don't think I'm her target audience."

"No, you're probably right."

I spend the next thirty minutes reading to Mr. Darcy, getting lost in the story with him. He grunts or mumbles during certain parts, but for the most part he just listens with a small smile on his lips.

"I'm sorry I can't read longer, but I should get back to work."

"Who is your young man?" he asks, ignoring my other comment.

"What young man?"

"Don't try that with me, Lauren. I know better. I hear it in your voice."

I swallow and frown, thrown. "Really?"

He just nods and waits for me to talk.

"Ty Sullivan."

He nods slowly and taps his lips with his finger. "Ty's a good kid. Despite that time I caught him and the King boys toilet-papering my maple trees in the front yard."

I laugh. "Not so much a kid anymore."

"You're all kids to me, girl." He reaches over to pat my hand. "He treats you nice?"

"Better than I probably deserve."

"Good." He nods once and takes the book from me. "Get to work."

"I'll see you next Monday." I kiss his cheek and hug him hard before leaving his room and heading home.

When I pull my phone from my purse, I see I've missed two calls and have three texts.

The first call is the pool guy; the second is Ty, as are all the texts.

Ty: **Just got to your house.**

Ty: **Your front door was standing wide-open. Where are you?**

Ty: **Lauren, answer me.**

Shit! I dial Ty's number as I pull out of the hospital parking lot toward home. I don't live far, just on the other side of town.

"Where are you?" His voice is hard and panicked.

"I just left the hospital."

"What?! Are you okay?"

"I'm fine, Ty. It wasn't for me. I go there every week to see a friend of the family."

"Are you on your way back?"

"Yes, I'll be there in ten minutes."

"Drive safely."

He hangs up and I toss my phone on the seat. Why was my door wide-open? I know I set the alarm.

When I pull into my driveway, Ty is waiting on the porch, his hands in his pockets, looking as delicious as ever in his white button-down with the sleeves rolled up. I just saw him a few hours ago and I want to jump him again.

"What's going on?"

"When I pulled up, your front door was standing wide-open and you weren't here." His eyes are blazing, making me stop short.

"Are you mad at me?"

"Hell yes, I'm mad at you. Why didn't you set your alarm?"

"I swear I did." I frown as I think back. "I was preoccupied with the story and with getting over to see Mr. Darcy."

I march past him and into the house.

"I think we should call the cops."

I glance around and sag in relief when I see that nothing has been touched. "Ty, it's been windy today. It probably just blew the door open."

"We don't know that."

"No one has been here."

"How do you know?" He's exasperated with me now.

"Because I can feel it! Nothing has been touched."

"You can *feel* it?"

"Yes." I shrug and continue back to the kitchen. "I probably forgot to set the alarm and the wind blew the door open."

"I'd feel better if someone came out to check the house out."

"Ty." I take his hand in mine and kiss his palm before nuzzling it with my cheek. "I love how worried you are, but I'm quite sure this was just a mistake on my part. I'm sorry that I scared you. I didn't do it on purpose."

He exhales deeply and pulls me against him, holding me tightly. "I was scared."

"I'm sorry." I hold on tight. "I'll be more careful."

He tips my chin up to look him in the eye. "If something happened to you, it would kill me, Lauren."

"Nothing happened. I'm fine."

"Oh, hi, Lo." Michael the pool guy saunters in through the mudroom, startling both of us.

"What the fuck are you doing here?" Ty demands.

"Ty, this is Michael, the person who maintains my pool." I pull away from Ty and prop my hands on my hips. "I thought you were coming tomorrow."

"Didn't you get my message? I had time today, so I came by. I got the glass out of the pool and you're ready to go. It's all clean. I did cover it, though, until you get that glass replaced so it doesn't get leaves and crap in it."

"How did you get in?" I ask.

"The front door was open. I've cleaned the pool when you were gone before. I just assumed you left the door open for me, so I called to let you know I was here." He frowns and looks between an angry Ty and me. "Was I not supposed to?"

"I swear I locked the door," I murmur. "It's okay, Michael, but in the future, if I'm not home, I'd rather you didn't come in."

"No problem." He holds his hands up like he's surrendering. "I didn't mean to scare you. My fault."

"Was the door standing wide-open when you got here, or was it just unlocked?" Ty asks.

"It was unlocked."

"Did you close it behind you when you carried your supplies through?" Ty crosses his arms over his chest and looks every inch like the lawyer he is.

"I thought so, but I could be wrong. Hey, I didn't mean to scare anyone. I'm sorry, Lo."

"It's okay." I offer him a smile. "Thanks for cleaning up the pool."

"It was a bitch." He shakes his head and lifts his toolbox from the floor, then looks Ty up and down before turning his smile to me. "He's hot."

"I know."

"The hot ones are always straight," Michael grumbles, and walks to the front door. "Call me if you need me!"

"You're hot." I grin as I turn to Ty, but he's not amused.

"He comes and goes as he pleases?"

"He's come to service the pool when I've been gone before, yes." I scowl and cross my own arms, mirroring Ty's stance. "What's your problem?"

He shakes his head and curses under his breath before muttering, "Nothing."

"I don't have time to deal with your weird mood, Ty. I have to work. Stay if you want to stay, go if you want to go. I'll be in the office."

I march away, but before I reach the door to the office, Ty spins me around and kisses me hard, then pulls away. "I have work to do too. I'll be in the living room."

With that he stomps away.

And men say women are moody.

CHAPTER

Twelve

TY

She's gorgeous when she's asleep. For the first time since I've begun staying with her all night, she's still asleep when I wake up, and it is a sight to behold. She's curled on her side, facing me, her hands tucked under her chin. She's breathing deeply as I gently brush her hair off her cheek and kiss her forehead.

I want nothing more than to pull her under me and wake her up with my cock inside her, but unfortunately, that's not in the cards for this morning.

I have a surprise.

I move gently, careful not to wake Lo, pull on my jeans and T-shirt, and pad down to my car to pull the poster-size prints along with my tools out of the back of my Jeep.

I hope she likes this. It could go either way.

As carefully as possible, I hang the three pictures

on her office wall and stand back to admire my handiwork. Whoever did these covers is an amazing artist.

Now to go get her.

She's still curled up on her side when I walk back into her bedroom and crawl onto the bed. I wrap my arm around her, lining my body up with hers, and kiss her cheek, breathing her in.

"Wake up, sweetness."

"Mmm." She wiggles closer to me, snuggling against me.

She's so fucking sweet. "Hey." I push my hand into her soft auburn hair and gently caress her scalp. "You need to wake up."

"Okay." She sighs and wraps her arm around my waist and goes right back to sleep.

"I know you're sleepy, but I have something for you, baby."

"Sounds good." She grabs onto my back and then frowns and opens those amazing blue eyes. "Why are you dressed?"

"Because I have something for you." I grin.

"Do I have to get out of bed?"

"Yes." I chuckle and kiss her forehead. "Come on."

"Why don't you get undressed and we'll try out that whole morning-sex thing you've been talking about?"

"Very tempting, sweetheart." *So fucking tempting.*

"Okay." She rolls to her back and stretches, yawns, and flutters her heavy eyes. The blankets fall, revealing her pink-tipped breasts, and I can't resist leaning over and kissing one hard nub. "Keep that up and we'll stay here." She sinks her fingers in my hair.

"Fair enough." I pull away. "Let's go."

She takes my hand as I help her from the bed, and I wrap my white shirt around her, buttoning just the middle two buttons.

"No naked today?"

I laugh as I guide her down the stairs to her office. "I get distracted when you're naked." When we get to the doorway, I hold my hands over her eyes and guide her inside.

"Surprise," I whisper in her ear, and pull my hands away. Her hands cover her mouth as she turns a half circle, gazing at all three of her covers blown up and framed, hanging on her wall.

"When did you do this?" She turns to me and watches me with wide blue eyes.

"I had them made yesterday after you left my office, but I hung them this morning."

"I can't leave them up."

I step to her and tip her head back to look up at me. "Yes, you can. This is your home, Lauren, and you should have these on your wall. No one but you and me comes in here anyway."

"Why did you do this?" she whispers.

"Because I saw you looking at my diplomas on my office wall. You need to have these on display. It's a big deal, Lauren. Be proud of yourself. God knows I'm so fucking proud of you I'm bursting."

She jumps in my arms, wraps those long-as-hell legs around my waist, grips my face in her hands, and kisses the fuck out of me. I plant my hands on her ass and carry her over to the wall, where I can support her with my body and I can touch her freely.

"I want you, right now," she murmurs against my lips. Her hands are clenched in my hair, holding me still so she can continue to plunder my mouth with her own.

I let her set the pace. She's circling her hips against mine, pushing her naked pussy against my crotch, and my eyes roll to the back of my head.

I swear to God, her lithe body is going to fucking kill me.

She grips both sides of the shirt she's wearing and yanks hard, ripping the buttons free. "God, I can't get close enough to you."

"I fucking love your body," I growl, and pull a nipple into my mouth, tugging with my teeth, rolling my tongue over it.

"Shirt off," she orders.

"I kind of like this sexy bossy side to you, sweetness."

Her eyes are hot as she watches me jerk my T-shirt over my head and toss it aside.

Just when I thought I couldn't get any harder, she leans down, bites my shoulder, and makes me want to come out of my skin.

"I love your tats." She grins and traces the yin and yang with her fingertip.

"I've noticed." I laugh and plant my hands on the globes of her ass, hitching her up higher. I pull one hand around to her clit and then slide two fingers easily inside her. "You're so fucking wet, sweetheart."

"I want you right now, Ty." She leans in and kisses my ink, and I almost come right then and there.

I push my jeans down my hips and thank God that I didn't throw on any underwear as I position the head of my cock at her entrance and slide home.

"You feel so damn good, baby." I bury my face in her neck and push and pull, over and over, increasing speed, losing myself in her warmth, in her amazing body.

Her legs and her pussy tighten around me and I know she's about to come. Her chest rubs over mine, sending electricity straight down to my cock, and I'm right there with her.

"I'm gonna come," she whispers.

"Look at me."

She opens her eyes and pins me in her hot blue stare as we ride each other in a torrential storm of lust and pure, unadulterated passion.

She bites her lip and bears down, groans, and shivers, coming over my dick, in my arms against the wall, sending me over the edge right along with her. I can't stop rocking against her as my body continues to come endlessly inside her.

"You do things to me that I've never felt before," she whispers as she rests her forehead on mine. "It scares me a little."

"It scares me a lot, but you're stuck with me, sweetness. You're mine, do you understand?"

She offers me a small smile and drags her fingers down my cheek. "I get it. It's not such a bad deal."

"So glad you approve." I pull out of her as she slides down my body. "I have to get to work."

I don't want to leave her, but today is a court day, and I don't have a choice.

Jesus, Sullivan, grow a pair. You can survive without her during the workday.

She grins and pulls my shirt closed over her breasts as she licks those plump lips of hers, made even puffier from our rough kisses.

"I have to work too." She turns back to look at the book covers hung on her wall. "They look so beautiful."

"Is it okay?" I ask hesitantly.

"That you did this?"

I nod.

"It's obviously okay, Ty. I just attacked you."

Every Tuesday night from mid-May to mid-October, Cunningham Falls hosts a farmers' market in Frontier Park. Local farmers and businesses set up tents and tables to display everything from fresh seasonal flowers to jellies and jams and handmade crafts.

In the center of the park is a temporary stage where musicians set up and play for the evening as well.

"Oh God, these brownies are to die for," Lauren

moans as she nibbles on a sample from Mrs. Blakely's booth. "I'll take four."

"There are only two of us," I remind Lo with a laugh.

"These are all for me. If you want some, get your own." She elbows me in the side and tucks her wrapped baked goods tightly to her chest.

"I had no idea you were so selfish." I tug her hair back from her face and bend down to kiss her cheek as we walk past the next table. "I bet I could talk you out of one of those brownies."

"No way." She giggles up at me, her big blue eyes shining in the cool fall air. She's wearing an orange vest over a long-sleeved gray T-shirt and jeans. Nothing fancy at all, yet she completely takes my breath away.

"Way."

"I don't see how. These brownies are my favorite."

I wrap my arm around her waist and tuck her against me as we walk and whisper in her ear, "If you'll give me a brownie, I'll bury my face in your pussy and eat you out until you can't remember your own name."

Her jaw drops and her breath catches and then she smiles up at me. "I guess I could part with one."

"You're so generous." I kiss her temple as she laces her fingers through mine and leads me eagerly to a vendor selling fresh apples and apple cider.

"I need some of these." She grins at the man, Lane, behind the table. "We'll take three pounds, please."

"Sure thing. Hey, Ty."

"How's it going, Lane?"

"Can't complain." He measures the apples and then passes the bag to Lauren, but I reach over and take them before she can.

"I'll carry the heavy stuff."

"Yes, three pounds of apples is just too much for my fragile frame to carry."

"You guys should come check out the pumpkin patch this weekend," Lane says.

"It's opening already?" Lo smiles wide and claps her hands. "I love fall. This is my favorite time of year."

"Yep, we open this weekend. There will be hayrides and the corn maze is ready too."

"No haunted house this year?" she asks, disappointed.

"It's there. Gorier than ever."

"Yes!" She fist-bumps Lane and grins over at me. "I enjoy Halloween."

"So I see." I smile as we wave at Lane and carry on. "I take it we'll be at the pumpkin patch this weekend?"

She nods and grins. Her cheeks are pink from the cold air.

"Are you too cold?" I cup her cheek in my hand.

"No, I'm just right. We should invite Jill to come with us to the pumpkin patch."

"Yeah, that's exactly what I want to do: take my little sister along on a date."

Lo slaps my arm and scowls at me. "Be nice. It's the pumpkin patch, not a date."

"Easy, slugger." I offer her my most charming smile. "Every day is a date with you."

"That was really cheesy, Ty." She rolls her eyes.

"A bit too much?"

"Just a smidge."

"Oh, hey, Lauren." Our heads turn to see Jack, holding hands with Misty, Lo's former friend and the bitch of all bitches.

I look down at Lo to catch her reaction. Her eyebrows climb on her forehead and then she pastes a fake smile on her lips. "Hello."

"I was sorry to hear about your pool." Jack's lips curl, evidence that he's not sorry at all. "I know how much you love it."

"Aww, poor Lo can't swim." Misty offers a fake pout and then the two laugh together.

"It can be fixed." Lo shrugs and tilts her head, watching them scornfully. "You both look like you could use a swim. Have you gained a few pounds, Misty?"

Misty gasps and glares at Lauren. "You know I work hard every day to stay in shape."

"Don't worry, baby"—Jack wraps his arm around Misty—"she'll get what's coming to her."

"Are you threatening her?" I step toward him and get in his face, nose to nose.

"Ty, it's okay." Lo pulls on my arm.

I stand firm. "No. It's not."

"You might want to listen to her. There are a lot of people watching, and I'll press charges if you so much as touch me." Jack's eyes are crazy, staring into my own. I back away from him, and just as we're about to walk away, Jack just can't keep his mouth shut.

"So"—Jack looks over at me and looks me up and down scornfully. I want to punch him so bad I can taste it—"how does it feel to fuck my sloppy seconds?"

Lo's grip on my hand tightens and I want with all of my being to tackle this smug-faced motherfucker to the ground and make him bleed, long and hard. To feel the satisfaction of my knuckles breaking his nose.

But I can't. The last thing I need is this pussy pressing charges for assault.

Misty has begun to laugh, finding Jack to be the funniest thing she's ever seen.

Lauren's eyes glimmer as she turns them to Misty and, steady as can be, says, "I could ask you the same question."

Atta girl. I smile down at her and kiss her temple.

She grins up at me. I'm relieved that despite being afraid of Jack in the past, she doesn't allow him to bully her.

"Also, I do believe you're violating the protection order that I filed. I know you received it. You're not allowed to come near me—or my property."

Both Jack and Misty lose their smiles and glare at both of us.

"You used to be so much better than this," Misty spits out.

"Better than what?" Lo asks.

"Better than the bitch you are now." Misty flips her hair behind her shoulder.

"No, I was a doormat before, Misty. I'm never going to be that again."

"Just pay me my money," Jack sneers. "I don't give a shit about anything else."

"Wow, you two are just perfect for each other," Lo murmurs. "But then again, assholes should stick together. We have better things to do than waste our time with you." She looks up at me and grins. "Let's keep shopping."

"After you." I kiss her hand and follow her around a pissed Jack and Misty toward the heart of the market, where a band is set up on the stage, playing country music.

"I feel nothing for him." She sighs. "It's sad to me."

"It is?"

"Yeah. I once loved him with everything in me, and now when I look at him, I feel just . . . emptiness. Nothing." She shrugs and glances up at me with worried eyes. "How is that possible?"

"It's not just a matter of falling out of love with someone, Lo. He is cruel to you. I suspect he has been for a long time."

She just nods, and I want so badly to march back there and beat Jack bloody.

Instead, I pull Lo close to my side, my arm

wrapped around her back and my hand resting on her hip. We nod and wave at the people we know, and Lo buys a jar of huckleberry jam before we walk closer to the stage.

"I love this song," she says with a small smile.

"Blake Shelton fan, are you?"

"Have you seen his dimples? He's hot." She shrugs and bats her eyes up at me.

"Come on, smart-ass." I tug her to the grass before the stage, set our bags down, and pull her into my arms. We sway back and forth and she begins to sing along under her breath, more than a little off-key, to "Mine Would Be You."

"Mine *is* you, Lo." I kiss her temple and ignore the stares and smiles of our community as they watch us dance across the grass.

"Everyone is watching," she murmurs, but doesn't pull away.

"I don't give a shit. Let them watch."

She relaxes her tall, lean body against me and the music carries us away. Before long, other couples, young and old, join us.

When the song ends, Lo cups my face in her hands and pulls me down for a soft kiss, which shocks the shit out of me, but I definitely don't complain or try to pull away.

"Let's go home."

I grab our bags and Lo takes my hand, leading me toward the bridge.

"It's dark, sweetheart."

"The city installed lights over the bridge. There were too many kids getting into trouble at night, so it's all lit up now."

"How do you know this?"

"It's my bridge." She shrugs as we follow the path to the bridge, walking side by side and hand in hand. When we get to the center of the bridge, she stops and looks over the side; her hair fans around her face and she takes a long, deep breath. "I love it here."

"Me too."

She glances up and smiles. The music from the band in the park drifts to us in the cold fall night. "You're not looking at the water."

"I'm looking at exactly what I love about it."

She sobers and turns to me, presses her body to mine, from her chest to her knees, and loops her arms around my shoulders, staring up at me. "You say the sweetest things."

"I'm just being honest, sweetness."

She shivers as my lips meet hers, not moving, just resting lightly against hers. Finally, I nibble at the corner of her mouth and hug her close as the band begins to play a country duet. I slowly begin to sway back and forth, unable to stop myself.

Lo's body was meant for mine, and when she's pressed up against me like this and music is playing, I can't help but move my body with hers.

"You must love to dance," she says softly.

"I never cared about it either way until you. Now I can't seem to stop dancing. Or maybe you just feel incredible against me and this is as close as we can get to sex with our clothes on." I grin down at her. Her face is bathed in moonlight and soft light from the streetlamps, making her eyes and hair shine, and I'm pretty sure I've never seen anything else so fucking beautiful in my whole life.

"This is a really great bridge," Lo whispers against my neck as she rests her head on my shoulder and gives herself up to the song.

"Don't you wanna stay here a little while?" The words float around us, and for now, on this bridge, in this moment, I feel Lo letting go. Trusting me.

No, I don't want to stay here a little while. I want to stay forever.

CHAPTER

Thirteen

LAUREN

I wake to loud banging and pounding coming from downstairs.

"Ty!" I reach for him, waking him up. "Someone's trying to get in!"

"What?" He scowls as he jumps from the bed and pulls his sweats up over his naked hips, then pins me with his intense eyes and orders, "Stay here," before jogging out the door and down the stairs.

I get out of bed and pull on my own jeans and a bra, and am pulling my shirt over my head when he saunters back in the room.

"The work crew is here."

"No one is breaking in?"

"No, sweetness." He pulls me into his arms and hugs me tight before patting my ass and letting go. "Looks like your pool house is being fixed."

"Oh, thank God." I slide my feet into my shoes and head for the door. "I'm going down to make coffee."

"I'll jump in the shower and meet you down there."

Ten minutes later, the coffee is percolating and I'm leaning against the countertop, scowling as hammers and loud male voices come through my mudroom door.

"How am I supposed to concentrate like this?" Another buzz saw sounds as men walk around my windows, carrying wood and glass, as Ty walks into the kitchen. It's now Friday, two days past when the windows were supposed to be finished, but because the glass was late coming in, and the window frames needed to be redone, a crew couldn't come out until today.

Four days before my deadline.

"Go in your office, baby." Ty kisses my head as he pours himself a mug of coffee. "Put your headphones on and ignore them. They should be done later today."

"I don't write with headphones on," I say, pouting. I know I'm being ridiculous, but I can't help it. "Why did this have to happen so close to my deadline?"

"I don't know why you're worried," Ty responds calmly. "You'll finish on time."

"We hope," I reply. The truth is, I've been too pre-occupied with all things delicious lawyer and his friends to devote the time I should to my book. My deadline schedule is rigorous, but it's always been manageable because I've never had this many distractions to deal with.

Not to mention, I haven't been able to swim for almost a week, and it's really put me off my game.

"You'll be able to swim in the morning," Ty reminds me, as if he's reading my mind.

"Thank God." I sigh and give Ty a kiss on the cheek. "Not swimming has been rough."

"I know." His gray eyes are happy as he smiles at me. "If you'd rather not go to the pumpkin patch tonight, we can do it another time."

"I want to go. If I can get some words written this afternoon, it'll be fine." Just then the buzz saws fire up again, making me cringe. "Or maybe I won't get anything done at all."

"Go to your office."

"I need coffee."

"I'll get it. Go." He swats my ass as I scoot out of the kitchen to my office and drop my butt in the chair, resigned to being unproductive again.

Should I e-mail the editor now, begging for an extension, or spring it on her at the last minute?

I shake my head, determined that that will be a last resort, and open my Word document. Just as I'm plugging my headphones into my computer, my phone buzzes with a text from Emily:

How many words so far today?

Me: **Zilch.**

Emily: **Get crackin'!**

"Easy for you to say," I mutter, and set my music.

"You don't have five million construction workers milling about your house, causing all kinds of distractions."

The music helps to block out some of the noise, and before long I'm swept up into the story, my fingers tapping quickly across the keyboard.

Ty sets a steaming mug of coffee at my elbow and rests his hands on my shoulders, kneading them firmly and rhythmically. I lean back into his touch as I continue to type, his hands soothing rather than distracting me.

After a long moment, he pulls my headphones off my ears and says, "Did he really just spank her ass with a riding crop?"

"You're reading over my shoulder?" I laugh as I look back at him.

"Of course. I'm standing right here."

"Yes, he spanked her." I move to replace my headphones on my head, but he grabs them and leans over me so he can see my face.

"Does that turn you on?"

"It turns *her* on."

"That doesn't answer my question."

I lean away and watch his face. He's not smiling, and his eyes are hot, almost like when he's aroused.

"I don't like to be hit," I finally reply. "It doesn't turn me on."

"Okay." He nods and begins to back away, but I stop him.

"Would it turn *you* on?" I ask softly.

He squats on his haunches at my side, turning my chair toward him so I have his undivided attention.

"The thought of striking you does nothing for me, Lauren." He pushes my hair behind my ear and pulls his thumb down my jawline. "I might enjoy swatting your ass playfully while I fuck you from behind, but I'd never do anything to hurt you."

He's not Jack. I nod and take my headphones from his hands. "I know."

"Do you?"

I meet his intense gray gaze with mine and smile reassuringly. "I know, Ty."

"Good." He cups my face and kisses me hard, then stands and kisses the top of my head. "I have to go to work. Are you going to be okay here?"

"Yeah, thanks for the coffee. I'm just gonna work too." Hammering and men yelling can be heard from the back of the house. "Or try, anyway."

"Good luck." He kisses me once more and heads for the door. "I'll pick you up at six for the pumpkin patch."

I wave him off and dive back into the story, the music playing in my ears, which I'm not used to, but it's better than the ruckus coming from my pool house.

Just as I begin to get lost in the rhythm of writing, there's a tap on my shoulder. I jump and spin, pulling the headphones off my head and yelping in surprise.

"Sorry, Lo, didn't mean to scare you," Dave, the

head of the crew, mutters. "But I've been calling your name, and you didn't hear me."

"I'm sorry, Dave. What's up?"

"Can you follow me?" He leads me out of the office toward the pool.

The whole room is a complete mess. Sawdust and tools are everywhere. Thank God Michael covered the pool, or this would ruin my filtration system.

I prop my hands on my hips. "Why does it look like the whole wall has been torn down?"

"Because it has." Dave grimaces. "It was all rotten, Lo. Could be from the moisture of the pool, but the wood was bad. I don't know who your dad had install this, but they did a shitty job." He points to the pile of lumber that has been torn out and tossed on the lawn behind the house.

"So you have to rebuild it?" I ask with wide eyes.

"Yes, ma'am."

"How long will this take?"

"It's not big, so just a few days. I'll have the guys work through the weekend." He shrugs and grins. "It's better to find it now, rather than have it collapse under the weight of the snow this winter."

"True." I'm still in shock that my pool house doesn't have a freaking *wall*.

"We'll work here until about three today, and then I'll let the guys go while I go order more supplies and we'll start early tomorrow morning."

"Okay, sounds good. Thanks, Dave."

He waves, and I stomp back to my office, resigned that I'll have to live with this noise through the weekend.

Glancing at the clock, I see it's already midmorning, so the early rush at Drips & Sips will be gone, and I should be able to find a quiet corner to hole up in with my computer. I close my laptop and throw it, along with the power cord and some notes, into my old computer bag and set out for the little coffee shop.

Just as I suspected, the café is quiet. I can wear my headphones here as easily as I can at home, and since I'm tucked away, I shouldn't be bothered much.

Or that's the plan, anyway.

And it works fine for the first few hours. Half of the coffee sitting at my elbow goes cold because I completely forget it's there as I get absorbed in the story. I'm finally to the climax of the book, the part where we don't know if the hero and the heroine will be able to make it through with their relationship intact.

It's all dramatic.

Suddenly, I feel eyes on me and a shadow falls across my keyboard.

"Hey." Jill grins and waves, holding two fresh coffees. "Can I join you?"

"Sure." I shrug, save my file, and close the laptop. "It's time for a break."

"Are you"—she glances around and then whispers, "writing?"

I nod and gratefully accept the coffee she hands me. "Thanks for the coffee."

"You look like you've been here awhile."

I check the time on my phone and am surprised to see it's already early in the afternoon. "I guess I have. Time flies when the story is hot."

Jill laughs. "And your stories are hot."

"Thank you." I blush as I take a sip of my coffee, still surprised that I confided in Jill and Cara last week. "What are you up to?"

"I have a few hours between house showings, so I thought I'd pop in for some coffee. Just tell me if I'm interrupting."

"You're fine. I really needed a break. I got quite a lot done since I've been here."

"Why *are* you here?" She sips her coffee.

"The construction crew is at my place repairing the pool house, and they're noisy and distracting. I couldn't concentrate."

"But you can concentrate here?" Jill raises a brow and looks about the café at the waitresses clinking cups and working the loud espresso machine.

"I used to come here all the time to write when I was with Jack. I had to hide it from him, so this worked. The espresso machine is much better than hammering and buzz saws."

Jill laughs and nods. "I can see that."

"So we're all going to the pumpkin patch tonight?"

"Yes! I'm excited. But don't make me go through the haunted house. I'll pee myself."

"Oh, don't be a wimp. It'll be fun."

"I'm happy with my wimp status. I don't think Cara will go for it either."

"What about the corn maze?" I ask.

"I have a horrible sense of direction, but I'm up for that." Jill sips her coffee, finishing it, then leans back in her chair and watches me for a long moment. "So, you're in love with my brother."

"Huh?" *Did she just say that?*

"You heard me."

"I don't know that I'm in love with him." I slowly shake my head back and forth.

"Why not? What's wrong with him?"

"There's nothing wrong with him." I laugh, knowing that there is no way to win this conversation. "We're still learning each other."

"Ty's a good guy." Jill traces the sleeve on her coffee cup. "He's had some tough breaks, but haven't we all?"

"We have."

"Have you seen him in the courtroom?"

"No."

"Oh, girl, you should see him when he gets riled up. He's all stern and hard and quite the force to be reckoned with."

"Really?" I'm surprised. "He's only ever been sweet and kind to me."

"He's ruthless in the courtroom. People don't fuck with him there."

This is a new side to Ty that I don't yet know. He's always so gentle—loving, even—with me. But at some moments he's been pretty controlling and take-charge, so it shouldn't surprise me that he's a hard-ass in his job.

"I'll have to check it out sometime."

"I think you'd enjoy it," Jill agrees.

"You two look a lot alike." I blush when I realize I've said it aloud. But it's true: they both have black hair, blue-gray eyes, and olive skin. Their biggest difference is their height. Ty is tall and broad, while Jill is petite.

"We look like our mom," she responds softly.

"Does she enjoy Florida?"

"I think so. We don't talk often."

"Ty told me about your dad. I'm sorry, Jill. I had no idea."

Jill's wide eyes meet mine. "He did?"

I nod.

"Wow."

"Why are you surprised?" I ask, tilting my head.

"Ty just doesn't talk about him." Her tone is soft, but matter-of-fact.

"Ever?"

She shakes her head, her eyes narrowed as though she's deep in thought. "He trusts you."

I blink rapidly. "I trust him too."

A slow smile spreads across Jill's pretty face. A smug, happy smile. "I hope so, because I have a feeling you're gonna be stuck with him for a long time." She checks her watch and then jumps up. "I have to go. I'll see you tonight!"

With that, she's off, waving at the barista behind the counter on her way out.

He trusts me.

*   *   *

The drive home is quick. I wrote two chapters today, putting me back on track for my deadline. I'm excited to see Ty and the others in a few hours and spend some time at the pumpkin patch.

The vans and trucks that littered my driveway earlier have gone. I park and insert the key to unlock the door, but it's already unlocked.

The door opens easily.

The alarm is also not set, but that doesn't surprise me because I left it off for the workers.

But I know that I locked this door, and neither Dave nor any of his crew had any need to walk through the house.

The hairs on the back of my neck stand up. Something is just . . . *off.*

I set my purse and keys on the table by the door and walk inside the quiet house. From what I can see, nothing has been moved or touched: everything is as it was when I left this morning.

Then I walk back toward the office, and the door is ajar.

I always shut that door.

Always.

Without taking another step forward, I turn toward the front door, grab my purse and keys, and pull my phone out of my pocket as I lock myself inside my car.

My hands are shaking, my breath is coming in petrified pants as I dial Brad's number first.

"Hull," he answers.

"It's Lo. Are you working?" I hate how unsteady my voice sounds.

"Yes. What's wrong, Lo?"

"Someone has been in my house."

"Where are you?"

"I'm sitting in the car in my driveway."

"Stay there, I'm on my way." He hangs up, and I immediately call Ty.

"Turner and Sullivan," the receptionist answers. Ty's cell phone must be forwarded to the office.

"This is Lauren. Is Ty in court today?"

"Yes, he is, but he should be here in about ten minutes. Do you want me to have him call you?"

"Yes, please."

"Is everything okay?"

"I don't know. I just need him. Please tell him as soon as you see him."

"Of course."

I hang up and throw my phone in the passenger seat, waiting for Brad to arrive. I swear, time has never moved slower than it is right now.

Where is he?

Finally, Brad's car pulls into my driveway, but I stay where I am, even when he climbs from his car and walks to mine.

"You can get out now, Lo."

"How do you know? You haven't looked inside the house yet."

Just then, Ty's Jeep comes screaming into my driveway. He comes to an abrupt stop and throws it out of gear, then jogs to my side, opens the car door, and pulls me out of the car and into his arms.

"What's wrong?" He's breathing hard and his heart is beating a staccato against my cheek.

"Someone has been in the house."

"What?" Ty pulls me away from him and shoots a look at Brad. "Have you checked it out?"

"I just got here. I haven't gone inside yet. I want to hear the story first."

"What happened, baby?"

Brad's eyebrow rises at Ty's term of endearment, but we both ignore him as I begin the story of going to the café to write, my impromptu coffee date with Jill, and coming home.

"So, nothing has been touched inside?" Brad asks when I'm finished.

"Not that I can see, but I swear I locked that door, and my office door was ajar."

"You said yourself that you were preoccupied with work before you left, right? And that the crew was distracting you?"

"Yes, but I always—*always*—close the door to my office, Brad. I never forget."

"Okay, I'll go inside and take a look around." Brad leaves us, his hand on his firearm as he enters the house.

"I'm not crazy, Ty."

"No one is calling you crazy, beautiful."

"Someone who shouldn't be has been inside my house."

After five long minutes, Brad returns, shaking his head. "There's no one in there now. The crew locked the back mudroom door. Maybe one of them came through the house on his way out?"

I'm shaking my head no before he even gets through the first sentence.

"If Lo says someone has been here, someone was here, Brad. She's never cried wolf before."

Brad sighs and pushes his hand through his hair. "I know. I believe that you feel that something is off here, Lo. But there's no sign of forced entry, and you had a work crew here all day who had access to the house."

I sigh in frustration and glance back at the house. "Did you go in my office?"

"You didn't?" Ty asks me, surprised.

"No. When I saw the door ajar, it scared me and I came outside and called you guys."

"I did go in the office, but only you can know if something in there has been messed with."

"Come on." Ty grips my hand firmly in his own and leads me to the porch. "Let's go check it out."

The door to the office is closed now, thanks to Brad. When we walk inside, goose bumps break out on my skin.

"Is anything different in here?" Brad asks, and stands back as Ty and I walk in, looking around.

"It looks the same as it did this morning," Ty murmurs.

"It does," I confirm, but my voice is hesitant.

"But?" Ty asks.

"But I feel it. Someone has been in here."

Both men look at me dubiously, and I'm mortified to feel tears form in my eyes. *Am I going crazy? Has Jack finally pushed me over the edge?*

"Hey, don't cry." Ty kisses my forehead before he turns to Brad. "What do we do now?"

"The same that you've already been doing, unfortunately." Brad glances around the room, and his eyes stop on the large book covers hanging on the wall. "Hey, I recognize those."

I stiffen, but before I can say anything, Ty responds, "Those are Lo's favorite books, so I had them framed for her."

"Cool." Brad seems to accept the explanation and turns for the door. "I'm sorry I can't be more help, Lo. There's just no evidence. But if you do find that something is missing, let me know right away."

I nod and try to offer Brad a smile as he turns and leaves out the front door.

"Someone was in my house," I whisper, and sink down onto the chaise lounge.

"Why didn't you lock the front door?"

"I did! I told you, I'm sure I did. I know that I was preoccupied with this deadline, and the commotion out there had me all distracted, but with all the Jack shit happening, I'm sure I locked it. And I *know* I shut this office door."

"Okay, I believe you."

"You do?"

"Of course. You're not stupid, and you're not a liar, Lo."

I nod, relieved to know that he believes me, because I'm not so sure I believe myself anymore. It all seems so silly.

"Maybe it was one of the construction guys who came through the house on his way out for the day." I shrug, then rub my hands briskly over my face.

"So you had coffee with Jill?"

"Yeah. She came into Sips and sat with me for a bit."

"What did you talk about?"

"Stuff." I shrug like it's no big deal.

Ty's eyes narrow. "What kind of stuff?"

"Girl stuff."

"I don't believe you."

I laugh and kiss Ty's cheek. "That's okay."

"You're not going to tell me?" His eyebrows are raised high on his brow.

"Nope."

He frowns, then smiles down at me. "Okay."

"I got the work I wanted to finished, so I can frolic through the corn maze tonight with no worries."

"Oh, great," he replies sarcastically. "You'll be frolicking without me."

"Why?"

"Honey, I'm a guy. I don't frolic."

"You have a tattoo of a princess tiara on your arm, big guy." I slap his shoulder and stalk past him to go change my clothes. "You'll frolic."

"I'll run, not frolic." His voice is right behind me on the stairs.

"You could romp through the corn," I suggest with a laugh.

"Do you remember earlier when we were talking about spankings?" Ty asks with a smile in his voice.

"I have no idea what you're talking about," I lie.

"You're about to remember, sweetness."

CHAPTER

Fourteen

TY

"I don't want to take a dumb hayride," Seth, Zack's twelve-year-old son, murmurs as we all hop up onto the wagon, stacked with hay bales, being pulled by a big green John Deere tractor. "Can Thor and I run alongside you, Dad?"

"That's fine, but stay close," Zack agrees, and sits next to his brother, Josh, who has Cara snuggled in his lap.

Jill climbs aboard and waits for us to sit, then sits on the other side of me, far from Zack. I glance over at him and notice his scowl before he schools his features and watches his son and the boy's dog happily run alongside the wagon as we bounce over the field to the pumpkins and the corn maze.

"The haunted house is down tonight," the driver calls back. "They're fixing the wiring or something."

"Well, crap," Lo mutters beside me, disappointed. I wrap my arm around her and kiss her temple, breathing in the clean scent of her.

"Thank God," Jillian exclaims at the same time, making the others laugh.

It's close to seven in the evening, just approaching twilight, but the rows of pumpkins and the high stalks of corn are illuminated with tall stadium lights so bright it's almost the same as being out here during the middle of the day.

"Why are we at the pumpkin patch again?" Zack asks.

"Because it's tradition." Cara elbows him and Jill smirks at him.

"What, are you afraid that you'll get lost in the corn maze and you'll need your twelve-year-old to help you find your way back out?" Jill taunts him.

"No, I'm afraid I'm going to have to find *your* ass in there when you lose your way." He grins at her warmly. I glance down at Jill and see she's grinning back.

I'm not sure how I feel about that.

This farm opens to the public every year. Families and people of all ages come out to enjoy the maze, choose pumpkins, and buy fall produce offered here, but during one day of the season, all proceeds are given to an organization called Text No More, an organization that educates the community about the ramifications of texting while driving.

Mary and Eric Thomas own and run Wildfire

Farms, and six years ago their four-year-old daughter was killed when struck by someone texting and driving.

Most of the community comes out to support this cause.

"Holy crap, Dad!" Seth points to the thousands of bright orange pumpkins on the ground ahead of us as we approach the patch. "That's a ton of pumpkins!"

"Why do we need pumpkins?" Josh asks Cara. "No one is going to come trick-or-treating way out at our place."

"Because they're fun." Cara grins at him. "Get in the spirit of it."

Lo is quiet next to me, deep in thought.

"You okay?" I murmur into her ear, and smile to myself when she shivers.

"I'm fine," she responds softly.

I tip her head back to look in her eyes. "You sure?"

She just nods and leans her head on my shoulder, and I shelve the issue, reminding myself to ask her about it later.

"Hey, y'all are coming to our place on Sunday for football, right?" Josh asks us all. "Seattle is playing San Francisco."

"I'm there," Zack confirms.

I glance down at Lo and watch the small smile form on her lips. "You down?"

"Sure."

"We're in," I confirm.

"I hate football," Jillian says with her nose wrinkled.

"Oh, us girls will be eating snacks and gossiping while the guys watch football," Cara assures her.

"Then I'm in," Jill replies with a smile.

The tractor stops by the edge of the rows of pumpkins and we all disembark the wagon. Thor and Seth have run ahead into the rows and rows of pumpkins, playing fetch with a stick Seth found on the ground.

"Thor and I want to go into the corn maze!" Seth calls to Zack.

"In a bit! We're going to look at pumpkins first."

"Pumpkins are for babies," Seth grumbles.

"Whatever, brat." Cara catches Seth in a headlock and rubs her knuckles on his head, making him laugh. "Take it back!"

"Never! You're a baby!" Seth giggles and tries to twist away from the small woman, who is clearly much stronger than she looks.

"I'll make you eat those words!" Cara yells back.

"You don't scare me!"

Thor barks and jumps around them, wanting to get in on the fun. Finally, Cara lets go, panting with exertion, and leans over, bracing her hands on her knees.

"I'm too old for this."

Josh leans in and whispers in her ear, making her flush and grin at the same time.

I swear, they're like rabbits.

Lauren's face breaks out into a wide grin as she follows the others, picking through the vines to find the perfect pumpkin.

"Are you really going to carve these?" I ask her with a grin.

"Hell yes. I love Halloween." Her smile dims for a moment before returning as she squats by a large, oddly shaped pumpkin. "This one would be perfect."

"That one looks heavy." I eye it dubiously.

"I have faith in you." She laughs and winks at me.

Cara, a few rows over, calls, "Lo! Come help me pick one!"

Lo points to her pumpkin. "That one's mine, Sullivan!" Then she sets off in Cara's direction. "I'm coming!" Lo calls out, and jogs through the vines and piles of dirt to Cara. "How big do you want?"

The girls set off, picking through the pumpkins and laughing with each other, while Josh and Zack play with Seth and Thor.

Watching Lo with my friends, the people I'm closest to in the world, rocks me back on my heels. She fits with them. The most I ever dared wish for was that they'd tolerate each other, given their history when they were kids, but Lo has come to be a part of our little group, and I couldn't be happier.

Lo laughs at something Cara says, throwing her head back and tucking her thick auburn hair behind her ear. Her smile is wide and happy, and her blue eyes are shining in joy, and it's in this moment that I know without a doubt that I love this woman.

She's it for me.

I stagger back a step and sit on a hay bale, rubbing my hand over my chest just as Jill steps up beside me.

"I definitely like her," she comments casually, watching Lo and Cara.

"You do?"

Jill nods, then smiles down at me. "She's good for you." She turns her eyes back to the two women and tilts her head in thought. "And frankly, I think you're good for her too."

"Why do you say that?" I continue to rub my chest, unsure why there's an ache there.

"Look at her, dude. She's come out of her shell since she's been with you. She's quick to smile now. I think you make her happy." Jill nudges me with her elbow. "Not that I understand the attraction. You're ugly and a complete jerk."

"Obviously," I smirk. "Did you pick a pumpkin?"

"I'm not getting one. I'm going into the maze." She rubs her hands together in delight. "I'm gonna beat Zack through it if it kills me."

"What's up with you guys?" I ask casually.

"Nothing at all."

"That's a complete lie." Jill shrugs and stands to march away, but I grab her arm, holding her close. "So, you can ask about my love life, but I'm not allowed to ask about yours?"

"I don't have a love life, Ty." Jill pulls her arm out of my grasp and walks away. "I like it that way," she calls over her shoulder.

Lauren turns to me and waves her arm over her head to get my attention. As if I weren't already aware of exactly where she is and what she is doing.

I'm always aware of her. I can't get enough of her.

Jesus, I fucking love her.

"We're ready for the maze," she calls out to me. As I approach her, she links her fingers through mine and smiles at me, and I want so much to blurt out in front of all of our friends that I love her, but I know that this will have to be handled gently.

I refuse to have her run away on me now.

"Thor and I are going to kick all of your butts in the maze!" Seth taunts us all. Thor barks in agreement and they take off into the tall cornstalks. Josh and Cara jog in after them, and that leaves Jill and Zack eyeing each other dubiously.

"I'll go alone," Jill announces, and takes a step forward.

Zack pulls her up short. "Like hell you will." He glowers at her. "You'll go with me."

"If I'm with you, I can't beat you," she reminds him, her hands on her hips.

I glance down at Lo, who is trying, and failing, to hide a smile.

"Come on, you're with me." Zack takes her hand and leads her into the corn.

"You're such a damn caveman," we hear her mutter at him scornfully, making us both laugh.

"So that leaves you and me." Lo grins and takes a step, but I pull her back against me, into my arms, and brush my nose against hers. "You don't want to go into the maze?"

"Honestly? I don't give a shit about the maze. I want to hold you for a few minutes without having those yahoos watching us."

"'Yahoos'?" She laughs. "Who says that these days?"

I laugh with her and nuzzle her nose again before gently kissing her cold lips. "Me."

"Your lips are warm," she whispers.

"Yours aren't." I kiss her again. "Maybe I should warm them up."

"I have other parts that have gotten cold out here too." She grins and tugs at the hem of my shirt under my wool jacket and lays her cold hands on the small of my back, making me jump.

"Jesus, baby, you're fucking cold!"

She giggles and presses herself against me so I can't back away. Not that I would back away anyway.

"Do you want me to stop touching you?" She bats her eyelashes at me, making me chuckle.

"Fuck no. I don't care if your hands are cold or hot or somewhere in between, as long as they're on me."

Her smile fades as she watches me, and her breath begins to come in pants, visible in the cold air, and her eyes are sparkling with pure lust.

She rises on her toes and presses her lips to mine, brushing back and forth softly, and unable to handle it anymore, I pull her closer to me and kiss her like mad. My tongue slips between her plump lips and explores her mouth leisurely. When we have to pull back for air, I glide my nose down her jawline to her neck and place a tender kiss on her soft skin.

"You can't possibly know what you do to me, Lauren."

"Ew!" Seth exclaims as he and his dog bound out of the corn. "Yuck. Come on, Thor, you shouldn't have to see this."

Lo giggles and smiles up at me. I cup her face in my hands and kiss her once more, gently, before pulling back and taking her hand in mine just as Zack and Jill come out of the maze.

"You guys made it out already?" Jill asks with a scowl on her pretty face.

"You were too slow," Lo responds with a shrug, and winks at me. "Come on, counselor, let's go buy some apples and cider. And jam. And I have to go fetch my pumpkin. Oh! And I want some cornstalks for the front porch too."

"Is there anything else you need?" I ask sarcastically.

"Just you." She grins.

"The feeling is entirely mutual."

CHAPTER

Fifteen

LAUREN

"I want to bake a pie," I announce as Ty and I approach my front door upon our return from the pumpkin patch.

"Tonight?" Ty raises his brow and sets my pumpkin on the porch, then jogs back down to his Jeep to gather my cornstalks and leans them against the house under the cover of the porch.

"Yep."

"At"—he checks his watch—"almost ten in the evening?"

"Do you have somewhere you need to be?" I laugh. "Got a hot date?"

I unlock the door and key the alarm code into the pad on the wall and then lead Ty into the kitchen.

"Most people just don't start baking pies this late

at night." Ty takes the heavy bags of apples from me and sets them on the counter.

"My parents used to go with me to the pumpkin patch, even when I was a grown woman," I reply softly, my heart heavy. "It was tradition for my mom and me to bake a pie when we got home, so I want to bake a pie."

"Then we'll bake a pie." Ty kisses my head, then strips out of his coat, pushes the sleeves of his long-sleeved T-shirt up to his elbows, and washes his hands.

"Do you know how to bake a pie?" I ask as I also pull off several layers of sweater and scarf and then set apples on the countertop for peeling and gather the other ingredients, including a frozen pie crust, and set the oven for preheat.

"Frozen crust?" Ty grins.

"I have never been able to get them right." I shrug and wash my hands. "They always fall apart on me. My mom could make them with her eyes closed."

"I can make a decent pie crust." Ty's voice is non-chalant as he roots around in my pantry for the flour.

"You're gonna make a pie crust from scratch?"

"Sure. If we're gonna bake a pie, we're gonna do it right."

"Okay, you do that and I'll peel these apples and get them in the pot."

We work side by side for several minutes in rel-ative silence, brushing against each other as we pass by and grinning at each other. I get the apples peeled and sliced and into a pot with all the spices to boil.

"Where's your rolling pin?" he asks softly.

"Over there." I point to a nearby drawer and watch as he balls up his crust dough, spreads flour over my kitchen table, and begins to roll out the dough, his forearms flexing with his smooth movements. A lock of his hair falls over his forehead and he reaches up to push it back, leaving a streak of white flour across his skin. "That looks like a great way to get out some aggression."

"It is." He grins at me. "Wanna try?"

"Sure."

He passes the rolling pin to me and stands back as I coat it in flour and roll it over the already-flat dough on the table.

"Your ass looks fantastic bent over the table." A smile is in his voice.

I smirk and pinch some flour in my fingers and throw it at him. "Behave!"

"You just threw flour at me." He laughs.

"Observant, aren't you?"

I throw another handful of flour and giggle when he throws some back at me, making it snow over me with white powder.

"You're making a mess!" I cry, and run around the table to the other side and scoop some flour in my hand and toss it at him.

"You started it, sweetness." He throws a handful

back at me just as I hear the pot on the stove begin to bubble.

"Time out! I have to stir the apples." I laugh and run to the stove to stir the thickening mixture of apples and cinnamon and sugar. "It smells so good."

I grab a pie plate and turn around to find that Ty has moved the first pie crust and is rolling out the second one to lay over the top.

"Do you have a pizza cutter?"

I pull the tool out of a drawer and pass it to him, and he makes long strips out of the crust.

"You're fancy." I grin while I line the pie plate with the first crust and tuck it around the edges, then walk back to the stove to fill it with the bubbling apples.

He just smirks and raises an eyebrow when he sees me pull a squeeze bottle of caramel sauce out of the pantry.

"I like caramel in my pie." I squeeze the sweet sauce over the top of the apples.

When I've finished, Ty weaves the strips of the remaining crust over the top. "I need one beaten egg," he instructs me.

When I've beaten an egg in a bowl, he brushes it over the top of the crust. "This will make it golden brown."

"Okay, Martha Stewart."

He laughs as I push the pie into the oven and set the timer for forty minutes.

"Now"—he grabs the caramel sauce off the countertop and pins me with his sexy gray gaze—"I have plans for this."

"What kind of plans?" I tilt my head, watching him carefully.

"Come here," he says, instead of answering my question.

I cross to him and grin up at him.

"Take your shirt off."

I cock an eyebrow but wordlessly comply, whipping my shirt over my head and letting it fall to the floor. My bra follows.

Ty's eyes shine as they glide down to my chest and abdomen and back up to my face. "Pants next."

"Getting naked was never part of the tradition." I pull my jeans down my legs and kick them to the side.

"I think we should start a new tradition."

He loops his arm around my waist and boosts me up onto the countertop and takes several steps back, watching me. Flour still covers his hair and is smudged on his forehead and cheek. His lips quirk up into a grin as he watches me, sitting high up on the counter, my feet dangling and rocking over the side.

"Jesus, you're beautiful, Lo."

My cheeks heat as I grin at him. "Thank you."

"So we have"—he checks the timer on the oven—"thirty-six minutes to play."

"That's all you need?" I ask sassily, earning a laugh from him.

"I love your smart mouth." He leans in and kisses me softly, only touching me with his lips, and it's driving me crazy to sit here naked and not have his hands on me.

"Ty, I want your hands on me."

"Oh, they're gonna be on you, beautiful. Along with some other parts of me."

"Now," I whine.

He chuckles before planting a harder kiss on me. "Patience."

"We only have thirty-five minutes."

"Plenty of time." He tips the caramel bottle and draws a heart around my right nipple.

"That's cold." I smile.

"I'll warm you up." He laves my nipple and the surrounding area with his tongue, licking the caramel off my skin. "Delicious."

He pulls a line of sauce down my neck to my cleavage and follows with his tongue, licking it off. His eyes are tracking his every move as I lean back on my hands, giving him easier access to all of the skin on my torso.

Ty squeezes more sauce onto me, writing *Ty + Lo* on my skin, then surrounds it with simple flowers, all connected with stems that end just above my pubic bone.

For being drawn in caramel sauce, it's not half-bad.

"I'm gonna be all sticky," I whisper.

"Don't worry, babe, I'll clean you up." He squats and pushes my legs apart.

"Do not squirt caramel sauce on my pussy!"

"Your pussy is sweet enough without it." He draws lines down my thighs. My clit tingles, begging for his lips, but he plants a kiss at the innermost point of my thigh, avoiding my core altogether.

"You're such a tease," I accuse him with a laugh.

He just smiles up at me and continues the torture, only touching me with the caramel and his lips.

"Did you want me to kiss you here?" He brushes a fingertip lightly over my clit, making my hips come up off the countertop.

"Yes!"

"What about here?" He pulls that finger down through my folds, gently stroking my lips.

"Yes, please."

He leans in and plants a tender kiss over my clit, then moves down to my entrance, also planting a tender kiss there.

"Where else?"

"Here." I point to my navel. He leans in and kisses it softly, then looks up at me for additional instructions.

I point to my left nipple. He rises and pulls it into his mouth, watching my eyes with his bright gray ones. I point to my other nipple and he repeats the movement on the other side, gently tugging on my already-puckered nub.

"Ty," I whisper. "Please."

"What do you need, baby?" He nibbles his way down my torso, licking at the now-warm caramel.

"I need you to make love to me."

He kneels back onto his haunches and lays the bottle on the counter, then spreads my lips wide and leans in to pull his tongue through my labia to my clit, wraps his lips around it, and sucks in little pulses, making me go mad. I plant my feet on his shoulders and buck my hips against his mouth as fire shoots straight through me. His hands grip my hips firmly, holding me to him.

"Fuck, Ty, I'm gonna come."

He growls and pulls his tongue down to push it into my pussy and presses his thumb against my clit, and I scream as the world falls away. I shiver and shudder and push against his face, riding the wave of this incredible orgasm.

Finally, he stands and unzips his pants and kisses me deeply. I can taste the caramel and myself on him.

"This is going to be sticky as hell," I warn him. He grins and cups my face in his palms, kissing me like he's a man starved. I find his uncovered cock and stroke it firmly, brush my thumb over the tip, spreading the drop of dew over the top, and he growls again.

"God, I love your hands." He lifts me off the counter, sets me on my feet, and turns me around, so that I'm bent with my legs spread and hands braced on the edge of the island.

"This way we won't get stuck together." He massages my pussy with the head of his cock. "I need to be inside you, baby."

I push back on him as he slips inside me with a curse.

"I'm sorry, sweetness, I'm not in the mood to be gentle."

"Don't hold back," I beg. I want it hard and fast.

He groans and begins to move quickly, pushing in and out, his glorious cock pulling on the walls of my pussy in the most amazing way. I tighten around him and he grips my hips even harder.

"Ah, fuck, baby, your pussy is so damn tight."

"Harder!" I cry.

He grips my hair roughly in one hand and yanks back as he begins to slam in and out of me like a man on the edge of insanity.

He cries out as he bottoms out and rocks against me, coming long and hard inside me.

"You make me crazy," he whispers as he releases my hair and plants a wet kiss between my shoulder blades. "I'll never get enough of you, Lauren."

I grin as I try to catch my breath.

The timer on the oven dings just as Ty pulls out of me, watching the juices from his climax drip down my thighs. "So fucking hot."

I chuckle and walk to the oven, check the pie, and set it on a cooling rack. "Pie's done."

"Good." Ty takes my hand in his and leads me up the stairs to my bedroom.

I'm a sticky mess, covered in caramel and flour and Ty. "You don't want to have a piece of pie?" I giggle.

"I think we need to clean you up first." He leads

me to the bathroom and turns on the shower, leading me inside when it's hot and the room begins to fill with steam.

"That's right, you made this mess, you should clean it up."

He pulls me against him under the water and kisses me hard as he grips my ass and grinds his erection against my belly, smearing the caramel between us.

"Seriously? Already?"

"I swear I'm sixteen again whenever I have your sexy, naked body against me."

I pull back and soap up my hands and begin to glide them over his tight abdomen, enjoying his taut muscles.

"I thought this was my mess to clean up." He grins.

"I like touching you," I whisper, and watch my hands as they move up to his chest, over his shoulders, and down his arms. I lather my hands some more and return to his stomach. His belly quivers when I pull my fingertips down the V at his hips.

"Ticklish?"

"No," he lies.

I smirk and replay the move, skimming his sensitive skin with the pads of my fingertips.

He jumps again.

"Of course you're not ticklish. You're badass."

"Damn right." He watches me with hot eyes as my hand circles his semihard cock and gently washes him.

"I like this."

"Do you." It's not a question.

"Very much." I slowly lower myself to my knees. I tilt my head back to look up into Ty's gaze and brush my lips lightly over the head of him. He hardens instantly in my grasp; his hands fist and his stomach clenches, and when I pull just the head into my mouth and suck gently, he swears under his breath and watches me, waiting impatiently to see where I'll take him next.

I brace my spare hand on his stomach, reveling in the way his muscles move under my hand, and begin to pump his length. I pull him to the back of my throat and swallow, then pull up and roll my tongue around the rim and over the slit, then repeat the motion, slowly, until his hips are moving in my rhythm.

Finally, he grips my cheeks in his hands and pulls me off him and leans down to kiss me while he pulls me to my feet.

"Any more of that and I'll come in your mouth."

"That's okay with me," I reply breathlessly.

"No." He shakes his head and lathers his hands with my body wash. "I'm going to come inside you, after I've made love to you for about three days."

I laugh at his words, but then still as his hands glide over my body, cleaning me thoroughly. When his fingers reach my core, he slows his movements further, teasing me as he washes me, smiling when I gasp and pant and have to grip his arms to stay upright.

"You enjoy this." I lean in and tug gently on his nipple with my teeth.

"I enjoy you, more than you'll ever know, sweetness." His breathing has changed. He shuts the water off and wraps a towel around his hips before drying me off completely. Before he can do so himself, I pull the towel off him and dry him off myself.

"Come." He pulls the towel from my hand and tosses it aside and leads me to the bed.

With gentle hands, he guides me down onto the bed. The lover from the kitchen is gone and has been replaced by one with tender hands and soft, loving eyes. He rolls me onto my back and covers me with his warm, clean body, resting his pelvis against my own. My fingers glide up and down his back as he settles over me, brushes the hair off my cheeks, and nudges my nose with his.

"Do you have any idea how amazing you are?"

Rather than answer, I capture his lips with my own and kiss him long and slow, pushing my fingers through his thick raven hair, gliding my hands down his back and arms. I can't stop touching his smooth, warm skin everywhere I can reach.

His lips leave mine and travel up to my eyes, over to my cheek, and farther still to my ear as his hips move and his hard cock rubs against my wet, pulsing core.

"I love making love to you," he whispers, sending tingles through me as he rears back and pushes inside me, then stops when he's buried as far as he can go.

My heart stutters at the mention of *love*. It's too soon for love. Isn't it? I know that what I feel as he begins to move is bigger than anything else I've ever felt for anyone in my life.

Ty's nose drags down my neck as he begins to move in long, slow thrusts. He pushes his pubic bone against my clit, then pulls back slowly and repeats the motion over and over. My legs hitch up around his hips. He reaches down and pulls my left leg up over his shoulder, spreading me wider, and pushes in even farther, stealing the breath from my lungs.

"God, Ty, you feel so good."

"This is all you, beautiful." He moves just a little faster, increasing the friction. My body tightens around him, and I can't stop the wave of ecstasy that moves through me, settles in my belly, and shoots out in all directions.

"That's it, love, let go."

There's that word again. My back arches off the bed as another wave moves through me. Ty pulls my nipple into his mouth and tugs, watching me intently as he moves over me, making love to me more tenderly than he ever has before. His eyes clench shut as he pushes in and comes silently, shaking with the force of his climax.

"I—" He buries his face in my neck.

"What?" I ask breathlessly, stroking his back with my fingertips.

"You're just—"

I chuckle and kiss his cheek, not caring in the least that the bulk of his weight is on me. "I need pie," I whisper into his ear.

He pulls up onto his elbows and watches me, his eyes serious and mouth grim.

"What's wrong?"

He shakes his head and kisses me softly. "Not a damn thing."

"Are you sure?"

He pulls out and rolls us over so I'm lying on top of him. "I'm sure."

I sit up and begin to roll off him, but he pulls me back into his arms.

"What's wrong?" I try again.

"I like having you in my arms." He pushes my hair over my shoulder and kisses my arm.

"It's definitely one of my favorite places to be." I grin and kiss his chin. "It feels safe here."

"You *are* safe here, Lo." He reverses us again, so he's leaning over me and looking down into my eyes. "I promise."

"You're good to me."

"That'll never change."

I grin up at him and rub my palm over his cheek, enjoying the way the short stubble there feels against my skin.

He turns his face and plants a kiss in the center of my hand before pulling away and helping me to my feet. "Now, about that pie."

"The last one downstairs has to sweep up the

flour mess!" I sprint ahead of him, giggling like a maniac as I fly down the stairs with Ty hot on my heels.

"You're a cheater! You got a head start!"

I beat him to the kitchen, panting and laughing as I hand him a broom. "You sweep and I'll cut the pie."

Rather than take the broom from my hands, he pulls me against him and kisses me long and hard, then lets go just as quickly and turns toward the mess on the floor as he pulls the broom from my grasp. "I want ice cream with mine."

The weekend has been the perfect combination of work and relaxation, especially after the disaster of a week we just had. Ty stayed at my place and was content to catch up on his own work while I dove into mine. Now, all too soon, we are driving out to the Lazy K Ranch for Sunday football.

"You know, you could have just come and spent some time with the guys. You didn't have to bring me," I say as Ty turns onto the driveway that leads down to the ranch.

"Cara and Jill are there." He shrugs. "It's not really a guys' night out, and besides, I want you there." He steers us down the windy tree-lined driveway. "I spend a lot of time with these people, and I want you to be comfortable with them too."

"I am comfortable with them." I smile. "I like them."

"Good."

He parks, and as we approach the front door, it flings open and a barking, excited Thor comes racing out of the house, stops to sniff us and get a pat on the head, then races to the side of the house.

"He has to pee!" Seth announces as he runs out after his dog, wearing a Seattle football jersey. "Hi, Ty! Hi, Lauren!"

"Hey, buddy," Ty replies, and leads me into Josh's home.

"Oh, good! They're here!" Cara claps happily from the kitchen, where she and Jill are bustling about. "Lo, come back here with us. The living room is full of testosterone."

"This is where we part ways, babe," I say to Ty, and kiss his cheek; but before I can walk away, he grips my arm and pulls me back against him for a long, hot, searing kiss, earning grumbles from both Zack and Josh, who suggest we get ourselves a room.

"This is football," Zack informs us as Seth and Thor storm back in from outside. "There is no kissing during football."

"Go watch your game," I say, and pull out of Ty's embrace. "I'll be the tall one in the kitchen if you need me." I wink and saunter away toward my friends. "I brought hot wings!"

"Wow, you made wings?" Jill asks.

"No, I *brought* them." I laugh. "I picked them up from the Bulldog in town."

"They have the best wings." Cara takes them from me to pop them in the oven to keep warm.

"What's the score?" Ty asks the guys as he hangs our coats and settles in on the couch.

"Seattle's up, seven to nothing, still early in the first quarter," Josh says.

"So, how's it going?" Jill pops a chip full of guacamole in her mouth.

"Good." I nod and then grin when they roll their eyes. "We just saw you Friday night. How are *you*?" I ask Cara.

"I'm good." She shrugs and stirs a Crock-Pot full of chili.

"How are you adjusting to being so far out of town?" I ask.

"It's been . . ." She purses her lips, searching for the right word. "Interesting. Ranch life is new, that's for sure. Oh! We have some fresh eggs to send home with you guys if you want them."

"Sure, we'll take some," I answer as Jill nods. "Thanks. Nothing like farm-fresh eggs."

"So true," Jill agrees. "Are you still going to plant a garden in the spring?" she asks Cara.

"Yes, look," she says excitedly, and points out the kitchen window to the backyard. "Those four stakes mark the area that Josh is going to fence in when the ground dries up a bit in the spring."

"You have to fence it?" I ask.

"If we don't want deer and rabbits to eat the veggies before we do, yes." Cara laughs.

"Ah, makes sense." I nod just as the guys shout from the living room.

"That ref is fucking blind!" Josh exclaims. "The ball was in! Sorry, Seth."

"It's okay." Seth shrugs. "It's football day."

"As I was saying"—Cara laughs—"I'm going to plant lots of veggies and herbs, and I'm sure there will be more than we can eat, so you guys are welcome to some of them too. Also, Josh has decided to expand to raising pigs for butchering, so we'll have eggs, chickens, pork, and beef, along with the veggies."

"Are you preparing for the zombie apocalypse?" Jill asks with a laugh.

"No, grain-fed meat is so much healthier." Cara giggles and then shrugs. "But we will be able to survive the zombies too."

"I'm so happy that you love it," I murmur. "I don't know if I could do it."

"We're city dwellers," Ty agrees as he joins us in the kitchen. He wraps his arms around my waist and kisses my neck before pulling away and opening the fridge.

"Yes, Cunningham Falls is such a bustling metropolis." Jill rolls her eyes at her brother.

"It's not fifteen miles from town in the middle of nowhere," Ty reminds her, and kisses me one more time.

"Dude!" Zack yells. "Stop kissing Lauren and bring us our beers!"

Ty laughs and returns to his friends.

"How's the real estate business?" Cara asks Jill.

"It's always good around here. Tourists move in and out. Winter's always slow, but I'm doing fine."

"Holy fucking shit!" The men all jump from their seats, their arms raised above their heads. "Go! Go! Go!"

"Montgomery's running the ball!" Zack yells. "Holy fuck, an eighty-yard run for the touchdown!"

"That's right, baby!" Ty yells, high-fiving everyone, including Seth.

"Did Josh and Zack just bump chests?" Jill asks as we stare at the spectacle before us.

"Yeah," I reply, and giggle when Thor begins barking and jumping around the cheering men.

"Montgomery is on fire today!" Josh cries. "Whew!"

"Who is Montgomery?" Jill asks Cara.

"I think he's the quarterback."

"Huh," Jill replies. "Okay."

Ty glances over with a wide smile and winks at me before settling back on the couch, taking a sip of his beer.

"How does watching football turn normal men into cavemen?" Cara asks. "I expect them to start belching and ordering us to bring them more beer any second."

Just then, Seth lets loose with a huge belch courtesy of his cola.

"I rest my case." She laughs.

"Good one," Zack says, laughing rather than admonishing him.

"Men are gross," Jill whispers, and shakes her head.

"They are predictable," I agree with a laugh. "And I have to admit, mine is sexy."

"So is mine." Cara sighs.

"Ugh, okay, I'm changing the subject." Jill pulls the wings from the oven. "Let's eat."

CHAPTER

Sixteen

I slip through the courtroom doors late Monday afternoon and find a seat on the aisle, about halfway up to the front of the room. This is one of only four courtrooms in town, and the spectator area is about half-full.

I'm not sure what the trial is about, other than it's a custody battle. The father is trying to take his kids from his ex-wife, who is Ty's client.

Brad Hull is currently in the witness chair, and Ty is questioning him. Ty didn't see me come in, and I'm relieved. I want to watch him when he doesn't know I'm here.

"When was the last time you were called to Ms. Jones's home due to Mr. Jones breaking the protection order?" Ty asks.

"One week ago," Brad responds.

"Can you please tell us what happened when you arrived on scene?"

"Mr. Jones was clearly intoxicated—"

"Objection!" the opposing counsel calls out. "Officer Hull couldn't possibly know from looking at him if Mr. Jones was intoxicated."

"*Lieutenant* Hull is a police officer who has vast experience with intoxicated citizens," Ty responds, speaking to the judge.

"Did you test Mr. Jones to assess his status?" Judge Wilkins asks Brad.

"Yes, sir."

"Overruled."

Brad continues, "The kids were crying, huddled on the front porch, and Mr. Jones was standing over Ms. Jones with his fist cocked back, ready to strike her."

"To the best of your knowledge," Ty continues, "had he already struck her before you arrived?"

"I'd had reports that he had hit her. Her eye was already blackened when I got there."

"What happened next?" Ty leans on the podium in front of him.

"I approached Mr. Jones and tried to speak with him calmly."

The voices become a monotone in my head as I stare at Ty's back, watching his economy of movement, marking notes with his pen, flipping papers. He pulls a large photo out of a folder and holds it up for the judge to see, then to Brad, and finally turns to share it with the opposing counsel.

His eyes meet mine for just a brief moment. There's a flicker of surprise, then they heat before the side of his mouth turns up and he looks away, moving without breaking his stride, unfazed by my presence here.

He's amazing.

Fucking amazing.

His demeanor is completely different from anything I've seen from him before. I've been with the friend, the brother, the lover, but I've never witnessed the lawyer, and I have to say, it's hot as hell.

He's calm and cool, even when Mr. Jones gets riled up at something Brad says and jumps to his feet, yelling obscenities at his ex-wife.

Geez, and he thinks he's going to *win* this case?

Thank God I never went off birth control, despite Jack's wanting me to. I would never want to put children through anything like this.

Ty doesn't even flinch as the judge calls for the bailiff to restrain Mr. Jones. I sit in awe for the next hour and watch Ty call two more witnesses. What Jill said is clearly true: he's a shark in the courtroom. Even the judge values his opinion.

Ty is going to go far in the legal world.

Pride spreads through me, warming my chest and igniting butterflies in my belly, and I find myself grinning from ear to ear. Last night in bed he was so tender, so loving. It's obvious that he's in love with me, and as I sit here, watching this complex man in his element, remembering how kind, loyal, and playful he is in other facets of his life, it occurs to me that I'm 100 percent in love with him as well.

The thought of ever being without him fills me with so much grief it's debilitating.

Now, how do I tell him? Because the thought of that also fills me with absolute fear. I'm not worried that my feelings aren't reciprocated; it's just the idea of the whole thing, because I decided long ago that I'd never put myself in this situation ever again.

Ty walks across the gallery to his chair, his eyes once again seeking out mine before he sits next to his client.

"I think we'll wrap things up for the day," Judge Wilkins announces. "Mr. Jones will remain in custody due to the current charges against him. We should be able to wrap this up tomorrow."

With that, the judge rises, and everyone else in the courtroom rises and waits for him to leave, then the room begins to empty.

I stay seated and wait for Ty to speak with his client, gather his papers into his briefcase, and walk back to me.

"Hey," he greets me, with soft gray eyes.

"Hi." I grin and stand. He takes my hand in his as he leads me out of the courthouse. "I hope you don't mind that I came to watch."

"I don't mind." He smiles down at me and leads me down the sidewalk toward his office. "What did you think?"

"I think you're badass." I swallow, wanting so badly to tell him that I love him, but instead I simply say, "I'm proud of you."

"For what?" He's surprised.

"You're awesome at your job. This is definitely what you should be doing." I shrug and turn my head to kiss his shoulder through his suit jacket. "I'm just proud of you."

"Thank you."

He opens the door to his building and waits for me to precede him inside. Cary is talking with Sylvia, but grins when he sees me.

"Just the person I was talking about."

"Me?" I ask.

"Yeah, I was going to have Sylvia call you. Do you have a minute?"

"Come into my office with us, Cary." Ty stops himself and glances down at me. "Unless you'd rather speak in private."

"Come with us." I smile and lead the guys into Ty's office. "There's no reason to have private meetings." I turn to Cary as I lean back on Ty's desk and cross my arms over my chest. "What's up?"

"So, I was talking to Jack's lawyer."

Just like that, my good mood evaporates. I sigh and rub my fingertips vigorously over my forehead.

"And?"

"And now he wants fifty million."

I blink at Cary, clearly having misheard him. "Excuse me?" My voice is thin.

"What the fuck?" Ty asks loudly, coming around his desk to meet Cary square on.

"Why? The trust fund was only two million." My

entire body breaks out into a cold sweat as it occurs to me that Jack must have found out about the books. My eyes widen and a sob escapes through my lips as I stare at Cary. "He knows."

"The lawyer didn't say anything about the books," Cary begins in a soothing voice.

Ty swears ripely and paces across the room. I watch him, and as I do, calm comes over me. Jack can't hurt me any more than he already has. I have Ty, and he's all I need.

"He can kiss my white ass," I mutter. "He's not getting a dime of anything. *Anything*."

"I agree," Cary responds, "but I don't want to make that clear out of the gate here, Lo."

"Go ahead and tell him," I respond defiantly. "What's he going to do?"

"Lauren, this is the man who threatened to rape you less than a month ago!"

"What?!" Ty roars, his face a mask of utter rage.

Cary blanches and shakes his head. "I'm sorry, Lo. I thought you told him."

I take a deep breath, trying to gather my thoughts. *Fuck.*

"Tell me what, Lauren?" Ty's voice is cold, and I recognize his stance. I saw it not thirty minutes ago in a courtroom.

"Cary, can you please leave us alone?" I ask, my gaze not leaving my angry man. Cary backs out the door, shutting it quietly behind him.

"What didn't you fucking tell me?" Ty asks in a low voice.

"Jack threatened to rape me that day he showed up at the house," I say matter-of-factly. I'm running on adrenaline now, almost defiantly. If Ty wants a fight, I'll give him one.

"And you didn't think it was important to tell me?"

"I was too embarrassed to tell you."

"Let me get this straight." Ty shoves his jacket angrily down his arms, throws it on top of his desk, and rolls up his sleeves. "Some asshole threatened to fucking *rape* my girlfriend, and she didn't tell me because she's embarrassed?"

"She wasn't your girlfriend then," I whisper.

"Have you lost your fucking mind?" he roars.

"Don't you dare yell at me!" I roar back. "Jack doesn't want me, Ty! He wanted to scare me, and it worked!"

Ty scrubs his scalp with both hands and paces away from me, then returns to me, standing two feet away, but doesn't touch me.

"What, exactly, did he say?"

"I'm not telling," I whisper.

"Oh, yes, sweetness, you are."

"You're not my husband and you're not my lawyer, Tyler Sullivan."

"I'm the *one* person in your life who cares about you above everything else, goddamnit!" His eyes are hurt as he watches me, and I feel like such a shit. Ty is the last person I ever want to hurt. I swallow hard and mentally pull up my big-girl panties.

"He said that if I didn't give him what he wants, he'd come back and remind me what it feels like to have him fuck me." The last five words are whispered so softly I don't know if Ty can even hear me. Bile rises in the back of my throat, but I swallow hard again and meet his eyes. "It's mortifying that I was ever connected to someone like that, Ty. Why would I tell you that?"

"Because I've been going through all of this shit *with you.*" His voice is still hard. "What else aren't you telling me?"

I shake my head and laugh humorlessly. "You know what? I don't have time for this." I move away from him, hitching my purse over my shoulder. "I have a deadline to meet in"—I check my watch—"thirteen hours, and I still have two chapters to write."

I turn to leave, but he halts me with a quiet "Stop."

I turn to face him. He hasn't moved. He's watching me with his arms crossed over his chest. "We are too important for you to just walk away, Lauren."

"I'm not walking away from you. I'm irritated with you and I need to go home. I'll call you tomorrow."

"You don't want me to come over tonight?"

I shake my head. "Let's just take a night off from each other, Ty. I'll be working all night anyway."

He nods, still angry, but his eyes have softened. In relief? I'm not sure.

I leave his office, ignoring Sylvia as she calls out

to me, asking if I want to make an appointment with Cary.

I can't deal with this right now.

I took the afternoon off because I missed Ty and I wanted to see him in action in the courtroom. Now I have a good eight hours of work ahead of me before I can e-mail the manuscript to my editor. She wants it by the time she gets to her office at 9:00 a.m. eastern time.

I can do this.

I push thoughts of Ty and his hurt eyes out of my head as I pull up to my house and let myself in and march straight back to the my pool house. The men finished up yesterday, thank God, and I can finally swim again. Seventy-five laps or so should get my head back in the game.

I strip naked and swim. I love the feel of the water over my skin, the sound it makes as it rushes past my ears.

Fuck, I even love the way it smells.

After the last lap, I climb out and brace my hands on my knees, panting and dripping water all over the concrete floor. I reach for a towel, dry off, and pull my clothes back on. I stop in the kitchen to grab an energy drink on my way to my office.

Two hours later, there's a knock on my door, pulling me out of the story. I save the document and walk to the front door, surprised to see Jillian standing there, white plastic bags dangling from her hands and a big grin on her pretty face.

"I've come with provisions, per Ty's orders."

"What did you bring?" I step back and let her breeze past me, shut the door, and follow her to the kitchen.

"He said you're writing tonight, and you forget to eat, so he made me bring you some homemade soup from Mrs. King, sandwiches from Mrs. Blakely's deli, and chocolate-chip cookies that I baked, but don't get too impressed because they're the ones you buy in the store and just bake in the oven."

"Thank you." I'm amazed at the spread before me. I'm mortified to feel tears gathering in my eyes as I remember how frustrated I was at Ty earlier and how I ran as soon as things got rough. "I wasn't very nice to him earlier."

"He'll be okay." Jill waves and unpacks her bags. "I know you're busy, so I'll get out of your hair. Just eat the soup while it's hot. The rest will keep until later."

She kisses my cheek and bustles back toward the door. I hear the door shut behind her.

I take the soup and the plastic spoon that Nancy King remembered to include back to my office and reach for my phone.

Thank you, I text to Ty.

You're welcome.

I eat the soup quickly, not wanting to lose the momentum of the story and eyeing the clock. I have nine hours to finish.

I flick on the desk lamp, pull my feet up under me in my chair, and dive back into the story. I'm vaguely aware of my phone pinging with incoming texts, but I ignore it and focus on the task at hand.

When I'm in this mode, there is no interrupting me.

I work without moving for the next two hours, until I type the words *The End*. Then, without a pause, I scroll up the document to the very beginning and read it straight through, looking for typos and awkward words, tweaking here and there until I'm completely happy with it.

There will be edits and revisions after my editor reads it, but for now I'm content knowing that it's as perfect as I can make it.

I open my e-mail and compose a note to her, attach the book, and send it off, then check the time.

It's five in the morning here in Montana, so I managed to sneak it in two hours early.

Go me!

I mentally give myself a high five and stand, stretching my arms high above my head and then down to my toes, trying to loosen my muscles.

I should have installed a hot tub long ago, for moments just like this.

I check my phone and see that I've missed texts from Cara and Jill. Nothing from Ty.

Cara: **I don't have class until 9 tomorrow. Meet Jill and me at Sips for coffee at 7:30?**

And the next one is from Jill an hour later: **Meet us for coffee at 7:30 or I'll come find you!**

I chuckle and quickly type a reply, hoping I don't wake them.

Me: **See you there!**

I pad into the kitchen and pour myself a glass of celebratory wine, raise the glass in salute, and take a long sip.

I wish Ty were here.

If Ty were here, he'd celebrate with me, most likely while we're both naked and he's inside me, rather than with just a glass of wine that tastes like it's on its way to being stale.

I think about calling him, but then quickly dismiss the idea. He's probably still asleep, and we have some talking to do before we are okay again.

Taking my glass with me, I turn the kitchen light out, and as I walk toward the stairs, there's a loud banging on my front door.

I grin to myself. Ty must have decided he couldn't wait any longer to see me and come over before work.

Without looking out the peephole, I unarm the alarm and swing the door open wide. "I was hoping I'd see you—"

I come up short when I see that it's an angry, snarling Jack standing on the porch.

"I fucking hate you," he growls, and backhands me square across the cheek, sending me flying back into the foyer and the glass in my hand crashing to the floor. "Did you think I'd never find out?"

His words are slurred and I can smell the whiskey coming off him in waves as I try to scurry backward on my hands, unable to pull myself to my feet. I'm still seeing stars, for fuck's sake.

He kicks me in the ribs twice, then pulls me to my feet by the hair and punches me in the nose before he pulls my face up to his. "Answer me, cunt."

"I don't know what you're talking about." I can't breathe. I think my nose is broken. I can barely see the three Jacks standing right before me.

He bares his teeth in a snarl and pulls me, his hand still buried in and gripping my hair, behind him to my office. He holds me up and points to the book covers on the wall.

"Peyton Adams, Lauren? Really? You made your fucking pen name the one we planned to name our daughter and your mom's maiden name?"

I flinch and clench my mouth shut. *How do I get out of this alive?*

"I'm going to kill you, you selfish motherfucking bitch," he breathes into my face, making me gag on his horrible, foul breath. "But first, I'm going to make you fucking suffer."

"Being married to you was suffering, Jack." My voice is raspy and my vision is tunneling quickly, but I pull myself together as much as possible. If I pass out now, I'll never get out of here.

He balls his fist and punches me on the jaw, snapping my head back. I can taste the coppery essence of blood as I pull my head back around to glare at him, blinking furiously.

"You owe me a whole fucking slew of money." He spits on me, then pushes me back against my desk. I brace myself with my hands, panting, tears rolling down my face from the shot to my nose, and watching him as he turns away and tears one of my covers off the wall, shattering it on the ground. "I can't believe you like to write books about fucking," he sneers, and laughs over at me before he pulls the next cover off the wall. "You were a fucking joke in bed."

"Pot, kettle," I mutter viciously, and feel around the desk for my letter opener. It's the only weapon I have here in the office.

He turns and glares at me, then stomps toward me and slaps me across the face again, on the opposite cheek this time. I move quickly, flailing out with the letter opener in my hand, doing my best to cut him, but he laughs as I stumble about and grips my wrist in his hand, wrenching the tool away from me.

"God, you're so pathetic." He shoves me back, then narrows his eyes on my laptop.

Dear God, he's going to destroy my laptop.

I lunge for it, but he's faster, scooping it up off the desk and throwing it with all his might against the wall. I stand, dumbfounded and numb, as I watch it shatter into about a dozen pieces.

Thank God I sent the book to the editor before he got here.

I laugh hysterically, finding it ironic that my first thought automatically goes straight to work. Jack could conceivably kill me this morning, and my biggest concern is losing my book. My ribs scream with the effort of the laughter, but I can't seem to stop it.

"Why are you laughing?"

"Just remembering how tiny your dick is," I rasp. If he's going to hurt me, I'll get my own hits in, even if they are verbal. My face is swelling as I search furiously for a way out of this room, but Jack is blocking my path to the door.

"You're a fucking bitch."

"So you've said," I wheeze.

He advances and swings, intending to punch me, but I duck out of the way, infuriating him even further.

Suddenly, he pulls a long knife out of his back pocket and holds it in front of him.

"Oh my God," I whisper. "You're nuts."

"You're a whore. Get on the floor."

"Just lie down and let you carve me up?"

My phone rings, distracting me, and he lunges, punching me with the handle of the knife in the temple. I fall to the floor, blinded, crying out. Jack lands three more kicks in my ribs and I throw up uncontrollably, propped on my side, as he continues to kick me in the ribs and down my back.

"Do you like it when I beat on you, you little whore?" Jack asks maliciously. His voice is pure evil. "I'm gonna fuck you before I kill you, Lo." He pulls me onto my back and holds the knife to my neck with one hand while he unbuttons his jeans with the other. "My cock inside you is the last thing you're ever going to feel, you stupid cunt."

"Your cock is so small, I never could feel it anyway," I growl.

He bares his teeth in fury and, throwing the knife aside, grips my hair in both of his fists, lifts my head, and smashes it against the hardwood floor of my office.

The only thought I have just before the darkness settles in around me is that I hope Ty doesn't find me like this.

CHAPTER

Seventeen

T Y

"Court is adjourned for lunch."

Thank God.

I rise and leave the courtroom, fishing my phone out of my pocket. I tried to call Lo early this morning, unable to stand being away from her any longer, but I couldn't reach her. She was probably either sleeping soundly or still working.

I should have said *Fuck it* and gone over there to be with her, hold her. Make her breakfast.

Reassure both of us that we're okay and remind her why she needs to be honest with me when it comes to her asshole of an ex-husband.

I turn my iPhone on and wait impatiently for it to wake up. When it finally does, I have twenty-two texts.

Twenty-two.

They're all from Jill, Cara, and the guys. Nothing from Lauren, and my blood runs cold when I start from the beginning and begin to read them.

Jill: **Lo didn't come to coffee. Know where she is?**

Cara: **J and I are gonna go check on Lo. She's 30 mins late.**

Jill: **We need you, Ty! Lo's hurt. Going to hospital.**

Josh: **Man, check your phone. Come to the hospital ASAP.**

I'm running toward my house now, cursing myself for walking to work today. I continue to check messages as I run, not paying attention to what's happening around me.

It's a wonder I don't either get hit by a car or fall on my ass.

What the fuck has happened to Lo?

Jill: **Call me! Now!**

My phone rings in my hand. It's Zack.

"What the fuck is going on?"

"Thank God you're out of court." Zack's voice is low and tight. "You need to come to the hospital, man. Lauren's been hurt."

"How bad?" I unlock the Jeep and throw my shit in the backseat, start it up, and peel out of my driveway.

"Bad. The girls found her. They went to her place to check on her when she didn't show up for coffee. Since we've been at the hospital, they won't let us back to see her because we're not her family." Zack's voice is filled with frustration.

"They'll let me in."

"How?"

"I'll lie and say she's my fiancée." It's not much of a lie anyway, since I plan to make her exactly that as soon as she'll say yes. "I'm almost there. Where are you?"

"ICU."

I hang up and shove my phone in my pocket as I find parking and run into the hospital. The ICU is easy to find. This hospital isn't that big, and I find the whole gang sitting in the waiting room.

"Ty!" Jill jumps up and runs to me, throws her arms around me, and lets loose with a long sob.

"Hold on, sweetheart." I pass her off to Zack, who wraps his arm around her and pats her back as she cries into his chest, and I turn to the receptionist. "Lauren Cunningham, please."

"Are you family?"

"I'm Ty Sullivan, her fiancé."

"I'll call back to the doctor. He'll come out to you in a few moments."

I nod and back away, and Jill throws herself back into my arms.

"Hey, princess, I need you to calm down and tell me what happened."

"Jack almost killed her," she cries, dabbing at the tears coming out of her eyes.

"What?" I jerk my gaze up to Zack and Josh, who both nod.

"They've already arrested him," Josh confirms. "He bragged all about it to Misty, and she may be a bitch, but she had the brains to call the cops."

"When we got to Lo's house," Cara begins, her own eyes red from shedding tears, "her door was standing wide-open. When we went inside, we found her in her office, beaten bloody. The room was torn apart."

"It was so much worse than anything Dad ever pulled, Ty. A hundred times worse," Jill whispers, and clenches her eyes shut against horrible memories from our childhood.

"Where is the doctor?" I pace back and forth, watching for the man to come out of the door that leads to the patient rooms. I need to see her. I need to hold her, make sure she's whole.

I need her.

"She was breathing, but she never woke up while we were with her," Jill adds.

"What time was this?" I ask as I pull my phone out of my pocket and text a note to Cary, asking him to take care of court for me for the afternoon.

"Around eight," Cara responds softly.

Shit, it's noon now! "When did he . . . ?" I'm unable to complete the thought.

"We don't know," Cara replies. "The blood was dried on her face when we got there, so she'd been lying there for a while."

My heart drops to my knees. Jesus, she was lying on the ground, hurt, and I wasn't there to stop it.

To protect her.

"Stop it, man." Zack plants his hand on my shoulder. "This isn't your fault."

I shake my head and walk away, shoving my hand through my hair. "I need to see her."

A tall gray-haired man in a long white lab coat walks into the waiting room, holding a chart. "Mr. Sullivan?"

"Yes, that's me. Call me Ty."

"I'm Dr. Black. Would you like to come somewhere private to discuss your fiancée's condition?"

"No." I shake my head. "We can talk about it with this group of people. They're our family."

"Okay." He nods. "Lauren has been severely beaten, Ty. Her eyes are both swollen shut and her nose is broken."

My hands fist at my sides and blood rushes to my head. I drop into a seat, my legs unable to continue holding me, as the doctor continues.

"She was obviously kicked in her side and back, and she is lucky to just be bruised. He didn't break her ribs. We were worried about her kidneys, but the MRI didn't show any bleeding." Dr. Black sighs and sits down next to me. "The most concerning injury is her head."

"What happened to her head?" I whisper.

"I think he must have either hit her in the back of the head with something hard, like a bat, or he could have slammed her head against the floor." The doctor swallows hard, obviously upset by Lo's condition. "Her skull is fractured, and her brain is swollen. That's why she hasn't woken up. Her body's automatic defense mechanism kicked in and shut down, trying to recover on its own."

"How long will she be asleep?" I hate the sound of my voice breaking.

"We don't know for sure. We have given her medicine to keep her in the coma until the swelling on her brain eases, and after that, it's up to her."

We're all quiet as we take it in. Jesus, Jack did a number on her. Cara is wrapped in Josh's arms, slowing rocking back and forth. Jill is sitting next to Zack, leaning on his arm, hiccuping from her sobs.

"I need to see her."

"I can take you back, but, Ty, I'm warning you, she doesn't look like herself. She's heavily bandaged, and bruised. Swollen. And she's hooked up to a ventilator."

"She's not breathing on her own?" I ask incredulously.

"Not while she's in the coma, no."

I blanch, nod once, and take a deep breath as I stand. "Can they come back as well?"

"One at a time, but only people you approve."

"Jill?"

She nods and takes my hand as we follow the doctor to Lauren's room. It's quiet back here and smells of antiseptic. The lights are dim in Lo's room. She looks so small in the bed, her head elevated and eyes closed. Bandages cover her nose and her neck.

"What happened to her neck?"

"She has a shallow cut. We suspect he held a knife to her." Dr. Black's voice is low.

I'm going to kill that motherfucker with my bare hands.

"She actually looks better than she did when we found her." Jill sniffles.

I can't move. My world is in this bed, unconscious and broken. The machines beep softly—measuring what, I'm not sure—and Lo's chest rises and lowers with each breath from the machine.

"Is she going to be okay?" I whisper.

"I believe so," Dr. Black murmurs. "But it's going to be a painful recovery. I need that swelling in her brain to go down, and then we need her to wake up before we'll know for sure." He pats me on the shoulder and backs away. "I'll leave you with her."

"You can touch her." Jill squeezes my hand once. "Do you want me to leave you alone with her?"

I nod and feel Jill kiss my hand, then she leaves the room, the door shutting softly behind her. Finally, my feet move and I lower myself slowly into the chair at Lo's bedside. I reach out and take her soft hand in mine, relieved to feel how warm her skin is, and it's my undoing.

I pull her hand up to my mouth and the tears come. Why didn't I tell her yesterday how much I love her? Why didn't I show her more often how fucking amazing she is?

"Baby, I need you to get better for me, okay? I have stuff I need to say, sweetness, and I need you whole and strong and with me for a very long time. So you just sleep and get better."

The tears continue to flow as I watch her still body. I sit for long minutes that stretch into hours, just watching her face. Nurses and doctors come and go, checking on her, asking me if I need anything.

I just need her well.

"Hey, man," Josh whispers as he comes in the room, then swears under his breath when he sees Lo. "Fucking Christ."

"I'm going to kill him."

"I'll help you," Josh replies grimly. "How are you?"

"Pissed off and devastated. Imagine how you'd feel if this was Cara."

He shakes his head and shoves his hands in his pockets. "I get it, man. I just wanted to let you know that we're going to go get some food and some sleep. It's already almost nine."

"I had no idea." There is no sense of time in here, just the measure of Lo's heartbeat and the breaths the machines give her. "You guys should go."

"Do you want me to bring you back anything?"

"No."

"We're going to come stay with you in shifts. Zack and Jill are coming back after we eat, and then Cara and I will be here in the morning."

"You don't have to do that." I feel tears form in my eyes as I gaze up at my best friend.

"Yes we do, Ty. You're our family. My parents were here for a while, and they'll be back tomorrow. My mom will probably bring you food, so just eat it and save yourself the argument."

"Thank you," I whisper.

"She's going to be okay. She's strong."

I nod and brush Lo's hair off her forehead, barely grazing her warm skin with my thumb. "I pray you're right."

"Good morning." Cara pokes her head in the doorway two days later. "Zack and Jill just left, and Josh and I are here."

"Come on in." I've been staring at the same article in the newspaper for the past thirty minutes. I still have no idea what it says.

"You look like shit." She sits across from me on the other side of Lo. She offers me a hot cup of coffee, which I take gratefully.

"I feel like shit."

"Well, you look like it."

"If this is your idea of a pep talk, you can just go now."

She shakes her head and looks down at Lo. Tears fill her hazel eyes. "I'm so sorry about this."

"It's not your fault, little one."

"Jack's being charged with attempted murder, Ty."

My head jerks up to meet her gaze. "Not just an assault charge?"

"No. He beat her with the intention of killing her." Cara shakes her head and takes a sip of her coffee. "He's crazy."

I swear under my breath and rub my fingers over my mouth as the doctor and nurse that just came on shift walk through the door. In the days since the incident, little has changed in Lo's condition.

I haven't left the hospital since I got here. Have barely left Lauren's side.

I want to be here when she wakes up.

The girls have taken turns sitting with Lauren, reading to her for hours on end. I've managed to tune out their voices, concentrating only on my girl, willing her to recover as quickly as possible.

"Mr. Sullivan," Dr. Shay nods at me and peruses through Lo's chart. "There is definite improvement on this morning's CT scan."

"There is?"

The doctor nods again and glances up at a monitor before making notes on the chart. "Her swelling is going down. I'm hoping to lessen the medication keeping her asleep today to see if she'll wake up on her own."

"Hear that, sweetness? You're doing great." I lean in and gently kiss her cheek. Her face is still battered, but the swelling there is going down too. Now she's just a riot of color, almost everywhere. When they gave her a sponge bath last night, pulling up her nightgown, it took everything in me not to run out and beat the shit out of Jack.

I don't give a shit that he's in jail.

"In fact, let's not give the next dose and do another CT scan this afternoon."

The nurse nods, takes notes, and they both smile at me before leaving the room.

"This is good news." Cara has a wide smile on her face. "Oh! I almost forgot! I have Lo's phone." She pulls it out of her bag and passes it to me. "Someone named Emily has been blowing it up."

"Shit, she's going to be worried. They talk just about every day."

I wake up Lo's phone and dial Emily's number.

"It's about damn time! Just because you're having naughty sex with the hot lawyer doesn't mean that you can just ignore me!"

My lips twitch and I clear my throat. "This isn't Lauren, Emily, this is Ty."

"What's wrong?"

I relay the story to her, and by the time it's over, she's crying. "I'm so sorry," she murmurs.

"It's not your fault, Emily. I thought you should know why she's not been responding to you."

"I'm coming out there." I hear her clear her throat and begin shuffling papers around. "I make a ton of money, there's no reason that I can't just pack up and come out. Let me talk with the nanny and my husband and make the arrangements and I'll call you back."

"You don't have to—"

"Yes I do. She's my best friend, Ty."

I look over to Lo and realize that she can use all the friends she has here with her. "Okay. Let me know when you'll be flying in and I'll make sure someone picks you up."

After we hang up, I see a few missed calls from a contact labeled MR. DARCY'S NURSE.

I dial it and am patched through to a nurses' station here in this hospital, in the extended-care wing, and it occurs to me that Mr. Darcy must be the family friend that Lo visits at the hospital.

"Oh, I'm so glad you called," the nurse replies when I tell her who I am and why I'm calling. "Lauren missed her standing appointment with Mr. Darcy this week, and he's been worried sick."

"Is there any way that someone can bring him to ICU so he can visit with her when she's feeling better?"

"Of course. Just call us and we'll bring him down to you."

"Just gonna surround her with people she loves, aren't you?" Cara asks, watching me carefully.

"She needs all the love she can get." I don't meet Cara's eyes as I set Lo's phone on the nearby table. "Will you please bring me some clothes? I'm going to take a shower here, shave, and change so I'm not such a mess when she wakes up."

"Look at me," Cara murmurs softly, and I raise my eyes to hers. "It's okay to love her, Ty."

"I do, with my whole heart."

"None of this is your fault."

"I wasn't there," I reply softly. "I should have been there, and instead I was home, not sleeping because we'd had an argument. I was lying in bed, overthinking a stupid disagreement, while the woman I love was being brutalized. I may not be at fault for putting her here, but I am at fault for not keeping her safe. Just bring me the clothes, please."

"Okay." Cara nods and rises from her seat. "This conversation isn't over. I'll be back in a while."

"Thank you."

Cara leaves and I'm left with Lo. I caress her hand, as I've done for the past two days.

I was lying in the comfort of my bed while the woman I love was being brutalized. The enormity of the past few days, the lack of sleep, the fear and dread, all come crashing down on me.

I want Lo.

The tears come again, and I lean in and bury my face in her neck, careful not to jar her, but needing to feel the connection to her.

"Wake up, baby," I cry. "I miss you so much. I need you to open those gorgeous blue eyes of yours so I can tell you how much I love you."

I hear the door open, but I don't look up as Josh takes the chair that Cara vacated not long ago.

Finally, when the sobs subside, I sit up and wipe my eyes, then glare at Josh. "If you say one word—"

"Hey"—he shakes his head slowly—"I would have broken long before this."

I nod and firm my lower lip, pissed that it's still quivering. Josh and I sit in silence until Cara returns with my clothing and some essentials.

"Will you two stay with her? I won't be long."

"Of course," Cara assures me as Josh nods. I step

out of Lo's room for the first time in two days and walk down to the nurses' station to ask for directions to a shower.

The hot water feels like heaven. I shave and dress quickly and shove the dirty clothes into the duffel bag Cara brought with her. I've been gone less than thirty minutes, but it feels too long. I need to get back to her.

When I return, Lo isn't in the room. "Where is she?"

"They took her for more tests," Josh responds. "They'll be back in a few."

"They took the ventilator out." Cara grins. "She's breathing fine on her own."

"Did she wake up?" I ask anxiously.

"No," Cara replies. "But hopefully she will this evening."

I nod just as they wheel Lo back into the room. "How did it go?" I ask worriedly.

"The doctor will be in with the results in just a few minutes, but she seems to be doing really well. There are no breathing issues, and she's reacting normally to stimuli, so that's all really positive."

Dr. Black bustles through the door with a smile on his face. "The swelling is going down further. We're not quite out of the woods yet, but this is a great sign. Now we just need her to wake up."

I sit back in my chair in relief, my body sagging as though the weight of the world has been lifted. "Thank you, Doc."

"It's all her, Ty. Your girl is strong. I hope you do actually ask her to marry you."

I look up in surprise, and Dr. Black laughs. "She's not wearing a ring, son. I wasn't born yesterday. Don't worry, your secret is safe with me."

He chuckles as he exits the room, leaving Cara, Josh, and me staring at each other. Finally, we all break out into laughter.

"You guys go ahead and go," I suggest as I lean over and kiss Lo gently on her uninjured temple. "We're good here."

"Are you sure?" Cara asks.

"Yes. Go eat and get some rest. I'll call if there are any changes."

They both nod and kiss Lauren on the cheek before leaving the room. With her hand in mine, I lean in to talk to her, to hopefully ease her out of sleep.

"I'm so proud of you, sweetness. You're doing great. Now just open those eyes for me and wake up."

"Need water," she croaks.

CHAPTER

Eighteen

"Baby?" I lean in close to her face, speaking softly. "Lauren, are you awake?"

She tries to move and scowls. "Fucking hurts."

"I know. Don't try to overdo it." I reach over and press the red call button.

"Can I help you?" a faceless voice asks.

"Lauren is awake. We need the doctor, please."

"Happened?" Lo opens one eye, trying to focus on me.

"I'll tell you everything. Just relax for now and rest, beautiful. You're in the hospital, but you're going to be okay." I kiss her forehead and gently caress the hair at her temple. "I'm so relieved to hear your voice."

"That was quick," Dr. Black murmurs as he bustles through the door with Dr. Shay on his heels. "Please stand back, Ty."

The doctors take over, taking vitals, checking her

pupils, asking her questions. A nurse stands at the end of the bed taking notes.

Finally, Dr. Black addresses me. "This is very encouraging, Ty."

"How is she?"

"She's going to be sore, and we're going to keep her for a couple more days to watch that head injury, but I think she's going to be just fine. We'll do another CT scan tomorrow morning to monitor the fluid on her brain." He grins down at Lauren and pats her hand. "You're a very lucky woman, Lauren."

"Don't remember anything," she whispers, and licks her lips.

"She asked for water," I say.

"I'll go get her some ice chips," the nurse offers, and hustles out of the room.

"You're going to be sleepy for the next day or two because we're going to keep your pain meds up," Dr. Shay informs Lauren. "You're going to be very sore for a few days, so be careful when you try to move around."

"Ty," Dr. Black says, "why don't you step out and make some calls while we remove her catheter and make her comfortable?"

"I don't want to leave her." I take her hand in mine.

"'S okay," Lo whispers. "Call everyone. I'll be here."

I kiss her forehead. "I'll be right back."

I hurry out into the hall and call Jill, then Josh and Zack, informing them that Lo's awake. By the time

I've called Cary and Emily, I'm itching to get back into that room to her.

I have things to say before she falls back to sleep.

I knock and wait impatiently for the nurse to open the door for me. Dr. Black is helping Lo back into bed.

"Why is she up?" I rush to her side.

"Had to pee." She winces as she eases back against the bed. "My ribs hurt like hell."

"How is your head?" I ask softly.

"Sore. Did I get hit by a truck?"

"No." I shake my head and press my lips to her forehead.

"Call if you need us. We'll be in for the next round of meds in about an hour."

The doctors leave and I drop into the chair beside Lo's bed, watching her carefully. "God, baby, I'm so happy that you're awake."

"What happened? All I remember is e-mailing my editor, and then waking up here."

"Maybe we should have this conversation after you've had time to recover a bit more." I don't want to upset her and make her hurt any worse than she already does.

"Just tell me." She raises her hand to cup my face. I feel tears in my eyes as I turn my face and press a kiss to her palm.

"Jack came to your house two mornings ago."

Her eyes register confusion as she watches me. "Two days?"

"You've been asleep for a couple of days, letting your body heal." I kiss her hand again. "Jack hurt you, sweetness."

She frowns and closes her eyes, then they open quickly, wide, and she stares at me in shock. "He destroyed my office."

I nod, waiting as it all comes back to her.

"He hit me." Her breath catches and she winces. "He was pissed because he found out about the books. How did he find out?"

"I don't know. I suspect he was the one who had been in the house while you were gone."

"He was going to kill me," she whispers, and a tear falls as the events of that morning play through her head. "He was drunk, and he had a knife."

I feel physically ill with the need to go after him and hurt him, but suddenly she blanches and tries to sit up, reaching for the call button. "I need a nurse."

"What's wrong?"

"I need to ask them something."

"Lauren, stop, you're just going to hurt yourself." I settle her against the bed and hold her shoulders in my hands, looking deep into her injured blue eyes. "What is it?"

"I should talk to a nurse," she repeats in a whisper.

"You still don't trust me?" I ask incredulously.

"I do!" She takes my hand in hers and holds it up to her cheek. "It's just—"

"Talk to me, sweetness."

"I don't know if he raped me." The words are barely audible.

"What?"

"He was holding the knife to my throat and was unbuckling his belt, and he said he was going to—" She can't finish the statement. Tears roll down her cheeks and she bites her swollen lower lip.

"Hey." I lean in and kiss her temple. "It's okay, Lo. We'll find out, okay?"

She nods and I press the call button, and before the nurse answers the call, Dr. Black walks through the door.

"What's up?"

"Was Lauren found dressed?" I ask bluntly.

The older man frowns and tilts his head in thought. "I'm not positive. I'm not an emergency-room doctor, so Lauren didn't come into my care until she was transferred up here." He scowls at both of us and then asks Lo, "Are you worried that you were sexually assaulted?"

She nods yes. "He threatened to, but then he knocked me out, and I don't remember anything after that."

Dr. Black leans back against the wall and crosses his arms. "Given the severity of the assault, and the fact that there were no witnesses and you were unconscious, we performed a rape kit, Lauren." He looks up at me with sober eyes. "There was evidence that you'd had sex."

"We made love not twenty-four hours prior," I confirm.

He nods. "But there was no evidence of violence or forced penetration. The rape kit was negative."

I sigh in relief and shake the doctor's hand in gratitude. "Thank you."

I sit beside Lo as the doctor leaves and caress her hand.

"Thank God," she whispers, her eyes drifting closed.

"Tired?" I ask softly.

"Yeah."

"Can you open your pretty eyes for just a minute more?" I lean toward her so she can see me clearly. She pulls her eyes open and offers me a small smile. "I love you so much, sweetness."

Her eyes flare in surprise and then soften and fill with tears again. I brush a drop away with my thumb and cup her face in my hand.

"I love you too," she whispers. "I'm so sorry."

"You have nothing to be sorry for. I just didn't want to go another minute without telling you that I love you and you're stuck with me. Nothing like this will ever happen again, I promise you that."

She begins to cry in earnest, wincing in pain.

"Don't cry, baby."

"He could have killed me and I never would have told you that I love you," she whimpers.

"You're right here, right here with me."

"He was so cruel. So evil. I was sure that I wouldn't

survive it. Thank God he didn't—" She shakes her head in misery. "I couldn't bear it if he'd done that."

"You're safe." I kiss her softly. "Go to sleep for a while, love."

She finally calms and slips into a deep sleep, and as each minute passes, I feel the rage building in me. Hearing how cruel he was to her, what he threatened to do to her, is the final straw in my resolve.

"Can we come in?" Jill asks softly as she opens the door and peeks around at us.

"Sure," I whisper back. "She's sleeping."

All four of them file in.

"Can you stay with her?" I ask the girls, my eyes pinned to Zack.

"You're leaving?" Jill asks, surprised.

"I have something to handle. We won't be long."

The girls nod and I motion for Zack and Josh to follow me out into the hallway.

"Are we going to do what I think we're going to do?" Josh asks with anticipation.

"Fuck yes," I reply. "Tell me Brad is on today."

"He is." Zack nods and leads us out the doorway to my Jeep, holds his hands out for my keys, and starts the engine. "You shouldn't be driving."

"How are you going to get to him, Ty? Just walk in and say, 'I want to kick the shit out of Jack'?" Josh asks.

"There are rooms in pretty much every jailhouse where attorneys and clients can speak without any kind of recording devices or monitors." I grin over at my friend smugly. "I'm thinking about taking Jack's case."

"Awesome." Zack rubs his hands together as he parks before the police station. "Let's go."

The three of us walk in, and I have one thing in mind: get to the motherfucker who hurt Lauren.

Brad meets us in the foyer and shakes our hands. "How is she?"

"Hurt," I reply. "I'd like to see Jack."

"In an attorney capacity?" Brad asks.

"We can call it that. I'm going to need a privacy room."

"I can do that. Follow me." Brad leads us down a hallway to a room with no windows and leads us inside. A table and two chairs are in the center of the room. "I'll be back with your client in a moment."

"Are you sure there's no camera in here?" Josh asks.

"I'm sure." I fold my arms over my chest, waiting impatiently for the piece of shit to be escorted in.

Finally, the door opens and Brad leads Jack inside. "Your lawyer would like to speak with you." Brad unlocks the handcuffs and backs toward the door. "Just let me know when you're done. I have some phone calls to make."

"You're not my fucking lawyer," Jack growls when Brad leaves.

None of us respond; we just watch Jack start to squirm.

"Sit." Zack plants his hand on Jack's shoulder and pushes him into the chair.

"You won't touch me," Jack sneers.

"You like beating on women?" Josh asks in a low voice.

"She deserved everything she got," Jack replies, his chin in the air.

"You like putting women in the hospital?"

"Oh, you mean she isn't dead?" Jack chuckles. "I guess I'll have to go back later and try again." He pins me with his gaze and leans forward in his chair. "Did she enjoy me fucking her again?"

Zack lunges, making Jack flinch, but I put my arm out. "No."

"See? You won't do shit to me. How will it look around town if I tell everyone that Ty Sullivan, the attorney who can do no wrong, and his cronies beat me up in jail?"

"I think you came in here already bruised up," Josh replies with a laugh. "You must have pissed off your cellmate. Did he fuck you too?"

Jack swallows and watches me, fear beginning to seep into his eyes. "Bullshit," he sputters.

Josh and Zack are circling the room menacingly, but what Jack doesn't know is that they aren't the ones he should be worried about.

They aren't going to touch him.

I'm going to make him wish he were dead.

"Where is that shithead of a cop?" Jack asks nervously.

"Oh, we're having an attorney/client consultation," I inform him quietly. "He won't come until I tell him to."

"So, what, you want a shot at me?" Jack stands and pushes the table out of the way. "Take your shot already."

"You're such a piece of shit," I reply deceptively calmly. "You're not a man. Real men don't beat defenseless women. Trust me, I know. I come from a man just like you. You're a pussy."

"I beat the fuck out of that bitch of an ex-wife of mine. She couldn't even try to fight back. That doesn't make me weak."

Zack growls and flexes his hands in and out of fists as he walks behind Jack, glaring holes through him.

"Let me tell you why I'm here." I lean against the wall, crossing my arms over my chest again. Jack's eyes bounce from me to the two large, intimidating men pacing about the room anxiously. "I'm here to make you wish you were dead."

"This is bullshit. I'm here for a stupid assault charge, and I'll be out in a matter of hours. I'll kill her later." He shrugs, but his hands are shaking as he wipes his mouth.

"Oh, they didn't tell you?" I laugh and shake my head at him. "It's an attempted-murder charge, and you won't see the light of day for years, you miserable motherfucker."

Jack's eyes go wide and then he frowns.

"But that's the least of your worries. Do you know what they do in prison to men who prey on children and women?"

I push away from the wall slowly and saunter over to him. "You'll be lucky if you survive the first year. You can bet that you'll be someone's bitch. You'll get your ass fucked on a regular basis."

"Fuck you!"

"You're not really my type," I reply as though we're having a regular conversation, and turn to walk past him—but then I pull back and punch him square across the jaw, knocking him on his ass.

Josh picks him back up again by the hair.

"And given that I know a lot of people, 'cause I do, I'm going to make sure that every fucking inmate in that prison knows that you like to bully women." I walk past again and thrust my elbow into his nose, sending a spray of blood across the room.

"Fucking A!" Jack yells, and doubles over in pain as blood pours out of his now-broken nose.

"Hurts like a bitch, doesn't it?" Zack growls into Jack's ear.

I land a hard punch to Jack's ribs and he doubles over, falling to the floor.

"Leave him there," I mutter to Zack when he makes a move to lift Jack. I kick him three times in the ribs. "You are most likely going to die in prison, Jack, which suits you." I pull him up by his hair and land a punch to his right eye, sending him crashing back to the floor.

"I'm going to ruin you for this!" Jack screams.

"Who's going to fucking believe you?" Josh taunts him. "I didn't see anything."

"If you ever"—I plant my heel into Jack's neck, holding him down to the floor and blocking his airway—"even so much as *think* her name again, I'll make sure you die in prison, and it'll look like suicide, you miserable piece of shit."

Jack throws up all over the floor, heaving from the threat and from the damage to his ribs, thanks to my foot.

"Put him in a chair." I stalk away from the evil man at my feet.

Josh and Zack each take an arm and roughly guide him into the chair.

"I should have waited until you were with her so I could kill you too," Jack sneers, one of his eyes swollen shut and blood pouring down his face and onto his orange inmate jumpsuit.

"Go let Brad know he's ready to go back to his cell," I direct Zack and Josh, keeping my eyes pinned to Jack's. When my friends leave, I push my face into Jack's and reach down, squeezing and twisting his dick in my hand. Jack cries out in pain and tries to push me away, but I hold firm and whisper, "I'll make sure you will die with your dick in your mouth if you ever try to get near her again. Are we clear?"

He makes a motion to spit at me, so I tighten my grasp on his dick and he cries out again. "We're clear!"

"Good." I stand back just as Brad opens the door.

"You done here?" He raises an eyebrow when he sees the Jack's condition.

"Yep. I'm not going to take his case after all. And it looks like his cellmate must not like him much either."

"Jack pisses everyone off," Brad agrees, and pulls Jack out of the chair and down the hallway toward the holding cells.

I walk out into the rainy fall night and join my friends at my Jeep.

"You okay?" Zack asks.

I nod and sit in the passenger seat. "I need to get back to Lo."

"We're on our way."

CHAPTER

Nineteen

LAUREN

"Everything still fucking hurts," I grumble as I slowly descend the stairs into the living room. It's been a week since I've been home, and Emily and Ty have been here every second of every day, driving me up the fucking wall.

I love them both, but they have got to stop hovering.

"Are you sure you won't take the pain meds?" Emily asks worriedly.

"No, just the ibuprofen." I settle into the deep cushions of the couch in the family room. "I'm sick of sleeping all the damn time."

Emily bustles into the kitchen to fetch the pills and water, then returns. "If you need me to stay, I'll make some calls and stay another week."

I swallow the pills and set the water aside. "I'm fine, Em. Honestly, I'm getting better every day, and I have Ty here. You need to get back to your family."

"What will you do when he's at work during the day?" Emily frowns. "Maybe it was too early for him to go back."

"He just went back today." I chuckle. "Life has to go back to normal. I'll probably work myself."

Emily nods and smiles at me softly. "I'm so happy for you, Lo. That man is totally head over heels in love with you."

"It's mutual." I sigh. "He's just . . ."

"Fucking hot."

"I was going to say *amazing*, but *hot* works too."

"You deserve to be happy." Emily grips my hand in hers and squeezes gently.

"I wish my parents knew about him." I sigh again and rest my head on the back of the couch.

"Did they know him?"

"Yes, they knew *of* him. But his parents didn't mingle in the same circles, and he and I didn't hang out together in school, so they didn't know him well. I wish they could know him now, as he is as a successful man."

"What else would you like for them to know about him?" Emily pulls her legs up under her and rests her head in her hand.

"How considerate he is. He's always putting my needs first. He makes sure I eat, for God's sake."

"And?"

I sigh and close my eyes, thinking of the man I love more than anything. "He's kind. Reliable. He loves his family fiercely." I open my eyes and meet her gaze. "He loves *me* fiercely. I wish they could see that."

"They know, Lo."

"I hope so."

"So where do you think this is all leading?" A romantic twinkle is in Emily's eyes.

"One day at a time, Em."

"Seriously, I want to know. I'm going to be two thousand miles away again in a few hours, so I need to get all the face-to-face dirt I can while I'm here."

"I love him," I reply hesitantly. "And that's unexpected, especially after my past."

"I get it." She nods. "What if he asked you to marry him today?"

"I highly doubt that will happen. He just said the *L* word a week ago. This isn't one of our romance novels."

"How can you write such beautiful stories and be such a cynic?" She tilts her head, studying me.

"I'm not a cynic, I'm a realist. We don't live inside a romance novel. I learned that lesson the hard way."

"You're right." A slow smile spreads across her lips. "But when you do get married, I get to be in it, right?"

I chuckle and shake my head. "If I say yes, can we change the subject?"

"You're no fun."

"I am too. I just think we're jumping the gun a bit to be picking out cakes and bridesmaids' dresses."

"I refuse to wear teal." She grimaces. "And no chocolate fountain. It's not classy."

"Oh my God, Em, stop!" I laugh and clutch my injured ribs. "Ouch."

"Oh, I'm sorry!"

"It's okay." I sigh and take her hand in mine, holding on tight. "Thank you for coming, and for being such a kick-ass friend."

"You're welcome. You can repay me by bringing me onto the movie set with you when the gorgeous men start acting in your movies."

"Done." Then I get sober. "I guess this means I can start telling people that I'm Peyton Adams."

"You should have done that from the beginning."

I shake my head sadly. "It's going to be weird to see myself in photos and give interviews and all the other things my agent has been begging me to do."

"It's going to be a lot of work."

"I know, but I'm tired of hiding who I am."

"Good girl."

The doorbell rings.

"That must be Cara and Jill. Cara's taking me to the airport and Jill is staying with you until Ty gets home."

"You're all a bunch of mother hens," I grumble, and follow Emily to the door.

She turns and pulls me gently into her arms, despite our vast height difference. "I'm so happy that you're okay, my friend. I love you."

"I love you too." Tears of gratitude and love prick my eyes. "Safe travels."

She pulls away and opens the door for the girls. "She needs to go back to bed," Emily informs them as she gathers her bags. "And she won't take the pain meds anymore."

I roll my eyes and push her out the door. "Goodbye, *Mom*."

"Take care of her, Jill!" Em calls right before she sits in Cara's Honda and waves through the window.

"How are you really?" Jill asks as I close the door and set the alarm.

"Tired. Sore." I shrug. "The usual."

"Why no pain meds?"

"Because I'm sick of sleeping all the time, and I'm ready to get back to my life." I prop my hands on my hips and glare down at her. "Are you going to lecture me too?"

"Nope." She grins. "You're a big girl. But promise that if you need them, you'll take them."

"I will." I yawn widely and then chuckle. "Ironically, I think I will go nap until Ty gets here. I'm sorry I'm such a horrible hostess."

"I'm used to fending for myself. You go nap. I'll be down here answering e-mail and setting up appointments."

I nod and wave as I trudge up the steps to my bedroom. Jesus, I'm exhausted just from climbing this flight of stairs. My ribs are singing and my head is pounding as I strip out of my clothes and lie on the soft bed.

I'll just nap for a few minutes, until the headache goes away.

"Wake up, my love."

Ty is kissing my forehead gently and brushing his fingers down my cheek. This is the best part of the day, waking up next to him, feeling him beside me.

"You're home," I whisper without opening my eyes.

"Mmm." He kisses me again. "And I need you to wake up. I have some things to show you."

"Would rather just feel you," I mumble.

Suddenly, I hear something purr and I open my eyes to find a tiny orange kitten curled up in the crook of Ty's elbow. "Who is this?"

"This is your new friend." Ty grins. "I figure he can hang out with you while you work and be a companion for you when I'm not here."

"He's not much of a watchdog." I scoop him out of Ty's arm and snuggle him down against my neck. "He's so soft!"

"You don't need a watchdog. You just need someone to brainstorm story ideas with." Ty's lips twitch as he watches me with the kitten.

"What's his name?"

"Fuzz."

"Why?" I chuckle.

"Because he's fuzzy."

"Hmm, maybe he should have a more sophisti-cated name, like Sir Lancelot." I rub my nose against his soft head. "Do you like that name, little guy?"

"There's nothing wrong with Fuzz." Ty frowns.

"How about *Sir* Fuzz?" I grin at my sweet man. "Thank you."

He leans in and kisses me gently, backing away when I try to deepen the kiss. I growl in frustration.

"You are not healthy enough for me to kiss you the way I want to, sweetness. Once I start, I won't want to stop. I'm desperate for you, but I can wait until you're well so I don't hurt you."

"You won't hurt me."

"Never intentionally."

My eyes roam over his long, lean body. He's changed from his work clothes into his jeans and a T-shirt and has a bandage over the inner biceps of his right arm.

"What happened to your arm?" I ask, alarmed.

"I had a tattoo added today." He smiles nervously.

"I want to see." I struggle to sit up, hissing in a breath at the pull on my ribs, then settle back against the headboard.

"Are you okay?"

"Yes. Show me. Can you take the bandage off yet?"

"Yeah, I was waiting to show you." He peels off the bandage.

My eyes grow wide and find his. "What does it mean?"

His eyes fall to his arm and he smiles widely. "I decided on the rose of Sharon because it means something special to you, and for me because I'll never go another day in my life without thinking of you when I see these flowers. And it's blue because it's the color of your eyes."

"You tattooed me on your arm."

"Of course I did, sweetness. I love you." He raises his hand and brushes his thumb down my cheek.

"I love you too," I whisper. "Thank you for that, and for Sir Fuzz." I nuzzle the kitten against me. He purrs and settles in with a wide yawn to take a nap.

"I think you both need a nap," Ty murmurs against my hair as he gently pulls me against his chest.

"I slept all day," I protest.

"The only way you're going to get better is if you rest and let your body heal, Lauren."

"Have I mentioned that I'm not a patient person?"

"Once or twice." He chuckles. "Emily is gone?"

"Yeah, she left this afternoon. I love her to death, but honestly, I was ready for it to just be us again. I want to get back to normal."

"I do too, but I don't like the idea of you being alone during the day yet."

"Now you sound just like her. I'll be fine. I'm just sore now, Ty."

"I'll work half days for one more week."

"You can't keep taking time off of work!"

"Yes, I can." He kisses my head and reaches over to pet the sleeping kitten. "You come first, Lo. Always."

I grin happily and let the sound of the kitten purring and Ty's even breathing lull me to sleep.

"You're nothing but a fucking whore!" Jack backhands me across the face. "I'm going to kill you this time."

He slaps me again, sending me back against a guardrail. How did we get outside? We're up on the second floor now, on the balcony.

"Ty!" I yell, but Jack just laughs.

"He's not here, bitch. He can't save you. He'll never save you." Jack laughs long and hard, delighted with himself. "Should I beat you to death, or just throw you over this balcony?"

I begin to cry. How can this be happening again? Where is Ty? I look over to the window and see him beating on the glass, trying to get to me, but he can't reach me.

He's trapped.

"Ty!" I yell again, but he doesn't come. There is only Jack and his maniacal laugh. He keeps pushing me against the cement railing, over and over. It hurts my sore ribs. "Please stop," I cry.

"You deserve to die, you selfish whore." Jack grips my shoulders in his hands and pushes me over the side of the balcony. I fall and fall and fall in slow motion, my arms and legs flailing.

"Tyyyyy!"

"Lauren!"

I gasp and then cry out as the pain in my ribs shoots through me. Ty wakes me, calling my name and gently pushing his fingers into my hair. I'm sweating, my eyes are wide, and I'm panting uncontrollably.

"You're here." My eyes search the room, looking for Jack.

"Of course I'm here." Ty takes my hand in his, but I pull away and cower from him. "Baby, you had a nightmare."

"Jack was hurting me." I look around the room once more and then begin to cry as Ty pulls me back into his strong arms, rocking me gently.

"He can't hurt you, baby."

"Oh God!" I turn my face into Ty's chest and cry, trembling and afraid. "He pushed me over the balcony."

Ty glides his hands soothingly up and down my back, kisses my head, and comforts me. "He's not here. He'll never be here again."

I lie in Ty's arms for long minutes, relishing his strength. My heart and breathing calm until finally we're just lying together, comforting each other.

"You scared the fuck out of me," he murmurs against my hair. "Are you okay?"

"I'm sorry I scared you."

"I'm sorry you had the nightmare." His voice is hard and I pull back to search his face.

"What is it?"

"I'd very much like to kill him right now."

"That won't solve anything." I lay my cheek back on his chest. "You already beat the shit out of him.

He's not worth it, Ty." I'll never forget that day in the hospital when Ty, Zack, and Josh returned from being gone, and Ty's hand was swollen, his knuckles bloody from beating Jack.

I groan a bit as I shift my position. My ribs are screaming again. The ibuprofen doesn't last as long as the other pain medicines.

"Sore?"

"Always," I mumble grumpily.

"Why don't you just take the stronger medication at night? It'll help you sleep, and then you can stick to the ibuprofen during the day."

I consider his suggestion, then nod reluctantly. "Maybe that should be the plan for a few more days."

Ty slips from the bed and brings back some water and a small pill, which I accept gratefully.

"I love you for all of this," I murmur as he takes the water and sets it aside, then comes back to bed.

"Just for this?" he asks with a crooked smile.

"Well, you're hot too, so that helps."

"So you love me for the nursing skills and my body. I see how you are."

"I might also love your culinary skills and how bossy you are sometimes."

"Good to know."

I grin and press a kiss to his chest. "I miss making love with you."

His body stills before he sighs deeply and his heartbeat picks up beneath my cheek. "I miss you too, sweetness."

His fingers glide lazily up and down my back, soothing me from the pain in my ribs and my head. From the pain of the nightmare.

He is my solace.

He is my home.

CHAPTER

Twenty

"I can't believe it's been a month since the incident."
Jill navigates carefully through the snow, driving me
to my doctor's office.

"I can," I reply grumpily. "I'm fine. I don't know
why you had to drive me today."

"Because until he releases you today, you're not
supposed to be driving." She grins over at me. "I'm
so happy you're feeling better."

"Me too." I nod. "I'm horny as hell and Ty won't
touch me until the doctor says it's okay. If he doesn't
say it's okay today, I'll maim him."

Jill laughs as she pulls into a parking space. "That
sounds like Ty, always living by the rules."

"He's driving me crazy. I've felt good enough for
sex for weeks."

"Just think of all the hot fun you can have tonight."
Jill wiggles her eyebrows at me, then grimaces.
"Wait. That's my brother. Ew."

I lead her into the office building with a laugh and sign in, then take a seat and wait to be called back.

"You should do something special," Jill whispers to me as she thumbs through an old *People* magazine.

"That's what I was thinking." I purse my lips in thought.

"Lauren," the nurse calls with a smile.

"You think about it, and I'll think about it, and then we'll chat when I'm done." I stand and remove my coat, leaving it on the seat beside Jill before joining the nurse to be led back to a room.

"How are you feeling?"

"Much better."

"Good." She smiles kindly and takes my temperature, my blood pressure, and weight and makes notes in a computer. "Go ahead and change into this very stylish paper gown, and Dr. Greene will be in shortly."

With that, she leaves.

I've lost weight in the past month. Too much weight. I hope I can gain it back when I'm able to get back in the pool. I've lost a lot of muscle tone and stamina from not swimming, and I'm eager to get it back.

I'm eager to get my fucking life back.

"Good afternoon, Lauren." Dr. Greene smiles as he bustles into the room and signs on to the computer.

"Hello."

"How have you been feeling?"

"Much better."

"How are your ribs?" He motions for me to lie back so he can raise the paper gown and examine my ribs. "The bruises are pretty much gone."

"They haven't been sore in about a week or so."

"Good." He nods and motions for me to sit up so he can look at the back of my head. "And your head?"

"I get headaches when I'm really tired, but for the most part it's nothing that a couple ibuprofen won't cure."

He nods as he shines a light in my eyes, looks into my nose and ears.

"Do you tire easily?"

"It's getting better." I shrug. "My boyfriend makes me nap a lot, so it's not so bad."

"Ty's a good guy. I figured he'd be here with you."

"He had court today, so I had his sister drive me. Please tell me I can get back to living my normal life again."

Dr. Greene sits on the rolling stool by the desk and looks up at me. "I'm going to release you to normal activity."

I do a happy dance in my seat, but he interrupts me with "Under a few conditions."

"As long as I can drive, swim, and have sex, I'll do whatever you want."

He laughs and turns to the computer. "You can do those things. I want you to rest when you get tired. If the headaches persist, or worsen, I want you to come see me immediately. But it looks like your ribs have healed, and I'm happy with your progress."

"Thank God," I mutter. "Thank you."

"You're welcome." He grins, stands, and shakes my hand. "We're finished. I'll want to see you again in a month, and then I'll just see you yearly for your normal physicals."

"Great."

I dress quickly and join Jill in the waiting area.

She's on the phone. "She's finished. I'll call you later." She hangs up and tosses her phone in her handbag. "That was your man. He had a break in court and was checking in."

"He's always hovering." I roll my eyes, but can't help the wide smile that spreads over my mouth.

"And you love him."

"I know. I get to attack him later. I hope court gets out early today."

I practically skip through the snow to Jill's car.

"Did you come up with some good seduction ideas?" Jill asks.

"Yes. You?"

She chuckles as she buckles herself into her seat. "Despite it being my brother, yes. I do believe we have a few stops to make on our way back to your place."

"You read my mind." My phone chirps with an incoming text.

Ty: **Did it go well? I should have been there.**

"Your brother is a worrier."

"Only with those he loves, Lo."

Me: **Went well. Will tell you about it tonight. Love you.**

Ty: **Love you, baby.**

Dinner in the oven: check. Candles and flowers: check. Hot, barely there outfit: check and check.

I just about reach my bedroom when I hear the front door open and close and Ty call out, "Lo?"

"Upstairs!" I call out, and bite my lip in excitement. I lean against the doorjamb so I'm the first thing he sees when he gets to the top of the stairs. I'm wearing one of his white, dress button-downs, undone, and my favorite blue tie, hanging loose around my neck. White lacy panties and thigh-high stockings complete the look.

Ty's eyes are on the stairs as he reaches the top. He raises his head and his eyes widen when he sees me. He swallows hard and comes to a stop about three feet away from me, just out of arm's reach.

"Your appointment went well?" His eyes rake up and down my body.

"It did."

"What did Dr. Greene say?"

I take a step forward and grip Ty's loose tie in my hand and pull him forward. My lips hover inches away from his and my body instantly tingles in awareness. "He released me to normal activities."

Ty dips in to kiss me, but I pull away and lead

him by the tie to the bed. "I won't be able to stop kissing you once we start, and I have something very important to do first."

"You do?" He smiles widely. His eyes are on fire, watching me adoringly.

"Mmm." I flick the buttons open on his shirt. I loosen the knot in his tie and pull his shirtsleeves down his arms, letting the shirt fall to the floor. "I love your chest." I plant a kiss in the center of his chest, then move over to glide my tongue over his nipple.

He gasps and gently cradles my head in his hands. "You're driving me crazy, baby."

"That's kind of the point, counselor." I plant sweet kisses over his skin to his right shoulder, down to the freshly healed flower on his inner arm. "This is pretty."

"It's you," he murmurs softly.

"I love that you've been so patient and taken such good care of me."

"That's my job, sweetness."

"The fact that you see it as part of your role as my man makes me love and appreciate you even more."

"I would do anything for you." He pulls his fingers down my cheek softly.

My hands glide down his sides to his trousers. I slip my forefingers under his waistband, under the elastic of his boxers, and move slowly from his hips, around to his ass, and then change directions to his front.

"You have smooth skin," I whisper.

"Lauren, I'm about to rip my shirt off you and pull you under me on this bed." His voice is rough with want, making me grin at him.

"Hold that thought."

"You're killing me, sweetness."

"It's been a whole month, Ty. You can give me a few minutes to have fun, can't you?"

"A few short minutes." He watches me with hot gray eyes as I kiss my way down his torso. My fingers unfasten his pants and peel his underwear from his body, then guide them down his legs, unleashing his hard cock.

"Is this for me?" I ask innocently.

"Forever."

My eyes widen at that single word. *Forever.*

I sink to my knees, grip the base of his pulsing dick in one hand, and lick from his scrotum to the tip, slipping my tongue along the slit.

"Ah, fuck, baby," he growls. He gently threads his fingers into my hair, caressing me as I sink over him and suck him deeply into my mouth, gripping his length. "God, I love your sweet mouth."

"Mmm." I pull up, swirl my tongue around the head, then sink down again, setting a lazy rhythm, enjoying the smooth texture of his skin, the musky smell of him, the way he groans with each full up-and-down motion of my mouth.

His hands slip down to my neck and my shoulders, kneading them firmly, massaging me as I make love to his beautiful cock.

"Mmm," I groan, not lifting my mouth from him.

"Feel good?" he whispers.

I nod and look up at him as I fuck him with my mouth. He's smiling, watching me intently. His hands continue to caress and love me, his eyes pinned to the point where his dick disappears into my mouth.

"You are so beautiful, Lauren. It makes me nuts to see you in my shirt and tie."

"I know." I back away and lick my way across his hip to lap at the sexy V there. "I love this spot."

"You love my hip?" He laughs down at me, then groans as I pump my hand up and down his hard length.

"I love this line of muscle. Not everyone has it, you know."

"You do."

"You like that?" I climb to my feet.

"I love everything about your delectable little body, sweetness."

"I've lost some muscle this month," I pout, but he covers my mouth with his, *finally*, and rests his hands over my rib cage, inside the shirt.

"You'll get it back," he whispers as he kisses his way across my jaw to my neck. "Is it my turn now?"

"Sure, you can have a turn. This is a democracy, after all."

He chuckles. "You're funny."

His eyes warm as he pushes his shirt over my shoulders and off my arms; it pools around our feet.

His finger dips into the hem of my panties. "You're so damn sexy."

I let my eyes trail up and down his naked body. "Back at you."

"Do you know how hard it's been to keep my hands off of you?" His hands sweep up to cup my breasts; his thumbs brush lightly over my already-puckered nipples.

I'm damp and hot and squirming beneath his touch. "You can touch me now. You can do anything you want to me now."

His eyes catch mine as he leans in and places a tender kiss at the corner of my mouth. "I'm going to take this slow, baby."

"We could do it fast first and then go slow the second round," I suggest, eager to have him inside me.

"I need to take my time, to show you how much I love you. I couldn't do it before."

I take his face in my hands. "I felt it then, Ty. I knew."

"I should have said it."

I shake my head and kiss him chastely. "I knew," I repeat softly.

He lifts me into his arms and lays me in the center of the bed, then covers me with his warm, hard body. I trace the lines of ink in his skin with my fingertip and watch his eyes as he pushes my hair off my face and nuzzles my nose with his own.

"I'm a little nervous," he admits.

"To make love to me?"

"I don't want to hurt you." He frowns.

"You'll never hurt me. It's hurt to not be able to be with you like this."

He exhales and rests his forehead against my own, his pelvis resting in the cradle of my thighs. His hardness is pressed against my core, and I slowly circle my hips, inviting him in.

"If I hurt you, just say the word, and it'll all stop."

"Don't you dare stop, Tyler Sullivan."

His lips twitch as he pulls back and guides his dick to my entrance and then slowly, oh, so slowly, embeds himself inside me to the hilt, then stops, panting, muscles strained. "Okay?"

"So, so okay." I rotate my hips. "I need you to move, babe."

"Not yet. I want to just feel you."

He cradles my head in his palms and finally kisses me. His tongue licks across the seam of my lips, then sinks inside my mouth, dancing and exploring. My hands glide lazily up and down his back, over his shoulders and into his thick raven hair, holding him to me.

He finally begins to move, slowly and gently, all the way out until just the head is buried in my folds, then pushing back in, repeating the motion over and over.

"I'm not gonna break," I whisper.

"It's not about that." He shakes his head and buries his face in my neck.

"What is it?" I hug him to me as his hips move slowly.

"It's about reconnecting with you, my love. God, I missed you so much."

I feel tears prick my eyes at his words, at the tender way his body is making love to mine. He feels amazing.

"You're amazing," he mumbles, mirroring my thoughts.

I clench around him, my legs hitched around his hips, my arms wrapped tightly around his shoulders, and my pussy clamped around his dick.

Our bodies couldn't get closer together.

He rolls gently onto his back, taking me with him so I'm straddling him.

"Ride me, sweetness."

I brace myself on his shoulders as I rise and lower myself on him.

"Do your ribs hurt?"

"Not even a little." I grin as I increase the tempo. "This is so fucking good."

He sits up with a growl, grips my hips in his hands, and guides me up and down, increasing the speed even further.

My back tingles where his fingers caress me, up and down my spine over my ink.

"You like my tattoo." I grin against his lips.

"I fucking love your tattoo." He kisses me long and hard.

Finally, I can't stand it any more and I begin riding him in earnest, relishing the friction, hitting his pubic bone against my clit with every thrust. "Oh, fuck, babe, I'm gonna come."

"Come, sweetness." He's lifting and lowering me now, his hands gripped firmly on my hips.

He's going to leave fingerprints on me, and I love it. He's doing all the work.

He's so damn strong.

I grab onto his hair as I bear down and convulse around him, coming hard and long over him. "Oh my God!"

"That's it, baby, let go." He nibbles my neck, down to my nipples, where he grips one in his teeth and tugs hard, sending more sparks down to my core.

As I come down from my orgasm, he lies back on the bed, panting, eyes on fire, and watches as I begin to move again, my breasts swaying with the motion of my riding him hard, gripping him. I lean back and also cup his scrotum in my hand. His eyes cross and then roll back in his head as I feel his balls lift and tighten. He bucks his hips and cries out as he comes inside me, grinding against me, riding the long wave of his climax.

He's sweaty and panting as I press a kiss to his neck and lay my head on his chest.

"That was fun," I comment lightly.

"That was life affirming." He chuckles. "I hope you're not too sore because I plan to stay inside you for the majority of the night."

"I'm good with that plan." I bite his neck gently, then lick it before pressing an openmouthed kiss on the tender skin.

"Keep that up and I'll pull you under me and

begin round two right now." His voice is light, but rough with renewed lust.

"Easy, tiger. I'm hungry."

"I'll call for takeout."

"No need." I lift off him and pull the shirt he wore all day over my shoulders, leaving it unbuttoned. "I have dinner in the oven."

"You do?" He raises an eyebrow in surprise.

"I can cook."

"You can?"

"Just because I don't often doesn't mean I can't," I inform him haughtily.

"What else can you do?" He rises from the bed and pulls his shorts on.

"Lots of things."

"Name two."

"I can play the piano."

"Holy shit, I had no idea." He's watching me with a half smile and appreciative eyes. "And the other?"

"I can make you hard with one touch," I respond playfully, and cup his semihard dick through his underwear.

"Oh, sweetness, that was never a secret."

Epilogue

"Can I interrupt for a bit?" Ty asks as he saunters into my office.

I've been working all morning. I push back from the desk and grin at him as I stretch. Sir Fuzz is curled up in my lap and yawns, stretching his paws out before him at the intrusion, then curls up and falls back to sleep, making us laugh.

"Fuzz won't be pleased, but I could use a break." I lift the growing kitten from my lap and lay him on my warm vacated seat.

After the incident with Jack, Ty had my whole office redecorated. The furniture is new and arranged differently from before. Even the carpet and wall paint are new. The book covers have been repaired and are hanging on the wall again.

This office is brand-new, so I don't have any bad memories here.

He thinks of everything.

"What's up?" I cross to him and twine my arms around his neck, leaning in for a kiss.

"How do you feel about taking a walk? Getting some fresh air?"

I glance out the window and frown. "It's raining."

"I have an umbrella." Something in his eyes looks uncertain.

"Are you okay?" I kiss him softly.

"I'm great. I'd just like to take you for a walk."

"Okay, I'm game."

He grins and pulls me out of the office, then bundles us both into coats and scarves, grabs a big red umbrella, and leads me outside.

"It's so weird that all the snow melted off." I shuffle down the steps of the porch and wait for him to open the umbrella.

He holds it over us, grasps my hand with his free one, and guides me down the driveway to the path that leads to the bridge. "It's been an odd fall, that's for sure. When winter does finally set in, I'm afraid it's going to be a doozy."

"Doozy?" I tease him. "Who says *doozy*?"

"Okay, it's going to be a bitch." He laughs and kisses my forehead.

"As long as we have snow for Christmas, I'll be happy."

"I'm pretty sure you have nothing to worry about."

We slosh through the rain on the paved trail to the bridge. It smells like wet leaves and winter. Despite its not being cold enough to snow, my cheeks are cold and we can see our breath in the cool air.

"It could snow tonight, if the temp drops," I mention casually.

"Mmm." I glance up at him, and he's watching the path ahead, his eyes far away. I wonder what he's thinking, but rather than intrude, I fall quiet and enjoy the walk.

We finally get to the top of the bridge, my favorite spot, and we stop to lean on the stone railing, watching the water below, the mountain ahead. The world is silent around us, aside from the rushing of the water.

It's tranquil. Peaceful.

Perfect.

"I love this place." I take a deep breath.

"I know." He grins. He pulls me into his arms, hugging me in that special way he does, rocking us back and forth, still managing to hang on to the umbrella. "I have something to say, sweetness."

"Okay," I mumble against his chest, comfortable in his embrace. "Shoot."

He pulls back so he can see my face, tucks a strand of hair that has escaped my hat behind my ear. "I love being your friend, Lo. Having you in my life and choosing to be your friend is the best thing I ever did. But falling in love with you has been effortless."

I swallow hard as I watch him watch me, his mind moving a thousand miles a second.

He cups my face in his hands. "You have the best heart of anyone I've ever met in my life. You're kind. You make me laugh when I've had the worst day, and your voice makes me want to listen to you for hours. You're so fucking smart, Lo. What you've done with your writing makes me so proud, you inspire me to dream with my eyes wide-open."

He clears his throat, his eyes fall to my lips as I lick them, then he finds my gaze again. "Your touch brings me to my knees, and I know that I'll never, ever get enough of you."

He drags his knuckles down my cheek as he gazes down at me with so much love in his eyes, my breath catches and I can just watch him, struck dumb.

"Being in love with someone is an unconditional commitment. To love someone isn't just a feeling, it's a decision that you make every day, no matter what happens. It's a judgment. A promise."

He backs away, lays the umbrella on the ground, and falls to one knee, taking my hand in his.

"That being said, I'm asking you here, in this place that means so much to you, to marry me. Be my wife. My partner. I love you, Lauren, today and every day for the rest of my life."

He reaches into his coat pocket and pulls out folded papers and a black box, flips it open, and holds them up to me. "This is a prenup. I don't want anything but *you*, sweetness. Be mine, always."

Tears fill my eyes as I fall to my knees before him. I take the papers from his grasp, and rather than read them, I keep his gaze locked on my own as I tear them apart and toss them into the water below.

"My heart isn't just mine, you know. It belongs to you too. It always will, Ty. I don't need a prenup. I trust you with all of me. Of course I'll marry you."

He smiles down at me as he places the gorgeous round diamond solitaire on my finger, then scoops me up into his arms, rising effortlessly to his feet and spinning in a circle, kissing me firmly.

"I love you so much, sweetness."

"I love you too."

He nuzzles my nose as he sets me on my feet. "It's a good thing you said yes. Jilly's already put my house on the market."

"Pretty sure of yourself, weren't you?"

"Hopeful, my love." He picks up the umbrella, tucks my hand in his, and pulls me to his side, guiding me back toward home. "Very hopeful."

It's Jillian's turn for Love Under the Big Sky!

Turn the page for a sneak peek at
New York Times bestselling Kristen Proby's
latest in the Love Under the Big Sky series

FALLING FOR JILLIAN

Available February 2015
from Pocket Books!

JILLIAN

What is it about master bathrooms that make people hem and haw? I glance down at my watch and offer the couple from Ontario a wide smile as they browse through the multimillion-dollar home near the ski resort on Whitetail Mountain. In all my years in real estate, it's always been the master bathroom and closet that people get hung up on.

You'd think it would be the kitchen, and sometimes it is, but invariably, they want to take a second or even third look at the master suite.

"This home is beautiful," Mrs. Langton says with a smile. "I love it. What do you think?"

Her husband smiles and nuzzles his wife's ear with his nose, making my stomach turn. "You know I'll buy you any house you want, my love."

She laughs and takes another look around the great room as we descend the staircase, our footfalls echoing through the empty space.

"Out of all of the homes we've seen, this is my favorite. The view is fantastic. And we're just down the road from the resort."

I glance out the wide picture windows that overlook Whitetail Lake below and wince. The snow is coming down harder than it was this morning, so getting off this mountain in my little Honda sedan isn't going to be easy.

"Does that mean you've finally decided?" Mr. Langton asks his wife.

"I think so." She claps her hands and bounces on the balls of her feet. "We'd like to make an offer on this house, Jillian."

"Fantastic," I reply, and shake their hands. "I'll get the paperwork ready this evening and we can meet at my office tomorrow."

"The weather sure has decided to get nasty," Mrs. Langton comments as we make our way outside and I lock the door to the mansion behind us.

"They're calling for a storm," I reply. "We had a mild fall, but it looks like winter is going to be a doozy." I glance longingly at the sturdy 4x4 rental that the Langtons are about to climb into.

I really need to replace my car.

"I'll be in touch tomorrow." I wave them off as they pull out of the circular driveway and head up the mountain toward the cabin they've been renting at the resort.

And now I get to make my way *down* this mountain in my two-wheel-drive Honda with no studded snow tires.

Fantastic.

I wasn't exaggerating when I told the Langtons that we'd had a mild fall. Until about two weeks ago, we hadn't had any snow that stuck around for more than a day or two, and that's unusual for early December.

I'll bet it's seventy and sunny in LA right now.

I sigh and resign myself to struggling down the narrow road to the bottom of the mountain.

I adore my hometown of Cunningham Falls, Montana. I grew up here, along with my parents and their parents before them. It's a town that welcomes the tourists that flock in by the thousands during both the ski and summer seasons to explore the wilds of Montana. But despite the many newcomers each season, the locals pretty much all know each other, whether we like it or not.

And there have been many times over the years that I'd rather they not.

I bite my lip and turn left out of the driveway, taking it slow. The snow is coming down so hard, it's like a thick blanket draped all around my car, making it hard to see the road before me or the steep drop-off to my right.

If not for the dark trees, I'd be screwed.

I inch my way carefully down the hill and around two switchbacks, and breathe a huge sigh of relief when I safely come out at the bottom and, through the large snowflakes, see the stoplight marking the main road.

Just as I come to a stop at the light, I hear screeching tires and the unmistakable sound of rubber sliding on ice just before a Mercedes SUV comes to a stop against my rear fender.

Perfect.

I open my door and step out just as the driver of the Mercedes does too, and we survey the damage.

"Well, it could be a lot worse," I mutter.

"I'm sorry," the tall stranger says, kneeling by the wreckage. "I guess I took that corner too fast."

"I guess so," I agree with a nod. "You barely touched me, though."

"Looks like you have a bit of a dent there," he replies, and stands, then grins down at me. "Jillian Sullivan! You haven't changed a bit in all these years."

I feel my eyes widen and I cover my mouth with mitten-encased hands, then laugh and throw my arms around the tall, broad man who slammed into my car.

"Max Hull!"

He hugs me tight and then pulls away, offering me a wide grin. His blond hair is short and styled conservatively. His green eyes are happy, if somewhat guarded, and he seems to be distracted.

God, the Hull brothers are hot.

"Are you here visiting Brad and Jenna?" Brad Hull is a cop here in Cunningham Falls, and Jenna runs a beautiful bed-and-breakfast called the Hideaway on Whitetail Mountain. I grew up with all three of the Hull siblings.

"I am." He nods, frowns, and then adds, "Thinking about moving home."

"Really? Is this good news?" I ask, and then laugh, looking up into the snow that continues to fall around us. "Now that I think about it, maybe we should catch up when we aren't standing in a blizzard."

"Good plan." He grins and kisses my cold cheek chastely, and I pray with all my heart that I feel a tingle of awareness, but there is nothing.

Damn.

"Let's exchange numbers so I can at least have your car fixed." Max pulls his phone out of his denim pocket and begins typing away on the screen. I rattle off my number, then grin when I see a text come through from him and save his number to my contacts.

"My brother can probably just knock the dent out with a hammer, Max, but thanks. I'm more worried about your expensive Mercedes."

"Doesn't look like I got a scratch. We got lucky." He winks and backs toward his car. "How is Ty?"

"Good. He's engaged to Lauren Cunningham, you know."

"I had no idea. Speaking of brothers and dating, I heard you and Brad went out a couple months ago."

"Yeah, once. We decided we're better at being friends." *Because I'm a dating failure and I have too much damn baggage.*

"Sounds like there's lots of news to catch up on."

"Be careful, they haven't sanded that road yet. I'll see you later!" We wave and I climb back into my car, soaked through from the quarter-sized flakes. I shake my head and send snow spraying through the interior, put the car in drive, and make my way home.

I slide several times while turning corners, and curse myself for not replacing my tires before the snowy season arrived.

Truth be told, I should just get a new car. A bigger one, with all-wheel drive. Especially since I show homes all over this valley, which means I drive through snow, mud, and the elements every day. It hasn't been a matter of not being able to afford a new vehicle, it's been a lack of time. Between the move home, starting the new job, and my soon-to-be sister-in-law's horrible attack at the hands of her ex-husband, there just hasn't been time to car shop.

As I approach the little house that I rent from my best friend, Cara, I see the snowplow has thankfully been down my street already, but they blocked in my driveway.

I hit my fist on the steering wheel and curse a blue streak as I pull my car to a stop at the side of the road, jerk my ballet flats off my feet, and toss them in the passenger seat, then reach into the backseat for my boots and stuff my feet in them.

I have to shovel the goddamn driveway.

It's almost dark now and it's only 4:00 p.m. The days are so short this time of year.

I trudge through the knee-high snowbank that is currently blocking my driveway, grab my snow shovel from the front porch, and trek back, gazing over at Ty's old house, which now sits empty with a FOR SALE sign perched near the curb.

I miss having my brother close by.

I dig in, shoveling the clumps of snow left behind by the plow, throwing them into my front yard, and when I've finished, I pitch the shovel in the snow, standing straight up, and sit in my still-running car.

It takes me three tries to get it into the driveway.

I definitely need a new car.

Finally, I stomp up to my front door, wet, sweaty from the workout of shoveling snow, and bone tired. I knock the snow off my boots and shake my hair and coat out, shedding the snow that's fallen on me in the last fifteen minutes while I shoveled.

I push inside and frown at the cold air that greets me.

Did I turn the thermostat down that far?

I immediately cross to the thermostat and crank the heat, then rush into the bedroom and strip out of my wet clothes, replacing them with warm sweatpants, a T-shirt, and a heavy gray sweatshirt over that.

I pull on some wool socks and rub my arms briskly as I walk swiftly into the kitchen to warm up some soup in the microwave, hoping the heat kicks in sooner rather than later.

When the microwave dings, I stand over the sink and quickly eat my hot chicken noodle soup.

Damn, burned my tongue.

This day just gets better and better.

I wrap my favorite quilt around my shoulders, grab my laptop, and settle on the couch, ready to type up the paperwork for the Langtons.

The Langtons who can't keep their hands off each other.

I smirk and rub my cold nose on my sleeve, then sniffle. Damn, it's really cold in here.

Maybe I need something to help keep me warm, like a dog. Or a cat.

Not a man!

"Why am I in Montana in the middle of winter in a cold-as-hell house?" I ask the room at large, and stomp across the room to check the thermostat again.

Fifty-eight degrees.

No wonder I'm freezing my nipples off.

Maybe the pilot light thingy on the furnace blew out? I have no idea what to do. I dial Ty's number with numb fingers and curse when I get his voice mail. He's probably keeping warm with Lo.

Well, that leaves Cara.

"Hello?" she answers on the second ring.

"Hey, I think there's something wrong with the furnace in your house. It's fifty-eight degrees in here, and I've cranked the heat and nothing is happening."

"It's way too cold outside for you to be sitting in a house with a broken furnace."

"You think?" I roll my eyes and burrow under my blanket again. "I can't reach Ty. I know the roads are horrible right now, I'm just not sure who to call after 5:00 p.m. around here. Everyone has gone home for the day."

"I'm sure Josh can fix it," she replies, and I hear Josh laugh in the background.

"It's a long drive into town in the snow, Cara."

"Josh can handle the snow," she replies confidently. "He'll be there in about a half hour. Are you okay until then?"

"Yeah, I'm bundled up. If need be, I can shovel my driveway again and I'll be nice and sweaty in no time."

"Well, that sounds . . . gross," she replies with a giggle. "No sweating. Just stay warm."

"I'll try. Tell Josh thanks."

I hang up and walk into the kitchen, the brightly colored quilt hugged tightly around me, dragging behind me on the floor, and I fix myself some hot cocoa while I wait. Josh will fix the furnace and everything will be back to normal in no time.

Just as I'm settling back into the cushions of the couch, surrounded by all of my throw pillows and blankets, there's a knock at the door.

Thank God. I thought I was going to suffocate under all that fabric.

With my trusty quilt held around me, I jog to the door and fling it open.

"I'm so happy to see you!"

The man on the other side of the door offers me a slow grin, allows his chocolate-brown eyes to roam from the top of my messy hair to the soles of my wool-covered feet, and then steps inside out of the snow and takes his army-green beanie off his head, uncovering messy brown hair. He stomps the snow off his boots and sets a tool chest on my floor.

My brain has paused. I was ready for Josh.

I wasn't prepared for Zack and the damn tingle of awareness that zings through me at just the sight of him. The man is a good twelve inches taller than my five foot two and he's just . . . *big*.

And the sexiest thing I've ever seen in my life.

"Hey, Jilly."

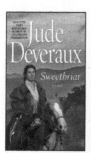

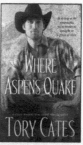